IN PERPETUITY

JAKE BIBLE

SEVERED PRESS
HOBART TASMANIA

IN PERPETUITY

ONE

"What you are holding in your weak little hands is called an A6 plasma rifle! Also known as a scorcher!" Master Sergeant Lawrence Kim bellowed at the fifty rows of fresh cadets that packed the antechamber to the combat simulator. There were twenty-five cadets per row, but Kim focused his attention on just a handful in front of him. "You will only refer to your rifle as a scorcher! It will not be called an A6! It will not be called a plasma rifle! If I hear any of you motherfucking pieces of shit referring to a scorcher as anything other than a scorcher, I will personally turn you all into bottoms! Am I understood?"

"Yes, sir!" the cadets yelled.

"Holy fucking moron crap!" Kim yelled. "Did you taint flakes just call me sir? Are you all retarded in ways that had yet to be invented until this very second? Have you never watched a training video in your life? Did you not all just complete your written exams administered by Central Space Command's most dedicated recruitment officers? My name is Master Sergeant Lawrence Kim! You will call me Master Sergeant or you will get my ten foot cock up your ass so fast that I'll be coming from between your gums before you can even register the intense tearing sensation that is your insides! Now, what is my motherfucking name?"

"Master Sergeant Lawrence Kim!" the cadets yelled.

"Jesus jumping on a laser! You are the stupidest motherfuckers I have ever had to train! Did I not just tell you sperm shits to call me Master Sergeant? Did I not just say that?" Kim roared.

He stomped up to a skinny young man, maybe twenty, maybe less, and thrust his chest against the cadet.

"What the fuck is your name, cadet?"

"Cadet Private Carlos DeSuezo!" the young man replied.

"What did I ask to be called, Cadet Private DeSuezo?"

"Master Sergeant!"

"Did you call me that?"

"I did not, Master Sergeant!"

"And why the holy fuck did you not call me by the name I just ordered all of you cunt scrapings to call me by?"

"It was confusing, Master Sergeant!"

"Do you know the difference between a pussy and an asshole, Cadet Private DeSuezo?"

"I do, Master Sergeant!"

"Which do you prefer to ram your itsy bitsy cock into, Cadet Private DeSuezo?"

"I prefer pussy, Master Sergeant!"

"Then would you not be upset if you were to whip out that one inch of yours and find that you are jamming it into a shit-crusted asshole? Would that not upset you, Cadet Private DeSuezo?"

"Yes, that would upset me, Master Sergeant!"

"Then you can understand how I felt when you piss dribbles referred to me by something other than Master Sergeant, can you not Cadet Private DeSuezo?"

"I can, Master Sergeant!"

"So let us try this again, you fucking snot licking, spooge drinkers! What is my name?"

"Master Sergeant!"

"I cannot hear you over the cocks and twats that are jammed in your mouths! WHAT THE FUCK IS MY NAME?"

"MASTER SERGEANT!"

"Very good," Kim grinned. "That's exactly what my name is. Now, your job, if your tiny little fucksticks for brains can handle it, is to name your scorcher. Can you handle that, you sphincter nibblers?"

"Yes, Master Sergeant!"

Kim turned and stalked over to a tall woman, close to thirty with shoulder-length brown hair and deep black skin. He shoved himself against her, mashing his muscled chest into her breasts. The woman did not budge, but her bottom lip started to quiver.

"What is the name of your scorcher, cadet private?"

"Master Sergeant?" the woman asked.

"You named your scorcher after me? I would be flattered if it wasn't so goddamned sad! There are a trillion names out there and you have chosen to name your scorcher after me? Were you born an abortion, cadet private?"

"No, Master Sergeant!"

"Then why did you name your scorcher after me?"

"I did not, Master Sergeant! I was asking a question!"

"I did not hear a question, cadet private, I heard my motherfucking name! Why is your head shoved up your cunt, cadet private? Now, that's a question!"

"Yes, Master Sergeant!"

"Yes? Yes what, you cum dumpster? At no point did I expect a response from that cock hole you speak with! What is your name, cadet private?"

"Cadet Private Nola Vklogg!"

"Cadet Private Nola Vklogg? You are not from Earth, Cadet Private Nola Vklogg, are you?"

"No, Master Sergeant, I am not!"

"Which piece of shit colony are you from, Cadet Private Nola Vklogg?"

"I am from Grafe, Master Sergeant!"

"Grafe? Grafe! Do you hear that, you pus bag whores? We have a Grafian here!" Kim shoved his face into Cadet Private Vklogg's, pressing his nose against her nose. "I bet you think you're better than all of us, don't you Cadet Private Nola Vklogg? I bet you think you can buy us all out with your riches and make us your slaves, right? When you go to the can, you probably shit diamonds and corphia crystals? Each time you flush, you flush my year's salary down the shitter. That make you feel special, Cadet Private Nola Vklogg?"

"I do not feel special, Master Sergeant! I am here to serve Central Space Command and fight against the Estelian threat to Earth and all of her colonies!"

"Is that so?" Kim laughed as he stepped back and looked Cadet Private Vklogg up and down. "A real patriot? Is that what we have here? Don't tell me you volunteered. Please don't tell me that."

Cadet Private Vklogg just stood there.

"Well, I'll be blown by a pack of wiccs," Kim laughed. "You did volunteer! Your parents must be very proud."

Cadet Private Vklogg winced at the mention of her parents.

"Uh-oh," Kim grinned from ear to ear. "I smell trouble in rich people land. Your parents aren't proud, are they? They're actually disappointed that the bribes they paid when you were born went to waste, am I right? All those credits just gone because you want to do your duty and kill doublegangers. They probably won't speak to you anymore, right? Am I right, Cadet Private Vklogg?"

"No, Master Sergeant!"

"I'm sorry, did you just say no?"

"Yes, Master Sergeant!"

"So your parents are speaking to you, Cadet Private Vklogg?"

"No, Master Sergeant! My parents were killed last year during the assault on the Benesheer, Master Sergeant! Along with my entire family! I escaped in a lifepod and was picked up by a CSC cruiser, Master Sergeant!"

"Well, fuck me standing on one leg," Kim nodded. "I have been corrected. Your rich fucking family died while vacationing on the most expensive spaceliner in the galaxy, you escaped with your black skin intact, and now you want to go out and get your tits blown off by doublegangers? Is that what you are telling me?"

"I want to do my duty and kill Estelians, Master Sergeant!"

"You want revenge, is what you want," Kim chuckled. "You know what revenge does to the mind, Cadet Private Vklogg? It warps it! It makes it do stupid things! Like fucking enlist in the CSC corps! That is the stupidest thing I have ever heard! You are a fucking moron, Cadet Private Vklogg! An A-one, prime moron!"

"Yes, Master Sergeant!"

"What is the name of your scorcher, Cadet Private Vklogg?"

"Nastua, Master Sergeant!"

"Was that your mother's name?"

"No, Master Sergeant!"

"Was it your grandmother's name?"

"No, Master Sergeant! It was the name of my baby girl, Master Sergeant! She was vaporized in the nursery during the first wave of the attack!"

"Now you want her to vaporize some doublegangers, is that it?"

"Yes, Master Sergeant!"

"Fucking-A right, you do! Now shut the fuck up and let me deal with these other shitstains! You! The fucking slant-eyed ginger!

How in the perfect science of genetics did you end up with slant eyes and curly red hair?"

"Good genes, Master Sergeant!" replied a short young man, looking exactly as Kim described him.

"Do you see my eyes, you little mongrel?"

"Yes, Master Sergeant!"

"Are they slant eyed like yours?"

"Yes, Master Sergeant!"

"Is my hair jet black?"

"Yes, Master Sergeant!"

"That's because my gene pool hasn't been pissed in by some Celtic mongoloid! My blood is pure, you fucking freak of nature! Who the fuck let an abomination like you join this elite fighting machine?"

"A recruiter outside of a bar, Master Sergeant!"

"That explains everything then!" Kim yelled. He reached out and grabbed the young man by his curly red hair. "The next time you stand in front of me, I want this red shit shaved off! If you ever desecrate my heritage by showing up with some fucking leprechaun looking hair again, I will let Cadet Private Vklogg take her size twelve boot and insert it up your anus to her ankle, do you fucking hear me?"

"Yes, Master Sergeant!"

"What is the name of your scorcher?"

"Mike, Master Sergeant!"

"Mike? You gave your scorcher a boy's name? Do you like boys, cadet private?"

"Todd Norlini, Master Sergeant!"

"What did you just fucking say to me?"

"I told you my name, Master Sergeant!"

"Jesus eating crackers, did I ask you for your fucking name?"

"Well, no, Master Sergeant!"

"Well no?" Kim asked. He shook his head. "Drop your trousers and bend over, Cadet Private Norlini."

"I'm sorry, Master Sergeant?"

"Yes, you are about to be," Kim smiled. "Cadet Private Vklogg?"

"Yes, Master Sergeant?" Cadet Private Vklogg asked.

"The second Cadet Private Norlini has exposed his anus, I want you to grip his tiny boy hips and shove your boot as far up his ass as you can. Are we understood?"

"Yes, Master Sergeant!" Cadet Private Vklogg replied.

"NORLINI! Why do I not see your brown eye?" Kim roared.

Cadet Private Norlini looked around, but no one would meet his gaze. He swallowed hard then unbuckled his trousers and let them fall to his ankles.

"Turn and spread them wide, Norlini," Kim chuckled. "Give Cadet Private Vklogg an open shot. Don't make this harder than it has to be."

Cadet Private Norlini slowly turned around, bent over, and spread his ass cheeks. Cadet Private Vklogg hesitated slightly then walked to the man, grabbed him by his hips and lifted her foot.

"Master Sergeant Kim? Combat simulator is now open. Please escort the cadets into the simulator for combat training," a voice said from a speaker above the cadets.

"Well, looks like you have been saved by the voice above, Cadet Private Norlini," Kim laughed. "NOW GET YOUR FUCKING ASSES INTO THAT SIMULATOR BEFORE I SCORCH RAPE EVERY LAST ONE OF YOU!"

Two

"Man, he loves his job way too much," the tech said as he initiated the training protocol once the last cadet had entered the combat simulator. He turned from the digital images floating in the air in front of his station and looked at the tech to his right. "We sure he isn't a doubleganger?"

"Why do you ask that?" the other tech asked, his eyes locked onto the set of images that floated in front of his work station. He waved his hand across one set and brought up a second set then dismissed that set for a third. "Why the hell would you think Kim is a DG?"

"Because he talks about assholes all the time," the first tech replied. "And you know how DGs are."

"Please don't tell me you believe that bullshit about DGs breathing from their asses," the second tech sighed. "How did you get cleared for this job?"

"No, I don't believe that," the first tech huffed. "I've just heard that they like to, well, violate their enemies in the ass."

"You are such an idiot," the second tech said. "And you are about to be late starting the next sim. Linklater will fire you in a heartbeat if you slow down today's schedule."

"Shit," the first tech responded as he hurried to initiate the simulator training protocol hovering in front of him. "Now, *he's* the DG. No way a human being can be wound so tight as Linklater."

"And yet I am," a voice snapped from the hatchway of the combat simulator control room. "100% human. And you are 100% fired."

"Sir, I'm sorry, I didn't mean—," the first tech blubbered.

"You didn't mean to stay gainfully employed? Good, because you aren't anymore," growled Lead Tech Officer Lieutenant Michael Linklater. He pointed towards the hatch behind him. "Out. Now. Report for cadet training. You blew your chance of staying out of combat, son. Too bad."

The tech started to argue then just lowered his head, stood up, and slinked past Linklater. The second tech kept his eyes glued to his station.

"What is he running?" Linklater asked as he sat down in the fired tech's seat.

"Planetary assaults," the second tech replied crisply.

"Good," Linklater said as he started whipping his hands back and forth in the air. "I prefer those to onboard fights. I get claustrophobic."

"Understood, sir," the second tech replied.

Linklater leaned forward into the image and spoke loudly, "Master Sergeant, your simulation is ready. Cadets may proceed at your discretion."

"They'll be doing both if they ever land on Stavroff," Linklater said. "I even gave the sim a solid option. This thing can actually chew them up and spit them out."

"Why the fuck would you do that?" North asked. "Never mind. Just don't activate it, okay Link?"

"Whatever," Linklater.

"Thanks." North's eyes flitted from one scenario to another, finally resting on a fighter skiff simulation. "How's the new TO doing?"

"How the hell should I know how the new Training Officer is doing?" Linklater replied. "You're the one that should be evaluating that. I'm just the guy that makes dumb cadet pilots think they are actually flying. You'll have to ask Captain Valencio yourself."

"You know you're supposed to be a help to me, Link, not be an asshole," North grinned. "I am second in command on this station."

"Not in here you're not," Linklater replied. "Know what would be a help to me? You getting the fuck out of my control room and being second in command somewhere else. I'm a little busy. Maybe go check on Captain Valencio in person and ask her how she's doing."

"I might do that," North replied.

"Good. She's in simulation bay one-oh-eight," Linklater said. "By the time you walk there her sim will be done."

"If I ever get transferred, you're going to have a hell of a time dealing with a new Chief TO," North said as he pushed off from the wall and stepped to the hatch. "You're lucky I know how good you are at your job."

"You're lucky I'm good enough to make up for the slack from the rest of these dipshits," Linklater said.

"Way to keep up morale, Link," North said as he shook his head, looking at the roomful of insulted techs. "One day they'll mutiny on your ass."

"Then I'd be the lucky one and finally be done with this hell," Linklater said. "Now get the fuck out of here. I have work to do."

Three

The cadet ran full out across the open field towards a large mound of burnt soil only a few meters ahead of him. He glanced to his left and saw six of his comrades get vaporized before his eyes, their bodies turning inside out and then to nothing in a blink. The cadet almost screamed, but forced himself to remember that it was all just a simulation; that the interface chip embedded in his brain only made it look like his fellow cadets had died.

A bright green flash of light hit the dirt in front of him and he threw himself to the right as a six meter swathe of ground was turned into dust. He rolled a couple more meters then tried to get up, but was knocked down by the crush of cadets that were all heading for the same small patch of cover.

"What the fuck is wrong with you?" a master sergeant screamed in the cadet's face. "Are you taking a nap? Do you think you can fucking kill doublegangers while napping, is that it?"

"No, Master Sergeant!" the cadet yelled as he was yanked to his feet.

"Then get to running, you fucking worm!" the master sergeant shouted.

"Yes, Master Sergeant!" the cadet shouted.

He gripped his scorcher and ran as hard as he could to the mound of burnt soil. A few hundred of his other cadets joined him as he finally made it to cover, their bodies jostling for protection. One by one, two by two, three by three, they were picked off, vaporized until only a third of their ranks were left behind the mound.

"You stupid fucknuts!" the master sergeant yelled as he stomped up to the pinned down group. "Look at you all! You think you'll win this war by hiding? Well, guess fucking what? You will not!"

The master sergeant pulled a pistol from his hip and aimed it at the frightened group of cadets.

"This is not a sim weapon," the master sergeant said. "There are only live rounds in this pistol. If I do not see every single one of you rush from this mound of coward dirt and take that DG bunker, then I will personally send the stragglers to meet their Makers! Am I understood?"

The cadets stared at him until he thumbed the safety off and the pistol let out a high-pitched whine. Then all of the cadets turned and bolted from the mound, their scorchers up and firing wildly.

More than a few cadets fell to simulated friendly fire.

Four

"Buddha in a hammock eating tacos, these new recruits ar stupid," Linklater said as he watched them get annihilated in th simulation before him. "Six hundred dead and not a single Estelian hit. How the hell are we going to win anything when we have morons like this fighting for us?"

"It's what the Perpetuity is here for," Chief Training Officer Major Bartram North said as he stepped into the simulation control room. Deeply tanned with a sharp nose and angular cheekbones, North looked wiry and fast, which he was. "We turn morons into killers."

"The problem is they are killing each other and themselves," Linklater scoffed as he swiped away the simulation image and brought up two others. "Look at these numbers, North. See this one? Three thousand dead in less than ten minutes. And here? Two thousand dead in twenty minutes. At least these idiots here obtained their objective and took the bridge of the Estelian destroyer. But I'm pretty sure it was dumb luck."

"Most of war is dumb luck, Link," North replied. "The brass just like to take the credit."

"Yeah, but we get the blame," Linklater smirked. "Fuckers."

North leaned against the wall of the room, careful not to put his shoulder against anything important, and studied the dozens of techs as they ran multiple combat simulations.

"What are you working on now?" North asked.

"Finishing touches on the Stavroff simulation," Linklater said.

"Seriously?" North asked, pushing away from the wall.

"Completely," Linklater said. "I'm even putting the lake country in there. The cadets that make the mistake of getting close to that water are going to be shitting themselves."

"We almost didn't make it out of there," North said. "Do me a favor and don't activate the wiltcha, okay? I want them focused on killing DGs, not fighting off a six-legged lake monster."

Five

"North! Hey, North! Hold up!"

North took a few more steps down the corridor then sighed and slowed. He turned and forced a smile onto his face.

"Hey, Metzger. Need something?" North said as Sergeant-at-Arms Coop Metzger came running up to North.

Thick of neck and arms, Metzger wore an all black uniform with Training Station Perpetuity's symbol of Earth with interwoven rings of colony planets swirling about it, emblazoned on a patch over his heart. He had a slung scorcher on his back and a pistol on each hip with a smile almost as wide as the corridor.

"You are not easy to track down when you have your comm off," Metzger said. "You know the security protocols, North. You have to have your comm on at all times."

"Just taking a walk to bay one-oh-eight, Metzger," North said. "Clearing my head a bit before the next batch comes in."

"That's what I need to talk to you about," Metzger said. "The next batch is double what you told me and I don't have the security personnel available to handle fifty thousand dumb assholes. You need to split the induction into two batches."

"Double? That can't be right," North said. He pressed a small patch on the inside of his wrist until an image of a young woman appeared. "Corporal Ngyuen? Why is Metzger in my face telling me the new cadet numbers are double what we were told by recruiting?"

"I have been trying to call you, Major North," the young woman replied, her image flickering slightly as it hovered above North's wrist. "CSC gave recruiting permission to clear out the slums in Metro London and Metro Moscow. Two sweeps and the numbers were doubled. I just found out as the transports docked an hour ago."

"Where the hell are we going to put the extra twenty-five thousand cadets?" North asked. "The next class does not graduate until Thursday and we already have two to a bunk as it is."

"Yes, well, Commandant Terlinger says to make it three to a bunk for the new cadets and be prepared for—," Ngyuen replied. She looked off to the side and cleared her throat. "Yes, Commandant, I will tell him. Uh, Major North? The commandant would like to speak with you personally about the increased numbers. At your earliest convenience, of course."

"I was about to do a surprise inspection on Captain Valencio," North growled. "Let the commandant know I'll be there directly after."

"He says now would be your earliest convenience," Ngyuen stated. "His office in five minutes."

"Son of a..." North sighed and squeezed his eyes together for a second. "Fine. I'll be there in five. North out."

He pressed his wrist again then rubbed his skin with the tips of his fingers and the image of Ngyuen vanished.

"See?" Metzger said. "Double. What the hell do you want me to do about it? That many scared wimps in one place is going to be trouble."

"Nothing I can do," North said. "I can't grow new security guards for you. Do your job and figure it out, Metzger. Spread them out and make sure they are paying attention. The second a cadet panics or gets out of line then shove a stun baton up his or her ass and make an example of the pussy."

"You know I'm your pal, right North?" Metzger smiled. "I'm on your side. You don't have to bark at me all the time. I'm just trying to keep us all safe on Perpetuity."

"Metzger, none of us are safe," North sighed. "Not ever. If we were then we wouldn't need a training station like Perpetuity, now would we?"

North didn't wait for an answer from Metzger, just turned and stalked off towards the lift to the station's top level and Commandant Lawrence Terlinger's office.

Three

The cadet ran full out across the open field towards a large mound of burnt soil only a few meters ahead of him. He glanced to his left and saw six of his comrades get vaporized before his eyes, their bodies turning inside out and then to nothing in a blink. The cadet almost screamed, but forced himself to remember that it was all just a simulation; that the interface chip embedded in his brain only made it look like his fellow cadets had died.

A bright green flash of light hit the dirt in front of him and he threw himself to the right as a six meter swathe of ground was turned into dust. He rolled a couple more meters then tried to get up, but was knocked down by the crush of cadets that were all heading for the same small patch of cover.

"What the fuck is wrong with you?" a master sergeant screamed in the cadet's face. "Are you taking a nap? Do you think you can fucking kill doublegangers while napping, is that it?"

"No, Master Sergeant!" the cadet yelled as he was yanked to his feet.

"Then get to running, you fucking worm!" the master sergeant shouted.

"Yes, Master Sergeant!" the cadet shouted.

He gripped his scorcher and ran as hard as he could to the mound of burnt soil. A few hundred of his other cadets joined him as he finally made it to cover, their bodies jostling for protection. One by one, two by two, three by three, they were picked off, vaporized until only a third of their ranks were left behind the mound.

"You stupid fucknuts!" the master sergeant yelled as he stomped up to the pinned down group. "Look at you all! You think you'll win this war by hiding? Well, guess fucking what? You will not!"

The master sergeant pulled a pistol from his hip and aimed it at the frightened group of cadets.

"This is not a sim weapon," the master sergeant said. "There are only live rounds in this pistol. If I do not see every single one of you rush from this mound of coward dirt and take that DG bunker, then I will personally send the stragglers to meet their Makers! Am I understood?"

The cadets stared at him until he thumbed the safety off and the pistol let out a high-pitched whine. Then all of the cadets turned and bolted from the mound, their scorchers up and firing wildly.

More than a few cadets fell to simulated friendly fire.

Four

"Buddha in a hammock eating tacos, these new recruits are stupid," Linklater said as he watched them get annihilated in the simulation before him. "Six hundred dead and not a single Estelian hit. How the hell are we going to win anything when we have morons like this fighting for us?"

"It's what the Perpetuity is here for," Chief Training Officer Major Bartram North said as he stepped into the simulation control room. Deeply tanned with a sharp nose and angular cheekbones, North looked wiry and fast, which he was. "We turn morons into killers."

"The problem is they are killing each other and themselves," Linklater scoffed as he swiped away the simulation image and brought up two others. "Look at these numbers, North. See this one? Three thousand dead in less than ten minutes. And here? Two thousand dead in twenty minutes. At least these idiots here obtained their objective and took the bridge of the Estelian destroyer. But I'm pretty sure it was dumb luck."

"Most of war is dumb luck, Link," North replied. "The brass just like to take the credit."

"Yeah, but we get the blame," Linklater smirked. "Fuckers."

North leaned against the wall of the room, careful not to put his shoulder against anything important, and studied the dozens of techs as they ran multiple combat simulations.

"What are you working on now?" North asked.

"Finishing touches on the Stavroff simulation," Linklater said.

"Seriously?" North asked, pushing away from the wall.

"Completely," Linklater said. "I'm even putting the lake country in there. The cadets that make the mistake of getting close to that water are going to be shitting themselves."

"We almost didn't make it out of there," North said. "Do me a favor and don't activate the wiltcha, okay? I want them focused on killing DGs, not fighting off a six-legged lake monster."

"They'll be doing both if they ever land on Stavroff," Linklater said. "I even gave the sim a solid option. This thing can actually chew them up and spit them out."

"Why the fuck would you do that?" North asked. "Never mind. Just don't activate it, okay Link?"

"Whatever," Linklater.

"Thanks." North's eyes flitted from one scenario to another, finally resting on a fighter skiff simulation. "How's the new TO doing?"

"How the hell should I know how the new Training Officer is doing?" Linklater replied. "You're the one that should be evaluating that. I'm just the guy that makes dumb cadet pilots think they are actually flying. You'll have to ask Captain Valencio yourself."

"You know you're supposed to be a help to me, Link, not be an asshole," North grinned. "I am second in command on this station."

"Not in here you're not," Linklater replied. "Know what would be a help to me? You getting the fuck out of my control room and being second in command somewhere else. I'm a little busy. Maybe go check on Captain Valencio in person and ask her how she's doing."

"I might do that," North replied.

"Good. She's in simulation bay one-oh-eight," Linklater said. "By the time you walk there her sim will be done."

"If I ever get transferred, you're going to have a hell of a time dealing with a new Chief TO," North said as he pushed off from the wall and stepped to the hatch. "You're lucky I know how good you are at your job."

"You're lucky I'm good enough to make up for the slack from the rest of these dipshits," Linklater said.

"Way to keep up morale, Link," North said as he shook his head, looking at the roomful of insulted techs. "One day they'll mutiny on your ass."

"Then I'd be the lucky one and finally be done with this hell," Linklater said. "Now get the fuck out of here. I have work to do."

Six

"Sit down, North," Commandant Terlinger ordered as North stepped into the sparse office. "Take a load off."

"I don't have time to sit, sir," North replied, standing at attention. "I'm already behind on my simulation inspections and I'm about to speak in front of fifty thousand cadets instead of twenty-five thousand. I really should be down level working, sir."

"Sit your smug ass down, Bartram," Terlinger snapped. "And can the attitude. You aren't the only person that works his ass off on this station."

"Sir, with all due respect—," North started.

"Sit the fuck down," Terlinger growled, hooking his thumb over his shoulder at the wide window behind his desk. "That's an order or I'll toss you outside the station myself. Understood, Major?"

North hesitated then stepped to the single chair in front of Terlinger's desk and sat down.

"How can I help you, sir?" North asked, his back ramrod straight. "I live to serve."

"You are a piece of work, North," Terlinger sighed as he sat down in his own chair and swiped his hand across his desk, bringing up a schematic of the Perpetuity. "You are lucky you're the most efficient Chief TO we've had or I wouldn't be willing to put up with half your shit."

"Thank you for the honor, sir," North replied.

"Shut up," Terlinger said.

He was a heavyset man, in his late sixties with thinning white hair that he kept slicked back against his scalp. He licked his lips incessantly, making them bright red and almost as slick looking as his hair.

"Level eighteen has been used for extra storage, but we are now converting it into cadet quarters," Terlinger said as he pinched part of the station image with his fingers and enlarged it. "Most of the crap stored in there is old and outdated equipment, but we cannot afford to just toss it all out an airlock. With CSC quintupling recruitment, we'll need every old suit, scorcher, and pair of boots we have on hand."

"Quintupling?" North exclaimed. "What are you talking about, sir? I haven't heard a word about this."

"You are now, North," Terlinger said. "Sorry I didn't deliver the news on a lace doily."

"Sir, my TOs and drill instructors are stretched thin already," North protested. "There is no way they can handle five times the training load. There isn't even enough time in the day to do that."

"You'll figure it out," Terlinger replied. "I have faith in you. I have already informed CSC that you will double the numbers per training group and are cutting training time down from two weeks to one week."

"One week?" North shouted, jumping up from his chair. "Sir, most of these cadets are backwoods colonists! The most time they've spent in space is on the trip from their hick worlds to Perpetuity! Not to mention the ghetto kids and lowlifes the CSC is shipping in from Earth! They need at least two weeks just to get acclimated to life in space, let alone being trained not to blow their feet off with their scorchers!"

"There are twenty-four hours in a day, North," Terlinger said. "Use every single hour. Jam these men and women full of pharma and churn them through the sims. They don't have to be perfect little soldiers, North, just able to fire their scorchers at DGs and not at each other."

"I can't guarantee that last part, sir," North said. "Pharmaed-up cadets don't learn nearly as well as straight ones."

"You aren't teaching ancient history, Bartram," Terlinger snapped. "They don't need to learn shit except how to fire and run in a straight line."

"Sir, do we even have enough pharma on board?" North asked, his left eye twitching slightly.

Terlinger watched him for a second then looked towards the hatchway of his office. "Ngyuen!"

"Yes, Commandant?" a voice called out from the reception room.

"Did you check in the new shipments of pharma CSC sent us?" Terlinger asked.

'Personally, sir," Ngyuen replied.

"See," Terlinger said to North. "Thank you, Ngyuen!"

"My pleasure, sir," Ngyuen called back.

Terlinger swiped the image of the station from his desk and then brought up a swirling mass of stars. He pinched in again and again until he zoomed into the image of a cluster of planets orbiting a blazing blue star.

"Show battle lines," Terlinger said and a set of bright yellow and bright blue lines appeared, splitting the star system in half. "Do you see those lines, North?"

"Yes, sir," North nodded. "That's Quel System, yes?"

"It was," Terlinger said then grabbed the yellow lines and yanked them from the image. "It's all Estelian territory now, so who knows what those abominations are calling it now."

"Sir, that's only five systems from us," North said. "When did this happen?"

"Three days ago," Terlinger said. "CSC is sending in a counter offensive to retake the system, but they are not optimistic. That's why we need more troops, North. We are losing the ship battles, but we excel at the ground campaigns. They can fly around in their cruisers and destroyers all they want, but we are now going to carpet bomb each of their planets with green cadets and kill every last Estelian we come across."

"Sir, but if their ships get past Boone System, then they are only one punch away from our solar system," North replied. "It doesn't matter how many of our outer planets we retake or how many of their planets we invade. If we lose Earth, then the war is over."

"Now you see why we need to crank out cadets," Terlinger said. "We have to not just to swarm the other systems, but keep the Estelians from swarming our home planet. If CSC has its way, they'll turn every man, woman, and child on Earth into killers. I would like to avoid that. Let's churn out some cadets and get them out to the other systems. The idea is the Estelians will back off from their course to Earth when they see they are losing everything they leave behind."

"What if they don't care?" North asked.

"Well, major, then Perpetuity will be the new front in this war," Terlinger frowned. "We stop being a training station and become a command base. I'd prefer if that doesn't happen."

North rubbed his face and gave the commandant a weak smile. "That, sir, I can agree with 100 percent."

Terlinger eyed North carefully. "You look like you could use some pharma yourself, North. Make sure you are up to the task I'm giving."

"I will, sir," North said.

"But do not take it too far," Terlinger said. "I am well aware of your file, North. Let's not have another Mendel situation, alright?"

"I have it all under control, sir," North said.

"Good," Terlinger smiled then waved at his office hatchway. "Dismissed."

Seven

"Bank left, Cadet Pilot Mnuki," Fighter Skiff Training Officer Captain Deena Valencio ordered. "Reduce thrusters to half and then turn a sharp right. Once you have their squadron in sight, then hit thrusters and take the fight to them."

Valencio sat in the seat directly behind Cadet Pilot Mnuki, her eyes watching the young man struggle with his orientation and control of the fighter skiff. It wasn't a large vehicle, only about thirty feet long by fifteen feet wide, with two plasma cannons mounted to each short wing and a battery of missiles locked into the undercarriage. But the cadet pilot was having a difficult time keeping the fighter skiff aimed in the correct direction.

"Cadet Pilot Mnuki, are you listening to me?" Valencio snapped, her voice harsh and raspy over the comm system. "Bank left! LEFT!"

The fighter skiff careened through open space, banking right then diving sharply, headed straight for the squadron of other CSC fighter skiffs flying directly below it.

"Mnuki! Pull up! PULL UP!" Valencio yelled. When the young man didn't respond in time, she switched control of the fighter skiff to herself and yanked hard on the flight stick in front of her.

The fighter skiff pulled up fast, but it was too late. The tail end of the skiff smacked into one of the other fighters, causing it to lose control and crash into the rest of the squadron. The screams of dying pilots echoed over the comm system as one by one the fighter skiffs erupted into silent explosions.

"You stupid fuck," Valencio snapped. "Did you hear a word I even said?"

All sensation of movement in the fighter skiff came to an abrupt halt and the bloody scene that surrounded them blinked out, replaced by the sterile walls of the massive fighter training simulator.

"Hey!" Valencio shouted as she shoved open the cockpit hatch and pulled herself out of the skiff. "I didn't say to end the sim! I still have forty-nine cadet pilots running scenarios!"

She jumped down from the skiff and looked at the other mock fighter skiffs that sat on the simulator bay's floor. One by one, cockpit hatches started to open and cadet pilots began to pull themselves out and look around.

"Did I say to get out of your seats, you morons?" Valencio barked. "Sit your asses back down and prep for the next sim!"

"There's no next sim," North announced from the hatchway as he stepped into the simulation bay. "I need this bay cleared so Linklater can refit it for ground troops."

"For what? Ground troops? Where the hell am I supposed to run simulations?" Valencio barked as she stalked over to North.

A woman of average height, weight, and musculature, Deena Valencio turned heads because of her shock white hair and bright pink eyes. A true albino, Valencio gravitated to the comforting darkness of space at an early age, honing her skills in cargo skiffs and transports until she was of age to join the CSC fighter corps.

Her pink eyes glared daggers at North.

"Why the hell do you need another sim bay for ground troops?" she snapped as she yanked off her helmet and tossed it at North's feet, causing the man to jump a couple feet back.

"New focus from CSC," North said, bending over to pick up the helmet. He offered it to Valencio, but she swatted it away, sending it flying against the closest simulator skiff. "Okay. Don't take it. It's not my call, Captain. I'm just doing what's needed to get the Perpetuity ready for the influx of recruits that's about to overrun us."

"I could give three shits about your influx," Valencio growled. "I have cadet pilots to train. You do know that we are fighting a space war, not just a ground war, right? Can't really fight a space war without fighter skiffs! And fighter skiffs don't fly themselves, North!"

"Come here," North snapped and grabbed Valencio by the arm.

He pulled her away from the prying eyes of the fresh cadets, through the simulation bay's anti-chamber, and out into the bright lights of the corridor. Valencio squinted her sensitive eyes then removed a pair of glasses from her uniform's chest pocket and put them on. As soon as they were on her nose, the lenses darkened and blocked out the harsh corridor lights.

"Take those off," North ordered. "I want to see your eyes when I'm talking to you." He pressed his wrist. "Corridor ninety-three, dim to half light."

The lights above dimmed on command, but Valencio did not remove her glasses.

"I'll smack them off your face," North warned.

Petulantly, Valencio yanked the glasses from her face and began to twirl them in her fingers by one of the stems.

"You're new here, Captain," North said as he glared down at the woman. "It takes some time to get used to how things run, I get that. But this is still CSC, Valencio, so what shouldn't take time to get used to is the chain of command. It goes from CSC to Commandant Terlinger to me. If I tell you to do something then you do it. It is not that hard. Did the commandant give you contrary orders to mine?"

"No, sir, he did not," Valencio grumbled.

"Then we shouldn't have a problem," North said. "I want those cadet pilots out of that bay this second so Linklater can get his techs in there and dismantle those simulation skiffs. I have neither the time nor inclination to get into a pissing match with you, Captain. So either comply or quit. Those are your options."

"Where am I going to train my cadets?" Valencio asked, her face nothing but cold stone.

"Outside," North said. "In actual skiffs, in actual space, in actual reality."

"You've lost your fucking mind," Valencio gasped, pointing at the simulation bay. "Did you see what I'm dealing with? All it took was one moron to choke and an entire squadron was wiped out."

"A sim squadron," North said. "With sim psychology. Get those cadet pilots out into real space and I bet their concentration will increase considerably."

"No way. Not going to happen," Valencio said, shaking her head back and forth. "You might as well just call their mothers and give them the bad news, because these cadet pilots will be dead before supper."

"I have aptitude scores right here," North said as he brought up an image of a testing roster over his wrist. "I believe you have the same information. Figure out who is best suited to pilot and who should be copilots. Pair them up and get them in the vacuum. Take them out as far as possible so the screw ups can't crash into Perpetuity. Once you're a safe distance then put them through the paces."

North wiped the roster away and crossed his arms. He leaned in close to Valencio and grinned a mirthless grin.

"Do your fucking job, Captain," he hissed. "Or you'll be back in the shit with the other burnt out fighter jocks. Is that what you want? Back in the battle where every second that ticks off is just another second closer to dying? I can easily arrange that."

"Do you know what I sacrificed to get here?" Valencio snarled.

"Do you know how much I don't give a fuck?" North replied. "Do your job or get the fuck off my station."

North turned and stomped off then hesitated and pressed his wrist.

"Corridor lights to full," he said then looked over his shoulder at Valencio and winked.

She quickly put her glasses on, took several deep breaths, and restrained herself from sprinting at North's receding back and tackling the man to the floor. After a couple of seconds, she got herself under control then turned and marched into the simulation bay.

"Clear out, you pieces of shit! Sim time is over! Time to pop your space cherries, you little cunts!"

Eight

"Keep it moving, recruits!" Metzger shouted as the new arrivals poured through the transport airlocks and into Training Station Perpetuity's recruit holding bay. "Do not slow down! Do not stop! Follow the colored lines above your heads! If you are in the wrong line then move your ass into the correct line! You do not want me to move you myself!"

There were thousands of faces, from all walks of life, that looked about the station as they jostled for room in a space designed to hold a fraction of their number. From the barely legal to the barely ambulatory, the recruits kept moving, urged on by Metzger's shouts and his security guards' constant prodding and herding.

"Invalid chip detected. Invalid chip detected," a computerized voice rang out from the loudspeakers far above the crowd of recruits. "Invalid chip detected. Invalid chip detected."

A bright red beam of light shot down from the ceiling and focused on a short man in his mid-twenties. At first he didn't notice then as the crowd moved away from him he looked up and squinted into the light.

"What? No! I'm a citizen, vetted and true!" the short man shouted. "I ain't no doubleganger!"

"YOU!" Metzger roared. "MOVE FROM THE CROWD AND GET YOUR ASS AGAINST THE WALL!"

"I ain't no DG!" the short man yelled. "My chip is just fine! I'm from Loab! Loab is legit!"

"I don't fucking care!" Metzger shouted as he and two of his guards shoved people out of the way to get to the man. Metzger had his scorcher to his shoulder and the laser sight put a bright red bead directly between the short man's eyes. "Comply or die, fuckface!"

The short man threw his hands in the air and started to hurry from the crowd towards the far wall. As soon as he was clear of most of the bodies, two more guards grabbed him and nearly dragged him to the wall, throwing him roughly up against the dinged and pitted metal.

"Hold the fuck still," Metzger growled as he got to the short man and spun him around. He pulled a small scanner from his belt and pressed it to the nape of the short man's neck. "Recite the Earth pledge!"

"Do what?" the short man asked and received a punch to his gut for the trouble. "Okay, okay! For Earth we live, for Earth we fight. Earth is our home, Earth is our light!"

The short man continued through the eight additional verses of the pledge while Metzger watched the readings on the scanner. After a few seconds, the scanner beeped and a light turned green on the side.

"He's clean," Metzger said and shoved the man away from the wall and over to his guards. "Get him back in line and everyone back to their posts!"

The short man didn't protest, even as he was manhandled by the guards and thrown into the crush of bodies still pouring from the airlock. Metzger watched the throng of recruits swallow him up then turned his attention to the ceiling.

"Invalid chip," the computerized voice announced again. "Invalid chip.

"Son of a cocksucker," Metzger growled then activated his comm as his men hunted down the new anomaly. "Linklater? You there?"

"Busy," Linklater replied over the comm. "Call back later."

"No can do," Metzger said. "I am having a bitch of a time with the chip verification protocol in the main transport airlock. It's given me eight false readings in the last ten minutes. I can't do my job if I have to do this damned computer's job too!"

"Hold on," Linklater responded. "Let me see what's up."

A couple seconds went by.

"Linklater, you still there?" Metzger asked.

"I said to hold on!" Linklater snapped. Another two seconds. "Well, fuck, Metzger. The problem is you're overloading the system! Who the hell authorized that many recruits to come aboard at once? No wonder you're getting false readings. You'd be getting false readings if those numbers were half what they are."

"Well, fix it," Metzger said.

"Are you not listening?" Linklater asked. "The problem isn't the system or the computer, it's the numbers. There's nothing to fix because there's nothing broken. You're just pushing through too many recruits."

"No choice," Metzger said. "Terlinger wants all of these idiots processed and lined up within the hour. We have an even bigger batch coming this afternoon. I couldn't slow things down if I wanted to."

"Then you are fucked and on your own," Linklater said. "So let me get back to the work I need to do and don't call me again."

Metzger swore under his breath then moved into the crowd and started shoving people along.

"Move it!" he yelled. "Do not stop! Do not look around! Just move!"

Nine

Commandant Terlinger stood on the catwalk and looked out at the thousands of confused and scared faces. He gripped the metal railing, squeezing and releasing, squeezing and releasing, over and over as the last few recruits were marched into the huge space below.

"Where is he?" Terlinger asked out of the corner of his mouth. "I want to get this going and I can't start without him."

"He's on his way," Corporal Ngyuen said, her finger to her ear. "He's one corridor away, sir."

"He shouldn't be any corridors away," Terlinger grumbled. "He knew what time I wanted to start and he knows we don't have a second to spare anymore."

"Right here, sir," North said as he sprinted through a hatchway and onto the catwalk, his boots pounding on the metal grate, making the structure shake slightly.

Terlinger gripped the metal railing with all his might as the catwalk shook from North's footfalls.

"Stand at attention, Major," Terlinger snapped. "Show these people the discipline expected on TS Perpetuity."

"Yes, sir," North said as he stopped next to the commandant, turned on his heel, and shot his back straight. He looked down at the massive crowd below. "ATTENTION CADETS! EYES FRONT, EYES UP!"

The crowd quieted and the majority of faces looked up at the major and the commandant. But many faces were still looking around the huge space, studying the walls of the station, the stacked crates of gear, the personnel that were running about performing their duties.

"Sergeant-at-Arms Metzger!" North yelled.

"Yes, sir!" Metzger called from below.

"Please have your men isolate those that did not obey my command!" North shouted.

"Yes, sir!" Metzger replied. He started pointing at the recruits that were looking this way and that, everywhere but up where they should have been.

There were loud protests from those that were singled out and pulled from the crowd and over to a row of stacked crates marked "RIMeals." Once all were separated, Metzger nodded to his men and they all pulled stun batons from their belts and jammed the ends into the backs of the recruits. The men and women screamed at first, but then the sounds stopped as thousands of volts coursed through their bodies, freezing the cries in their throats.

"Thank you, Sergeant-at-Arms Metzger!" North shouted. "Return the recruits to their places!"

"Move!" Metzger yelled at the barely conscious men and women that leaned against the crates. "I said move!"

The stunned recruits shuffled and stumbled their way back into the quiet crowd. People stepped aside, almost afraid to touch the wobbly recruits for fear of becoming pariahs themselves.

"Now, EYES FRONT, EYES UP!" North yelled then took two steps back as the commandant cleared his throat.

"Thank you, Major North," Terlinger said. "Welcome, new cadets. I am Commandant Terlinger and I am in charge of Training Station Perpetuity. The man directly behind me is Chief Training Officer Major North. I run this station and he runs you. Do not have any illusions that you retain any free will from your former lives. As far as Central Space Command is concerned, I own you, which means Major North owns you as well. You will each have one week to train and ready yourselves for battle with the abominable Estelians. In that week, you will be expected to learn all facets of ground combat, as well as protocols of space travel on board the CSC cruisers, destroyers, and battleships. Your days of riding public transports are over. You are now the property of the CSC and you will be so until you either die or this war is over. If there are any questions, please direct them to your master sergeant who will in turn take those questions and shove them down your throats. Good luck and Godspeed."

"Well said, sir," North whispered.

"I know," Terlinger said. "Be on time for the afternoon batch, North. If I have to ask Ngyuen where you are again then expect to be on the next cruiser to the front lines."

"Understood, sir," North said. "My apologies, sir."

"Shut up," Terlinger said as he walked away, Corporal Ngyuen right on his heels.

North waited for the commandant to leave then turned and looked down at the new cadets.

"You are being split into twenty groups!" North shouted. "Your group number should appear on your wrist! Look for the hatch with the corresponding number! Go through that hatch! Your master sergeant will be waiting to kick you cocks and twats into fighting machines! DISMISSED!"

Ten

"Son of a…"

"You stupid…"

"Damn whore-faced…"

"Oh for fuck's sake!" Linklater shouted as the simulation controls in front of him flickered then blinked out. "Dornan! What the hell did you do?"

"I didn't do a damned thing," Corporal Dornan replied as he watched one of his sim controls blink out as well. "We just have too many cadets in the sims, Link. We need to quadruple the memory for each bay and then reinforce each scenario. The programs are using old protocols and shutting down when the max numbers of casualties are reached."

"Who the hell let that happen?" Linklater barked. "Didn't I say to up the thresholds?"

"No," Dornan replied. "At least not to us."

Linklater looked about the control room at a dozen nodding heads.

"Like you'd say otherwise," Linklater grumbled. "Damned cowards. Someone take my spot while I go adjust the servers. I can't trust one of you fucks to do it right. Get the controls back up and just keep rebooting until I can increase the numbers."

"Aye aye," Dornan said.

"Fucking smart ass," Linklater snapped as he stood up and hurried from the control room.

He rushed down the corridor, dodging station personnel left and right, until he came to a hatch with "Server Tower" stenciled on it. Linklater pressed his wrist to the panel by the hatch. It opened instantly and he stepped into a small, circular space barely as wide as his shoulders.

"Sim bay servers," he ordered. "Now."

The floor lurched slightly then shot upward, propelling Linklater past bank after bank of blinking servers that filled the walls of the tower. The floor gave another lurch and Linklater braced himself as the lift slowed then stopped.

Linklater barely gave the work a thought as he pulled a small power driver from his belt and popped open the faceplates of the servers that surrounded him. He systematically went from one to the other, adjusting the processing capacity of each, until he knew they could handle the increased cadet load required of each simulation.

"Return," Linklater said once he'd locked the last server faceplate back in place. "Now."

The lift rocketed back down and Linklater had to swallow hard to keep his gorge from rising in his throat. He started to close his eyes against the vertigo the lift always brought on, but a shower of sparks got his attention and all thoughts of nausea left him instantly.

"Stop!" he shouted. "Now!"

The lift slowed then stopped.

"Up. Six levels," he ordered.

The lift obeyed and Linklater found himself staring at an entire server bank that was crushed so badly it would have taken an expert to recognize the technology as anything but scrap.

"What the holy fuck?" Linklater asked then activated his comm. "Dornan? Who do we trust the most in maintenance?"

"Wendt, of course," Dornan replied. "Damn fine maintenance chief, if he does say so himself. Why? Roaches get into the servers again?"

"If so then they are big fucking roaches," Linklater said. "Call him for me and have him ladder it to level three-fifty."

"Ladder it? You're still in the tower?" Dornan asked.

"You are such a fucking genius," Linklater replied. "Yes, I'm still in the tower and I just found a serious problem! Call Wendt and tell him to get his ass here now! I'm going to need an extra pair of hands for this shit!"

"On it," Dornan replied.

The servers sparked and sputtered, causing Linklater to jump back. The servers directly behind him sparked as well and he spun about, stunned by the severity of the damage. He pressed his wrist and brought up the schematics for the entire server tower.

"Okay, let's figure out what you do and see if we can reroute your systems before something important stops working."

Eleven

The cadets struggled with the heavy cannon, barely getting it upright in time before the wave of Estelian troops crested the opposite hill. Master Sergeant Sherfi Walla started screaming at the top of her lungs at the cadets as they continued to struggle with the massive weapon. The more she screamed, the more the cadets faltered, forcing her to shove several out of the way and take over.

"Secure the braces here and here!" she yelled. "Just like in the training vids! Then adjust the trajectory here, pull back the locking mechanism, and fire!"

"We didn't see the training vids on artillery," one of the cadets replied. "They only showed us the vids on scorchers and pistols."

"Did I ask for your lame excuses, Cadet Private Loser?" Walla screamed.

"It's Kline," the cadet replied. "Heather Kli—"

"I do not fucking care!" Walla yelled. "Braces here and here! Locking mechanism here! Fire!"

The cadets all looked from the cannon to her and back to the cannon.

"I FUCKING SAID TO FIRE!" she roared.

The cadets jumped into motion, secured the braces, pulled back the locking mechanism and fired.

Several blasts of concentrated energy shot from the cannon's barrel and flew across the landscape towards the oncoming Estelian troops. Half the first row of Estelians were shredded instantly, skin, bone and blood flying in all directions from the energy bursts.

"Holy shit," a cadet muttered.

"Fire again!" Walla yelled. "Do not stop firing until I fucking say so!"

The cadets pulled back the locking mechanism once more and fired the cannon, sending yet another wave of energy bursts towards the Estelians. They continued their assault until Walla held up her hand.

"There we go! That's how you kill some DGs!" Walla yelled. "Now break it down and hump it over to that ridge! We don't stop until we hit our objective!"

"What is our objective, Master Sergeant?" a cadet asked.

"To keep killing DGs until they kill us!" Walla shouted. "Is there any other objective you need, Cadet Private Fucknuts?"

"No, Master Sergeant!" the cadet replied.

"Good, then get to humping that cannon, you worthless piece of shit!" Walla yelled as she kicked the young man in his ass. "Or this boot goes all the way up there!"

Twelve

"Major North!" Captain Valencio called as she ran down the corridor. "Major North, I need to speak with you right now!"

North stopped and looked over his shoulder. He tapped at the tablet he held, placed his thumb against the screen then handed the tablet to the corporal waiting at his side.

"Use the print to sign the rest," North said. "Leave the tablet in my office, but send copies to my personal server. If I don't make it back to my desk today, I'll review them from my wrist as I go."

"Yes, sir," the corporal said, glanced at the oncoming Valencio, then saluted and hurried down the corridor away from the obvious confrontation.

"Major, you are a hard person to track down," Valencio said.

"You shouldn't be tracking me down, Captain," North sighed. "You should be getting your cadet pilots ready for real space. Is there a reason you aren't flying right now?"

"The flight deck was not prepared for the order, sir," Valencio said. "And I have to say, again, that neither are these cadet pilots. Half these kids can barely walk a straight line. If I take them out into the vacuum then more than likely I will not be bringing all of them back."

"This is war, Captain," North said. "Most of them won't last five seconds after their first launch from a carrier. Better to get the slackers out of the way now."

"Sir, you are intentionally sending innocents to their deaths," Valencio said. "In combat, that is expected, but in training? That's just murder."

"Only if you let them die," North said.

"Sir! I cannot—"

"Listen, Deena. It is Deena, right?" North asked.

"Yes, sir," Valencio nodded.

"Deena, you came highly recommended. I've told you that before," North said. "I brought you on to the Perpetuity because I needed a fighter skiff trainer that could handle it all for me. I can fly a skiff, but I'm ground combat. That's what I have the most experience in, which is why Commandant Terlinger brought me on. I didn't think it mattered before, but now that we are quintupling the number of recruits and halving the training time, it really fucking matters."

"Quintupling, sir?" Valencio asked.

"Yeah, quintupling," North replied. "I have thousands upon thousands of combat virgins about to step foot onto this station and I have to concentrate on them. What I need you to do is concentrate on your cadet pilots. As of this second, I am giving you full reign out there. Take every cadet pilot you can and get them into the vacuum. If you are afraid they are going to crash into each other then take them way out like I suggested before. Give them room to learn. As much as you need. Fly to fucking Mars, for all I care. Understood?"

"Free reign? Seriously?" Valencio asked. "What will the commandant say?"

"He doesn't care," North replied. "The CSC's focus is ground troops. That's what he cares about. It's my job to keep Terlinger happy and it's your job to keep me happy. The cadet pilots are all yours. Do with them as you wish. Just keep them out of my hair and let me focus on the ground troops. Got it?"

"Got it, sir," Valencio said. "You will not hear from me again, sir, I promise."

"Except for your nightly report," North said. "Don't fall behind on your reports. The CSC lives for reports."

"Yes, sir," Valencio nodded. "Thank you, sir."

"You are welcome, Captain," North smiled. "And sorry for ripping you a new asshole earlier. Hopefully your new autonomy will make up for the new anatomy. Now, if you will excuse me, I have the afternoon batch of recruits to scream at before I make the rounds with the master sergeants."

"Yes, sir," Valencio said and saluted.

North returned the salute then turned and walked off quickly, leaving Valencio to stand there in the corridor as station personnel hurried by her. After a couple of seconds, she shook her head and pressed her wrist.

"Warrant Officer Zenobia," she said.

"Paging Warrant Officer Zenobia," a computerized voice replied.

After a second, the image of a sleepy young woman came up on Valencio's wrist.

"Captain? What's up?" Warrant Officer Dusty Zenobia asked. Short, muscular, with almost pure red skin and close-cropped blonde hair, Zenobia looked just like her nickname of "Demon." She rubbed at her eyes and then adjusted her tank top, rolling her head on her neck. "I was grabbing some Z's before my next shift."

"Nap time is over, Demon," Valencio grinned. "We are hitting the vacuum."

"What? Why?" Zenobia asked. The flickering image showed her standing up and stretching as she turned and kicked her bunk, sending it folding back into the wall of her quarters. "The cadets aren't ready yet."

"North kicked us out of the sims," Valencio said. "Gave me full reign to take the skiffs out into the vacuum for live training. The flight deck has them up and running."

Zenobia scratched at her ass then pulled a wedgie out of her crack. "Well, that's cool. We leaving now?"

"Yeah, so get your pants on and meet me on the flight deck," Valencio said. "I'm getting Richtoff and London together for this too."

"London? Why him? He's support, not combat," Zenobia said. "Where the fuck are my pants?"

"Right behind you," Valencio said. "Get some pharma and wake up, okay? I need you alert for this."

"Roger that," Zenobia said, grabbing her pants and throwing them over her shoulder. "Don't need pharma, though. Just need to take a shit then I'll be ready to fuck."

"Just be ready to fly," Valencio laughed.

"Same thing where I come from," Zenobia smiled. "See ya in five."

"Five? You shit fast," Valencio said.

"I fuck fast too," Zenobia replied then waved her hand.

The image flicked out and Valencio started moving again, her new authority energizing her. She dodged the oncoming station personnel and pressed her wrist again.

"Get me Warrant Officer Richtoff," she said.

"Paging Warrant Officer Richtoff," the computerized voice replied.

Thirteen

The chime rang on Maintenance Chief First Sergeant Hal Wendt's wrist for the tenth time, but he ignored it once again, keeping his focus on his current task.

"You…had…better…get that," Corporal Niecey Coor gasped as she ran her fingers through Wendt's hair, his face buried between her legs. "Ten…times…means trouble."

"You really want me to stop?" Wendt asked as he pulled his mouth from Coor's crotch and looked up at the naked and flushed woman he had on his workbench. "I can stop if you want."

"Shut up," Coor's said as she shoved Wendt's head back between her legs. "Just give me five more seconds."

"That's what I thought," Wendt replied, his voice muffled.

Coor arched her back as Wendt returned to task. Her mouth opened wide in a silent cry as her fingers went from stroking Wendt's hair to tugging on it then outright pulling. She shuddered over and over then collapsed forward, wrapping her arms around Wendt's shoulders as a massive orgasm took all muscle control from her body.

"Holy shit," she gasped. "Holy shit, holy shit, holy shit. God, I needed that."

Wendt gently pushed back and stood up, licking his lips.

"Sorry it's been a while, baby," he said. "This station keeps falling apart which means I keep working double shifts."

"As long as we get to do this once a week, I'm good," Coor said as she leaned back on the bench, shoving various parts and equipment out of the way, and spread her legs wide. "Your turn."

"Damn right," Wendt grinned as he unbuckled his pants.

There was a loud knock at the locked hatch only a couple feet from the workbench. Wendt stopped unbuckling and looked at the naked woman right in front of him.

"Shit," he said. "Maybe I should have answered those calls."

"Hand me my clothes!" Coor snapped as she jumped down from the workbench. "Goddamn it, Hal! Get me my clothes!"

"Here, here!" Wendt said as he crouched and picked up Coor's underwear, pants, and shirt. He tossed her the shirt then held out the underwear. "Step in."

The loud knocking turned into hard fist pounding.

"Hold on!" Wendt yelled. "Come on, come on. Step in!"

Coor clumsily stepped into her underwear while she tried to get her shirt on over her head.

"Where's my bra?" she snapped.

The fist pounding got even louder.

"No time for your bra," Wendt said as he yanked Coor's underwear up her legs then bent and picked up her pants. "Get into these."

Coor shimmied into her pants then shoved Wendt away as she buckled her belt and started to search for her lost bra. "It was just right here. Where the fuck is it?"

"Wendt! What the hell?" a voice called through the hatch. "Open the hell up! Linklater needs you!"

"Oh, shit," Wendt said. "It must be bad if that asshole wants me." He looked at Coor. "You ready?"

"No! I can't find my fucking bra!" Coor snapped.

"Forget the damned bra!" Wendt replied as he reached out and unlocked the hatch then pulled it open. "Oh, hey there, Jeff. My comm must be out. I'll have a look at it right away. So…what's Linklater need?"

Corporal Jeff Diego glanced past Wendt to Coor then back to Wendt. His eyes glanced down then quickly away.

"Yeah, your comm isn't the only thing that's out," Diego said. "Zip it up, Sergeant. You outranking me doesn't mean I have to look at your cock."

Wendt glanced down and saw his pants were unzipped and he was at full attention.

"Fuck," Wendt said as he tucked himself back in and zipped up. "Shit. Don't say a word of this, okay?"

"I want that bottle of scotch you've got tucked away," Diego said then smiled at Coor. "Hey, Niecey. Didn't you get knocked back down to corporal because of something like this last Christmas? Damn, I'd hate to see you get reduced to private or even booted from Perpetuity all together."

"What do you want, Jeff?" Coor growled.

"I'll take that bra that's hanging from that hook there," Diego smirked. "Nice bottle of scotch and your bra should keep me happy on those cold, lonely nights."

"You're a fucking perv, Jeff," Coor said as she turned, yanked the missing bra from the hook over the workbench, and tossed it to Diego. "You tell anyone where you got that and your jerking off days are over, got me? I will slice your dick off."

"I know you will," Diego grinned, catching the bra and stuffing it into his pocket. He focused back on Wendt. "Dornan said you're to meet Linklater up on three-fifty in the server tower. You're supposed to ladder it up since Linklater is on the lift."

"Ladder it up to three-fifty? Fuck that," Wendt said.

Diego shrugged. "I'm just relaying the message." He patted his pocket and smiled at Coor. "Thanks for the gift, Niecey. I'll be thinking of you tonight." He reached out and lightly tapped Wendt on the cheek. "Have that scotch to me as soon as you're done with Linklater. I'm off shift tonight and I need to get tight and cut loose."

"Just use pharma like everyone else," Coor said.

"Nah, the new batch feels weird," Diego said. "Gave me the willies this morning. I almost ripped Barker's head off for taking a drink of my milk. I'd rather have the scotch."

"You'll have it. Now fuck off," Wendt said and closed the hatch in Diego's face. He sighed then turned around and looked at Coor. "Linklater's already pissed. Want to let me have my turn?"

"I don't think so," Coor said as she shoved Wendt out of the way and pulled the hatch back open. "Looks like Jeff isn't the only one that'll be jerking off tonight."

"Ah, come on, Niecey!" Wendt called after Coor as the woman hurried down the corridor and away from Wendt's workshop. "My nuts feel like lead! Niecey? Niecey! Shit!"

Fourteen

The injector clattered into the sink and North took a deep breath as the pharma worked its way through his nervous system. North stared at himself in the mirror and watched as his pupils dilated to almost full. He counted to fifty, and when his pupils didn't contract, he picked up the second injector by the sink, pressed it to the median nerve in his left forearm and pulled the trigger. The second dose of pharma was designed to smooth the edges of the first dose and he instantly felt his whole body start to relax.

Another glance in the mirror showed him almost normal pupils. Almost.

"Close enough for government work," he muttered as he tossed the injectors into the incinerator port in the wall. There was a flash and a whump. "Time to get back to it."

His wrist chimed and he pressed at it, surprised to see Linklater appear. More surprised by where he was.

"You're looking a little intimate with those servers, Link," North said. "What the hell are you doing?"

"I wish I knew," Linklater replied. "I'm waiting on Wendt to get here and help me with this shit. He knows the server tower better than I do."

"Then why are you messing with them?" North asked.

"Because the sim maxes needed to be upped," Linklater said. "Which I did just before finding this cluster fuck."

"What do those servers do?" North asked.

"Fucking HR, I think," Linklater replied. "Recruitment files for all of the cadets. With the volume we're bringing in, Terlinger is going to shit himself if the intake process collapses. I'm surprised it hasn't already."

"That's because we're bypassing the intake," North said. "No time. Metzger's guys are manually scanning the cadets whenever there's a glitch. So far all chips have passed muster."

"Yeah, I know. Metzger and I already had words," Linklater said. "Good thing I'm here to get it all back online because I told him it wasn't a computer issue, but just a volume issue."

"Why are you there anyway? I need you in the sim control room," North said. "Get some other tech to handle the work."

"Yeah, right," Linklater laughed. "What do you think is going to happen if Terlinger knows I found an entire bank of servers crushed and handed it off to a maintenance chief?"

"If it all goes right then he'll do nothing," North said. "If anything goes wrong then he'll toss you into the vacuum."

"Exactly," Linklater said. "So I'm staying. You can order me to go, but this is recruit intake, North. And recruit intake is Terlinger's current obsession, right?"

"Keep up the good work," North said. "Is that what you called about?"

"What?" Linklater asked.

"You called me, Link," North said.

"Oh, right, yeah, I forgot," Linklater said. "I was just calling to say I won't be in the evening briefing. Obviously."

"Gotcha. Not a problem," North replied. "If that's all then— wait? Did you say the servers were crushed?"

"Yep," Linklater said. "Looks like someone took a wrench to them. I'm guessing one of the maintenance crew decided to take his or her frustrations out in the server tower. Normally, intake servers would be pretty benign. Today, they are not."

"No, today they are not," North said. "I may send Metzger up to have a look after I scream at the afternoon batch of recruits. Which I'm late for! Fuck!"

"Metzger? I don't want that gorilla up—," Linklater started, but North cut off the transmission before he could finish.

"Fuck," North said as he rushed from his quarters and started sprinting towards the main recruit holding bay.

FiFteen

One hundred fighter skiffs flew from the Perpetuity's flight deck, followed by a bulky cargo skiff that was soon trailing far behind the much faster and more maneuverable vehicles ahead of it.

"Try to keep up, London!" Zenobia shouted as she flew her skiff around the fighters being piloted by cadets. "We'll be done with training before you even get to us at that speed!"

"Can it, Demon," Warrant Officer James London replied over the comm. "You just fly like a pharmaed-up weasel and I'll keep things slow and steady. I'll be there to refuel your cocky red ass when you need it, don't you worry."

"No need to get racist on me, James." Zenobia smiled as she cut off a skiff, sending the cadet pilot into a panic and almost crashing into the fighter next to him. "Watch where you're flying, cadet pilot!"

"You are having way too much fun," London said.

"You both are," Valencio interrupted. "Keep the chatter down until we get to the training point."

"Kinda going far out, aren't we boss?" London asked.

"You brought enough fuel cells for all the fighters like I asked, right?" Valencio responded.

"I did," London said.

"Then we are going just far enough," Valencio replied. "I want these rookies to learn how to fly. They'll need room for that unless you brought two hundred body bags."

"No need for body bags in the vacuum, boss," London laughed. "Bodies turn hard as rock in this deep freeze. I only need two hundred tow lines. I can drag them back to the Perpetuity and let the maintenance crew deal with the clean up."

"You're a prince amongst assholes," Zenobia said.

"I try," London replied.

"Will you all shut it?" Warrant Officer Millie Richtoff said over the comm. "I hate useless banter. Useless banter gives me a migraine. Can we stick to business?"

"Useless banter is business," Zenobia replied. "It's a long tradition amongst fighter jocks."

"It's a long tradition amongst egotistical assholes," Richtoff replied. "Professionals keep their mouths shut and minds focused."

"Captain? Care to weigh in?" Zenobia asked. "Useless banter or boring professionalism?"

"I don't really care as long as we get the job done," Valencio replied. "We keep these rookies from ramming into each other and you can have all the useless banter or all the boring professionalism you want. I just want results."

"Oh, you're going to get results," Zenobia said as she tapped at the control panel in front of her. "Hello, cadet pilots! My name is Warrant Officer Dusty Zenobia! Amongst friends, I am known as Demon, but you will call me God. I am going to show you how to fly these finely tuned machines like a real pilot! Try to keep up without dying, alright?"

Zenobia hit the thrusters and her fighter skiff shot past the entire group and out into the wide open vacuum of space.

Sixteen

Ngyuen glanced at her wrist as North stepped onto the catwalk above another massive crowd of fresh recruits.

"Ten seconds to spare," Ngyuen smiled. "Close."

"North! Get your ass over here!" Terlinger yelled from the railing. "You're late!"

"Actually he had ten seconds left, sir," Ngyuen said.

"Did he?" Terlinger asked. "Good. I didn't feel like climbing down there to one of the airlocks and ejecting his ass."

"I thank you for that, sir," North said. "How many are we looking at with this batch?"

Ngyuen pulled up a file on her wrist and scrolled through it. "Eighty-seven thousand, four hundred, and fifty-one."

"Eighty-seven thousand?" North gasped, looking at Terlinger. "That's more than we're scheduled for. Did CSC increase the recruitment again?"

"It appears so, North," Terlinger said. "Will that be an issue for you?" Terlinger looked at the major and frowned. "Jesus, man, you're sweating profusely. How much pharma did you take?"

"Enough so that nothing is an issue for me," North said. "I told you I had it under control."

"Better have," Terlinger nodded. "I can afford for cadets to burn out, but having you burn out on me will be highly inconvenient. Don't inconvenience me, North."

"Wouldn't think of it, sir," North said. "Do you want me to—?"

"Death to the Estelian impostors!" someone below shouted. "Long live the Earth colonies!"

"Who said that?" Metzger shouted from the side of the crowd.

"What the hell?" Terlinger asked, but no one had time to answer as a blinding flash erupted down in the bay below.

North's world turned upside down and inside out. He felt himself lifted up off the catwalk and thrown out into the open air. Everything was pink spots before his eyes, a shrill ringing in his ears, and a thought-shredding buzz saw of pain ripping through his brain. He knew he was screaming, as well as falling, but he couldn't truly grasp the importance of either.

Not until he slammed into a mound of corpses.

Then it was all black.

There should have been a lot more pain than there was when he came to, but the pharma kept the agony to a minimum as he slowly rolled off the pile of bodies that had saved his life. He hit the deck of the bay and pressed his forehead against the cool metal before pushing himself up to a kneeling position. Slowly, and with the reluctant caution of a beaten dog, North got to his feet and looked about at the bloody chaos that filled the bay.

Corpses littered the area. Arms, legs, heads, blood and offal were everywhere.

Of the eighty-seven thousand plus recruits, North could see maybe a quarter of that on their feet and moving with another quarter on the ground, wounded but not dead. The rest, close to fifty thousand, made up the grotesque detritus that was strewn here and there.

Something grabbed North by the ankle and he cried out, although the sound was a muffled squeak to his blast-damaged ears. He looked down and saw a three-fingered hand poking out of the corpse pile, blood squirting from the stumps where two fingers had been previously. North just stared at the hand as it weakly flapped against his leg then watched in stunned shock as it slowly went limp then stopped moving all together.

Far off, a lifetime away, someone was calling his name.

North raised his head from the less than complete appendage and tried to find the source of the hail. But all he could see was insanity. Death-laden, sanguine insanity.

"North!" A hand grabbed him by the shoulder and whipped him around. "Goddamn it, North! Where's the commandant?"

The words were filtered by fuzz and reverb, but North at least knew where they came from.

"Metzger," North said. "What happened?"

"What?" Metzger yelled.

"What happened?" North bellowed then closed his eyes against the resultant pain in the center of his forehead. "Fuck, my head."

"Lumen grenade!" Metzger said. "One of the recruits must have been a doubleganger and had it embedded internally!"

"Why didn't the scanners pick it up?" North asked.

"I don't know!" Metzger replied. "They should have!"

But North knew. He pressed his wrist. "Link?"

Nothing happened.

"Don't bother!" Metzger said as he tapped his scorcher. "Lumens work like an EMP, but molecularly!"

"I know how lumen grenades work!" North replied. "And they are nothing like an EMP!"

"Same result!" Metzger yelled. "They fuck shit up! Including people!"

"Yeah, I know!" North shouted.

"Then why did you bother trying to call Linklater?" Metzger asked.

"Habit!"

"Oh!"

The two men looked about at the carnage.

"Fuck me," North said.

"Ya got that right," Metzger nodded. "Where's Terlinger?"

"He was up there, the last I saw him," North said as he pointed up towards the catwalk.

"Jesus fuck, man," Metzger said, looking at North's right hand. "How are you not screaming?"

North lowered his right hand and stared at the fingers. The middle and ring fingers were bent at angles that fingers should not have been bent at. "Oh…"

"Here. I can fix those," Metzger said. He dropped his useless scorcher, grabbed North's wrist with one hand and the dislocated fingers with the other then twisted and pulled.

"Fuck!" North screamed.

"Yeah, you felt that," Metzger smiled as North pulled his hand away.

"Hard not to," North said then looked back up to the catwalk. "We should check on the commandant."

"I'll leave that to you," Metzger said, seeing some of his security guards come hobbling his way. "I'll coordinate down here. Looks like med has arrived." Metzger stopped and looked over at the men and women streaming into the bay.

"That was fast," North said.

"Fast?" Metzger yelled. "It took them twenty minutes."

"Twenty minutes? I was out that long?" North asked.

"I don't have a clue how long you were out!" Metzger said then grimaced as he glanced around at the corners of the bay. "Why aren't security claxons blaring?"

"Why aren't a lot of things working?" North asked. "I'll find the commandant then I'm going to get Linklater. Too much tech going down for this to be isolated."

"Or for it to be just one man," Metzger said. "There's someone inside."

"How do you know?" North asked.

"I know," Metzger replied. "It's my job."

"Shit," North said. "We're going to have to do a full personnel sweep."

"Not without the commandant's orders," Metzger said, nodding towards the catwalk. "Better get up there."

North started to respond, but Metzger was already moving off towards his people and yelling.

"Pharma up, people!" Metzger ordered. "We're gonna need the boost!"

The ladder to the catwalk wasn't an option as North's adrenaline counteracted the pharma and his hand started to sing. He made his way through the dead and wounded and out a side hatch. Medical personnel were sprinting at him, but he waved them on and shouted for them to focus on the truly wounded. A couple dislocated fingers were nothing compared to the damage thousands faced in the bay.

North reached the closest lift and took it up three floors to the catwalk level. He stepped out and found himself looking at a collapsed Ngyuen on the corridor floor.

"Kyly? Kyly, can you hear me?" North asked as he knelt next to Ngyuen and carefully rolled her onto her back.

The corporal moaned softly, but didn't wake up. North pressed his wrist, but his comm unit was still offline. He pressed Ngyuen's and was surprised to see it activate.

"Unauthorized biometrics," a computerized voice said. "Access denied."

"Medical emergency override," North responded. "Medical personnel needed at this location."

"Medical override acknowledged," the computerized voice said. "Medical alert sent. System locking down to prevent further use."

"Yeah, you do that," North said as he stood and moved towards the hatch to the catwalk.

He got to the open hatch and was surprised there was no sign of Commandant Terlinger. North stepped out onto the catwalk, keeping his eyes averted from the bloody mess below, and kept going until he reached the hatch on the far side. He pressed his wrist against the sensor, but the hatch didn't open.

"You have got to be kidding me," he muttered as he tried again. "No way."

He took a deep breath, looked at the wheel in the middle of the hatch, then gripped it with both hands and started to turn. Pain erupted in his fingers, but he ignored it as best he could until the wheel's resistance lessened and the hatch moved. North put his shoulder against it and shoved until it was open enough for him to fit through.

There was no sign of Terlinger, but there was certainly sign of his passage. A trail of deep red blood led from the hatch and down the corridor.

"Shit," North said. "Commandant! Commandant Terlinger!"

No response.

North followed the trail of blood, which became thicker and darker with every meter, until he reached a corner. He looked left and saw nothing, he looked right and gasped.

"Commandant?" North asked as he rushed at the man collapsed against the wall, a four foot metal rod protruding from his belly. "Commandant!"

"North?" Terlinger whispered. "Is that you?"

"It is, sir," North said. "Just be quiet and hold still. I'm going to call for help."

"Can't," Terlinger responded, shaking his head slightly. "I'm offline."

"Damn it, me too," North said. "Just stay put. I'll find a wall comm and call med."

"No, don't," Terlinger said as he looked down at the metal bar. "They won't make it in time. Just stay here and listen."

"Sir, I have to try," North argued. "I can't let you—"

"Shut up, North. That's an order," Terlinger coughed, sending a stream of black-red blood spilling out over his lips and down his chin. "There is something you need to know."

"Sir, med can still help," North said. "The bleeding is slowing, I can see that. If they get you in a pod then they can fix you right up."

"Can't fit this in a pod," Terlinger smiled through bloody lips and teeth. "Doesn't matter. I can feel how fast I'm fading."

"Sir, I—"

"Shut up, North!" Terlinger ordered. "Listen!"

"Sorry," North replied.

"This war," Terlinger said. "This war is not what you think."

"War never is, sir," North said then got a harsh look and closed his mouth.

"The Estelians, they aren't what you think either," Terlinger continued. "They aren't even..." He bent over and coughed hard, sending a shower of blood across the corridor floor. "They aren't..." More coughing, more blood.

"Sir, just rest," North said.

"This," Terlinger whispered, pulling a medal from his chest and handing it to North. "This will tell you everything..."

"Sir, this is your Medal of Valor," North said. "From your time in the Xenxo System."

"No," Terlinger said. "It's the truth... The truth..."

The commandant's eyes rolled up into his head and he sighed one last time.

"Fuck," North said as he checked for a pulse, but couldn't find one. "Oh, fuck."

North stood up, a medal in his hand and a million questions in his mind. He struggled for clarity, but all he found were Terlinger's last words wreaking havoc with his thoughts.

"What truth?" he asked then shook his head as he tucked the medal into his pocket. "Doesn't matter. He was dying, he didn't know what he was saying." North took a deep breath and shook his head. "I have to call in to CSC. That's something I do know. That's a hard truth right there."

Seventeen

"Everyone hold up," Valencio ordered as she slowed her fighter skiff. "I'm getting some weird chatter from Perpetuity."

"I'm hearing it too," London said. "There was an explosion or something."

"We heading back?" Zenobia asked.

"Not unless North calls us," Valencio replied. "If something is going down then the safest place for us is in the vacuum. We hold tight until I hear directly from North."

"So, what now?" London asked. "We sit here?"

"Give me a minute," Valencio said.

"Best call North and double check," Richtoff said. "You know how crabby that guy gets when he thinks you're going against him even when you're not. Better safe than sorry."

"Everyone shut up and let me think," Valencio ordered. "When we're in the vacuum, I'm in charge, not North."

Valencio stared out of her cockpit and watched the glinting dust particles that floated by her fighter skiff. There were more than a few times in her life where she felt just like those particles. Even with the structure of the military and the CSC, there was still tons of uncertainty and insecurity to deal with. The war against the Estelians was not a cut and dried campaign.

She had done things that she was not proud of. She had killed many that had stopped fighting and were just trying to flee. Just doing what she had been ordered to do. Even if they were doublegangers, they were still trying to run to safety, not attack her. She wasn't indoctrinated so much that she didn't know that innocents were lost on both sides of the war.

Valencio turned her head and studied the cadet pilots that waited for her orders. They weren't exactly innocents, but they were certainly ignorant. Ignorant of the realities of war and the realities of living with war. They'd been recruited in schools, at job fairs, on collectives, at recreation halls, more than few of them on the sidewalks outside bars.

Vids projected to their wrists from grinning, attractive CSC reps. Told that Earth needed them, that the colonies needed them, that if they didn't do it then who would? Who would stand up and fight the Estelians? Who would help against the monsters that had corrupted humanity? Who would lead the charge, follow faithfully, fight to the death against the doublegangers that threatened good, red-blooded earthlings every second of every day?

"We stay," Valencio said. "North wanted us off the station and out in the vacuum, so we stay off station and out in the vacuum. None of these rookies can do a damned thing on the Perpetuity except get in the way. Might as well keep to the schedule and teach these cadet pilots what it means to fly a fighter."

"Roger that," Zenobia replied.

"Sound decision," Richtoff said. "Best to stick to business."

"London? Agreed?" Valencio asked.

"Your call, boss," London replied. "I'll back whatever."

"Then we stay and train," Valencio said. "London, you monitor communications with the Perpetuity. I want strictly intracomm between fighters. No distractions. Let the station work out whatever is going on. If North wanted my help then he shouldn't have kicked us out of the sim bays."

"Harsh, but fair," London laughed. "I have the comm. You jocks just fly and scare the fuck out of these rookies. If at least a dozen don't have piss in their panties and shit in their drawers by the end of today then we haven't worked them hard enough."

"I fucking hear that!" Zenobia laughed.

"Richtoff? You take the lead," Valencio said. "Head an hour out. We'll train by the cannon debris field."

"That a good idea?" London asked. "You sure the Perpetuity won't be using it for target practice?"

"Not if you relay our position back to them," Valencio growled. "Did you not understand your responsibilities when I put you in charge of communications?"

"I'm on it, boss, I'm on it," London replied. "My bad."

"You sure you're on it?" Valencio asked.

"I'm sure, I'm sure," London said. "I'm initiating squadron intracomm now and calling in our position and training plans to the Perpetuity. If I don't get confirmation from them, I'll let you know."

"You better, London," Zenobia said. "I don't want to end up as space trash floating around the solar system because some idiot cadet back on station decides to take cannon pot shots at old wreckage."

"Everyone off my back!" London snapped. "Jesus, people, I know how to do my job!"

"Good," Valencio said. "Richtoff? Take us out."

"Cadet pilots!" Richtoff shouted over the comm. "We are taking a trip to the debris field exactly forty-four degrees from your center! Adjust course and follow me! We stay tight in sixteens! Not sure what your sixteens are then take a look at your formation map on your screens. Green is your sixteen, red is not your sixteen. Now break into formation and hit those thrusters!"

Valencio watched as the cadet pilots clumsily maneuvered their skiffs into fighting groups of sixteen. It took way longer than she would have liked, but no one had a mid-space collision, so she considered the effort a win. She tapped at her screen and began numbering and tagging each sixteen for reference. Once all the sixteens were formed, Richtoff's skiff shot ahead and the groups followed closely.

"Hanging back with me, boss?" London asked.

"I get a better view of the chaos from here," Valencio replied.

"I hear that," London said.

"We good with Perpetuity?" Valencio asked.

"We're good," London said. "Our location is noted. Not that the flight controllers could give two fucks. They wouldn't tell me what was up, but shit ain't good back there."

"Then staying out here sounds like the right call," Valencio said.

"I can't argue with that," London said.

The last sixteen followed in formation. It was a ragged formation, but workable. Valencio aimed her skiff after them and hit her thrusters, careful to keep a safe distance from the wobbly cadets.

Eighteen

North found Ngyuen in the medical bay, already up and about, helping the medical staff organize the triage process as the wounded that could be moved from the recruit holding bay were brought in.

"Corporal!" North shouted over the cacophony of shouting medics and doctors as well as crying, screaming, and moaning wounded. "Corporal Ngyuen!"

"Major North," Ngyuen replied as she handed a tablet off to a nurse and hurried over to the Chief Training Officer. "I was told I have you to thank for getting me here so fast."

North spotted the small bandage on Ngyuen's temple and raised an eyebrow. "Anything serious?"

"Small concussion," Ngyuen replied. "Nothing a couple doses of pharma can't take care of. Have you seen the commandant?"

"You don't know?" North asked. "Commandant Terlinger is dead. They just picked up his body which is why I came to find you."

"Dead? The commandant is dead?" Ngyuen almost shrieked then got control of herself and took a deep breath. "I hope it was quick."

"It wasn't," North said. "Listen, I need you to get me his access codes. I'm in charge of the Perpetuity until CSC tells me otherwise. I'll need your help navigating his command files so I can put the station under emergency watch."

"Are we not going into lockdown?" Ngyuen asked. "It would seem wise since this is an obvious Estelian attack."

"I don't know what this is," North answered. "Which is why I need the commandant's codes. I'll need to go over the surveillance vids from the explosion. See if anything unusual happened before that man set off the lumen grenade."

"Nothing unusual about a damned DG murdering real people," a medic snarled as he passed by, his uniform coated in blood and his eyes wild. "Those savages only know how to kill."

"We don't know that it's the Estelians, medic," North snapped. "Tend to your job so I can tend to mine."

The medic grumbled and muttered as he moved off to a hover stretcher holding an unconscious recruit with severe burns across her face and neck. North turned to Ngyuen and grabbed her by the arm.

"The codes, Corporal," North said.

"There is a protocol to handing them over," Ngyuen said. "We'll have to walk through it together. You are second-in-command on the Perpetuity, which gives you access to 75% of what you will need already. I'll take you to the commandant's office so you can get started while I receive authorization from CSC."

"Fucking bureaucrats," North said. "You'd think we are fighting to protect protocols and forms over fighting to protect Earth."

"I will warn you, sir, that for many in the CSC, they are one and the same," Ngyuen said.

The woman swayed slightly and North gripped her tighter, keeping her from falling over.

"Thank you," Ngyuen said. "Maybe I need another dose of pharma."

"Hold off until I have all access to the station," North said. "Can't have you fading on me when I need you the most."

"You sound exactly like Commandant Terlinger," Ngyuen smiled weakly. "He will be missed."

"That he will," North said. "You okay to walk?"

"I am," Ngyuen sighed.

"Then let's get a move on," North ordered.

Nineteen

The bead of sweat rolled down his scalp, across his forehead, and into his right eye. He blinked several times, but the sting of the salty liquid just would not go away.

"Son of a bitch," Linklater growled. "Hold this so I can wipe my eyes."

He handed Wendt a data scanner and wiped his face with the sleeve of his uniform. There wasn't much dry material left after how much he'd been sweating while working in the server tower, cramped next to the sergeant in front of the crushed servers.

"These servers better not be what handles climate control in this tower," Linklater said.

"They aren't," Wendt replied, handing the scanner back to the lieutenant. "Those are located at the top and bottom with several redundancies in between."

"I'd love to know what the redundancies to these damned things are," Linklater said. "Then we could just scan those and know what we are looking at because they sure don't seem to be just personnel files."

Wendt brought up the server tower schematic on his wrist for the umpteenth time and shook his head.

"Whatever fool forgot to label these in the system needs to be ejected into the vacuum," Wendt complained. "How can we not know what these are for?"

"They probably aren't for anything," Linklater said. "With my luck, I've been in this damned tower, sweating my balls off, for nothing."

"Is there ever a reason to sweat your balls off?" Wendt asked.

"I can think of a few," Linklater replied. "And none include you in the scenario."

"Sorry to disappoint," Wendt replied.

"Grab that one by the corners and just yank it out," Linklater said. "I'm done with being cautious."

Wendt grabbed onto the specific server and wiggled it back and forth until the broken apparatus came free from the bank. He turned it this way and that, checking the entire thing before he set it on the floor of the lift and scratched his head.

"There aren't any manufacture marks," Wendt said. "No indication of age, capacity, version number. Nothing."

"That's not regulation," Linklater said. "Gimme that."

"It's right there," Wendt said, nodding at the server on the floor before turning back to the bank. "I'm going to pull another one."

Sparks flew from the server bank and Wendt cried out as he pulled his hands back fast.

"Shit!" he cried.

"I told you to shut the power off to this bank," Linklater said. "Serves you right for not following through."

"I did follow through," Wendt barked as he yanked off his scorched gloves to check the burn marks. "I turned off the power to this entire level. I didn't want to since we have no idea what the servers actually serve, but I did it."

"Apparently not," Linklater said.

Wendt grumbled to himself as he pressed at his wrist and brought up the power grid for the server tower. He zoomed in on their specific level then thrust his arm under Linklater's nose.

"See!" he snapped. "Power is off!"

Linklater looked at the image then shrugged. "Except the power isn't off."

"The only way the power could still be on is if there is an off grid failsafe," Wendt said. "And the only way that could be set up is by you."

"Which I didn't do since I have no fucking clue what these servers are," Linklater replied. "Try again."

Wendt swiped the image away on his wrist and stood in front of the demolished servers, his eyes studying the hole where the one server had already been removed. He pulled a halogen from his belt and shined it into the empty space. Leaning close, he checked the framing first then the connection ports in the back.

"Well, this is interesting," Wendt said. "Check this out."

Linklater set the server aside and nudged Wendt out of the way, yanking the halogen from the tech's hand.

"What am I looking at?" Linklater asked.

"You'll see it," Wendt said.

"Just fucking tell me what— Oh... That shouldn't be there," Linklater said.

"No shit," Wendt said.

"Take this" Linklater said, handing the halogen back to Wendt.

Linklater pulled out a pair of thick gloves, crossed himself then reached into the empty space. He was all the way up to his shoulder before he could grab what he needed to. He frowned and looked at Wendt.

"Make sure you let my family know I loved them," Linklater said.

"You have family?" Wendt asked. "I thought they just found you under a bridge eating goats."

"I have parents," Linklater glared.

"No siblings?" Wendt asked.

"No," Linklater said, his face turning red as he started to pull. "Only child."

"That explains a lot," Wendt said.

There was a loud pop and a flash of blue fire. Linklater dodged to the side, avoiding getting hit by the freak flames, then started swatting at his uniform as the sleeve began to smolder.

"Ow! Fuck!" Linklater yelled as he danced back.

"Holy crap," Wendt said as he looked at the thick cable that dangled from the empty server space. "That is not just power but a serious wide open pipeline. This whole station could go dark and these servers would still run. An Estelian EMP could destroy every micron of tech in the Perpetuity and not even affect these guys."

"Yeah," Linklater said. "And it hurts, too."

"We have to find out where this comes from," Wendt says. "It's not the station's main generator, that's for sure."

"You're thinking backwards," Linklater said. "We have to find out where this thing goes, not where it's coming from. Take a look at the optics again."

Wendt leaned in and then gasped. "You have got to be shitting me..."

"That is an incorruptible data transfer conduit," Linklater said. "Not only do these servers have an off grid power source, but they have multiple backups somewhere. Look at all the optics. We're talking ten redundancies, at least."

Wendt rubbed his face then looked around at all the damaged servers.

"This is going to take us forever to track down," Wendt said. "We're going to need help."

"No," Linklater snapped. "No help. We have no idea what this shit is or who set it all up. We can't trust anyone with this."

"Can't trust anyone...?" Wendt asked. "You think this is Estelian?"

"I don't know what this is," Linklater said. "And until I do, it's just you and me."

"How do you know you can trust me?" Wendt asked. "I could be the traitor."

"I doubt that," Linklater said. "You're too lazy to be a traitor."

"Asshole," Wendt sneered.

"Now, I'm not saying you aren't compromised," Linklater smirked. "You do like pussy way too much. Any one of those women you screw could have you wrapped around their little fingers and you wouldn't even know it."

"Oh, I'd know it," Wendt said. "I give way more than I receive. I'd know a faker, trust me."

"Whatever," Linklater said. He started to speak again then closed his mouth and rubbed at his face.

"What?" Wendt asked.

"How many servers are there?" Linklater asked.

Wendt did a quick count. "Three hundred, easy."

"Three hundred," Linklater said. "With ten possible redundancies per server."

"Shit," Wendt replied, doing the math. "We could be looking for ten backups or three thousand backups if they aren't all housed together."

"Exactly," Linklater said. "We have to pull each server and see if they are all linked or individual. Only way to know for certain."

"You sure you don't want to call in help?" Wendt asked.

"I'm sure," Linklater said. "But I better let Dornan know I'm not coming back to the sims."

"You do that," Wendt said as he pulled up a hatch in the lift floor.

"Where the fuck are you going?" Linklater asked.

"To take a leak and get us some provisions," Wendt said. "We're going to be here a while. We'll need water and supper."

"Fine," Linklater said. "I'll call Dornan and then get started."

"Better call North as well," Wendt said. "He's in charge now."

"Until the CSC sends a new commandant in," Linklater said. "Which means we have very little time. New brass always likes to shake things up."

"Got it," Wendt said and disappeared through the hatch.

Linklater stretched then grabbed onto the next server and pulled.

Twenty

"With the commandant dead, it's up to us to keep things in order until CSC sends a new boss," Metzger said as he addressed the large group of security guards. "Not a single recruit gets onto this station without a full body scan. No more fast scans. I want each and every person that puts a foot on this metal to have a wand run up and down their bodies carefully. You even get a hint of something off and I want that recruit isolated and locked down tight."

"What about the recruits already on board?" a guard asked.

"We go over them again," Metzger replied. "Then we start in with station personnel."

"Station personnel?" another guard asked. "We think that crazy fuck had help?"

"We don't know," Metzger said. "But we are going to find out."

He looked about at the guards and realized he had nowhere near the manpower he needed to accomplish what he wanted. The looks on the guards' faces told him they knew it as well.

"We start with each other," Metzger said. "Everyone gets wanded."

There were some grumbles and Metzger held up his hand to silence them.

"You want to get blown apart because the guy next to you has a lumen embedded in his gut?" Metzger snapped. "You want to get ripped down to your molecules because you thought you knew the asshole that is supposed to have your back? Everyone gets wanded! Starting with me!" Metzger slung his scorcher and held out his arms. "Who wants to do the honors?"

No one stepped forward.

"Someone better volunteer or I'll make sure that not only do you get scanned externally, but internally as well," Metzger said. "Nothing like a scan wand up the ass to ruin your day."

Several guards grabbed scan wands from the crate next to the group and moved towards Metzger.

"That's more like it," Metzger grinned. "And bring me some more pharma! Gotta get right for this shit!"

Twenty-One

North could feel his body crashing already, but he knew if he pharmaed up too soon he'd blow his adrenals. He rubbed at his temples and took a couple deep breaths.

"Are you alright, Major?" Ngyuen asked from his side as they approached the hatch to Terlinger's office. "You seem shakier on your feet than me."

"Blood sugar," North said. "I skipped lunch and it's already supper time."

"I could have the mess hall bring you a tray while we work," Ngyuen suggested. "The commandant ate in his office all the time."

"I may take you up on that," North nodded. "I could use a hot and some water."

"I'll place the order as soon as we get inside," Ngyuen said.

She pressed her wrist against the panel next to the office hatch and waited, but nothing happened.

"That's strange," Ngyuen said. "It should respond. Even with the heightened security alert, my credentials should override. I'm the commandant's personal assistant."

"Let me try," North said and pressed his wrist to the panel. Still no response. "Locked from the inside?"

"Highly unlikely," Ngyuen said. "Only the commandant or myself could do that. You will be able to once we go through the protocols to get you authorized for the correct codes. But as of now, the only person living that can lock this hatch from the inside is me."

"What about Metzger?" North asked. "He's in charge of security."

"Yes, that is true," Ngyuen said. "Sergeant Metzger could do it."

North pounded on the hatch. "Metzger? You in there? Open up!"

There was no response.

North pressed his wrist back to the panel. "Emergency override."

Nothing happened.

"You try?" North ordered.

Ngyuen placed her wrist to the panel.

"Emergency override," she said.

"No emergency detected," a computerized voice responded.

"The hatch is jammed," Ngyuen said. "Manual override requested then."

"A repair request has been sent to the maintenance department," the voice replied.

"Cancel maintenance request and give me access to the manual controls," Ngyuen said.

"Request denied," the voice said. "Hatch has been locked internally. Manual controls not available."

"Fuck!" North yelled then pounded both fists on the hatch. "Metzger! If you are in there then you had better open up right now!"

Still no response.

"Is there any other way to get this hatch open?" North asked. "Maybe the old fashioned way?"

Ngyuen hesitated. "No, Major."

"You are a shitty liar, Corporal," North said. He pulled his pistol and shoved Ngyuen aside. "Cover your eyes."

North fired three times into the panel then holstered his pistol, grabbed the damaged panel, and yanked hard.

Most of that section of the wall came away. North tossed the debris aside as claxons rang out and red flashing lights turned the corridor into a disco from hell.

"Security, please report to Sector Eighteen on Administrative Deck One! Security, please report to Sector Eighteen on Administrative Deck One!" the computerized voice announced from speakers up and down the corridor.

"Yes, security, please do that," North said as he thrust his hand inside the opening in the wall. He tugged and pulled, pushing several cables out of the way until he found the release catch. With a hard twist and a shove, there was a loud clang from the hatch. "Get that open, Corporal!"

Ngyuen hurried forward and pulled on the hatch. It resisted then swung open. North pulled his arm free from the wall and shoved Ngyuen aside, his pistol back in his hand.

"Wait there," North said, glancing into the reception room of the commandant's office, his pistol up and braced by both hands. "Do not let anyone through."

"Alright," Ngyuen replied, her eyes wide and afraid.

North moved cautiously into the reception room. The lights above flickered on and he shook his head.

"I'm guessing Metzger wasn't in here," North said. "He's not this much of a slob."

The reception room was trashed. Framed recruitment posters had been thrown from the walls and left shattered on the floor. The spots where they had been were scorched by burn marks. Ngyuen's desk was overturned and all the drawers pulled out and tossed this way and that, most of them broken and warped. The hatch to the commandant's office was ajar and North tore his eyes from the mess and focused on the dark slit between wall and hatch.

"This is Major Bartram North!" North called out. "I will give you one chance to show yourself! Come out with your hands raised and you get to live! Keep hiding and I come in shooting! I am not in the mood for anything between those options!"

No response.

North moved forward slowly and pressed the toe of his boot against the hatch. He gave it a hard kick then moved quickly into the commandant's office. He swung left then right, his pistol covering the corners of the room. No sign of any intruder, but the commandant's office was just as trashed as the reception room outside.

North moved over to the desk, walked carefully around it, and aimed his pistol underneath. Still nothing.

"What the hell?" North muttered.

He started to turn and call for Ngyuen, but a shimmering from the corner of his eye caught his attention. He spun quickly in time to see something coming at him. It was as if what little light was in the room, and coming from the window behind the commandant's desk, was captured and reflected back at him.

Then the shimmer slammed right into North and his pistol went flying across the office.

"Fucker," North grunted as he and the shimmer tumbled over the desk and onto the floor.

A hard blow between North's eyes made him see stars, but he recovered quickly and brought his right knee up fast. The shimmer grunted and North thrust his head forward, slamming his forehead into the shimmer. Another grunt and the weight on North's body was gone.

He didn't hesitate for a second and rolled a couple meters away, shoved up onto his feet, then rushed the shimmer, diving at the thing's middle. A third grunt and then a cry as North and the shimmer slammed into the commandant's desk. North whipped his arm about, cracking his elbow across what he thought was the shimmer's face. He kept hammering at the thing, again and again, until a knee nailed him in the groin.

North was shoved aside easily and he fell to the office floor, his hands gripping at his crotch. He rolled himself and tripped up the shimmer. The office debris was crushed and moved as the shimmer hit the floor and North pushed the pain in his groin from his head as he reached out and grabbed the shimmer by the legs. He pulled hard, but then caught a boot to the face and everything was bright lights and pure agony as his forehead and nose took the brunt of the force.

"Fuck!" North gurgled around the blood that quickly flowed into his throat.

The shimmer was up and gone from the office while North struggled to get onto his knees then up onto his feet. He staggered across the office and out into the reception room, surprised to see Metzger running in from the corridor.

"Did you see it?" North asked, his hands to his face as blood poured between his fingers. "The fucking asshole was wearing a cloaking shield! He had to run right by you!"

"I didn't see a damned thing," Metzger said, his scorcher sweeping the room. "Only person out there is Ngyuen!"

"Corporal!" North called. "Did you see it?"

Ngyuen peeked her head into the reception room. "I didn't see anyone leave, Major. But if the person was wearing a cloaking shield then I could have easily missed them."

"She was all the way across the corridor with her back to the wall," Metzger said. "I'll check the office."

"Don't bother," North said. "I was just in there." He pulled his hands from his face. "That's where this happened."

"You'll want to cold pack that," Ngyuen said. "I'll go get you one."

"Make it two," North said. "I need one for my balls too."

"Ouch," Metzger smirked.

"Fuck you," North said.

Metzger looked around the reception room. "Terlinger's office look this bad?"

"Yeah," North said. "Whoever that was, they were looking for something."

"Any idea what?" Metzger asked.

"Not a fucking clue," North said. "I'm just glad the fucker wasn't a suicide bomber. Could have killed me and taken out half this administrative deck with that damned window in Terlinger's office."

"Never have liked that there," Metzger said. "Major security risk and weak point for Perpetuity."

"The old man always said that if there was ever an attack on the Perpetuity, he wanted to see it coming," North said. "I guess he didn't expect an attack to come in the recruit holding bay."

"Speaking of," Metzger said as he slung his scorcher and pulled a scan wand from his belt. "Spread 'em wide, major."

"You shitting me with this?" North snapped.

"I had my people scan me," Metzger said. "Only way to have transparency. So, if you don't mind?"

"I do fucking mind," North said, but he spread his arms and legs anyway. "Get it over with."

Metzger ran the wand up and down North's body then through his legs.

"You're clean," Metzger said.

"No shit," North replied. "You know, the best time to have done that would have been back in the bay just after the attack."

"I know," Metzger said. "I expect to get a reaming from CSC over that, but nothing I can do about it now."

Ngyuen returned and handed North a cold pack. "The corridor's med kit only had the one. Sorry."

"One is better than none," North said, looking at the cold pack. After a couple of seconds deliberation, he cracked the pack, activating the cold crystals, and gently pressed it to his groin. "Ahhhh. Much better."

"You wouldn't rather use that for your face?" Ngyuen asked.

"You obviously have never been clocked in the nuts," Metzger said.

"No, obviously I have not," Ngyuen replied.

"Let's get to work, Corporal," North ordered as he hobbled towards the commandant's office. He glanced back over his shoulder. "Give me search reports on the half hour, alright?"

"You got it," Metzger said. "Good luck with CSC."

"Gonna need it," North said.

"Sergeant? May I speak with you briefly?" Ngyuen asked.

"Right now?" North snapped.

"I'll only be a minute, sir," Ngyuen said.

"Go ahead," North said. "Just hurry it up."

Twenty-Two

The squadron was a mess.

Even moving the cadet pilots into groups of sixteen didn't seem to make much of a difference. Stragglers kept breaking formation and getting confused with what sixteen was theirs. Near collisions were so frequent that Richtoff's voice had become ragged from the constant warnings she was shouting. Zenobia had to invent new curse words to berate the cadet pilots with. And London had muted his comm because he was laughing so hard.

Valencio just waited in her fighter skiff and watched, demoralized and dejected.

"That's enough! All skiffs full stop!" Valencio finally yelled when two skiffs almost crushed a third between them. "How is this even possible? You have to have a basic aptitude for flying to even be considered for cadet pilot training! But I can swear to every Maker in the universe that I do not see a scrap of aptitude right now! I would personally be surprised if any of you even knew how to walk!"

A cadet mumbled something into the comm and Valencio had to keep herself from ramming his skiff with hers.

"Did you just say that you never wanted the job?" Valencio snarled. "Did I just hear you right, cadet pilot?"

There was silence on the comm as everyone waited for the cadet pilot to answer. When the young man didn't respond, Valencio flew her fighter skiff right up next to his, easily maneuvering around the haphazardly stopped squadron.

"I asked you a question, cadet pilot!" Valencio shouted. "Did I hear you say you didn't want the job?"

"Yes, sir," the offending cadet pilot replied. "I never signed up for fighter skiff training."

"You didn't?" Valencio asked, her voice dripping with venom and irony. "Oh, well I am so happy you alerted me to this mistake. What did you sign up for?"

"I, well, wanted to be a navigator on a cruiser or destroyer, sir," the cadet pilot answered.

"Really?" Valencio responded. "What's your name, cadet pilot?"

"Hogan, Captain," the young man answered. "Gaelan Hogan."

"Gaelan Hogan?" Valencio asked. "Your folks must really be into their Celtic heritage. Are they big fans of the former Irish Republic?"

"Yes, Captain," Hogan replied. "They have been tested and certified. Both are genetically 75% of Irish descent."

"Good for them," Valencio chuckled. "Always nice to know people are still holding on to the old ways of genetic segregation. Gotta keep those bloodlines pure, right?"

"Well, I wouldn't say that, Captain," Hogan replied quietly.

"You didn't, Cadet Pilot Hogan," Valencio responded. "I said it. But I'm sure your parents agree with me. Why go to the trouble of getting tested if you don't want to keep from dirtying the gene pool?"

"They just, well, are proud to be Irish," Hogan said. "The Unified Nations make it hard to know exactly where you come from. Can't tell by looks anymore."

"Can't tell by looks anymore?" Valencio asked. "Those words just came out of your mouth? Can't tell by looks anymore? Jesus H. Christ with a scorcher. You did not just say that."

"I didn't mean anything by it, Captain," Hogan said. "My parents just believe—"

"You've seen what I look like, right, Cadet Pilot Hogan?" Valencio asked. "You've seen my skin color, my hair color, my eye color, yes?"

"Yes, Captain," Hogan replied, his voice shaky.

"No way to tell what my ancestry is," Valencio laughed. "Albinos are just white. I look like I came from a family of lab rats. But you know what my genetics test out as?"

"Uh, well, no, Captain," Hogan said.

"I test out as nearly 85% Navajo," Valencio said. "Don't know how. Those people died out a thousand years ago. My father's surname is of European Spanish descent and my mother is about as mixed as it gets. And I'm a fucking albino! But according to CSC's intake tests, I'm 85% Navajo. Do you know who the Navajo people were, Cadet Pilot Hogan?"

"I'm afraid I do not," Hogan replied.

"They were natives of the southwestern region of what was once the United States," Valencio said. "I know you've heard of that place."

"Of course, Captain," Hogan said.

"Did I ask you a question, Cadet Pilot? I don't think I did. I told you what you know, I didn't ask for you to tell me. How about you keep your fucking mouth shut unless I ask you a question. You think you can do that, Cadet Pilot Hogan?"

"Yes, sir," Hogan said.

"Good. So the Navajo were a tribe of people that predated the European settlers of the Americas by a couple hundred years. Maybe less, maybe more. Hard to tell nowadays with our homogenous history. But they were a primitive people, yet culturally rich. Really fascinating stuff. You should read up on them sometime."

Valencio tapped her thrusters so her skiff was directly nose to nose with Hogan's.

"Do you know what skin color they had, Cadet Pilot Hogan?"

"No, sir," Hogan replied.

"Brownish red," Valencio said. "Like they'd been in a solarium for a month straight without leaving. They had to have skin like that to handle the intense sun that part of the world gets. Do I look like I can handle intense sun?"

"No, sir."

"You are right there, Cadet Pilot Hogan," Valencio said. "I can barely stand in front of a mirror for longer than five minutes without burning. My parents begged me not to be a fighter skiff pilot because of the exposure to solar radiation. My cockpit is specially designed to keep me from frying up in my skiff. I live a life of filters and lotions, Cadet Pilot Hogan. Yet, somehow, I am 85% Navajo. It's crazy."

Valencio stared from her cockpit and into Hogan's, her eyes locking onto the young man's tinted visor on his flight helmet. She stared and stared, quiet for a full three minutes before she spoke again.

"My parents don't have a drop of Navajo in them," Valencio said, finally breaking the silence. "Not a drop. Do you know what that means, Cadet Pilot Hogan?"

"You were adopted, sir?" Hogan asked.

"That's what I thought," Valencio laughed. "I got the CSC report back and I called my parents right away. Nope. Not adopted. They have the DNA tests to prove it. So, now that you know that, can you tell me what it means that my genetic testing came back as 85% Navajo and my parents don't have a single percent?"

"I'm not sure, Captain," Hogan replied, his voice thick with confusion. "I'm not a geneticist."

"Neither am I, Cadet Pilot Hogan," Valencio said. "So, not understanding what it all meant, I thought they'd just made a mistake with mine. So I got tested again. Nope. Came back the same. In fact, being a thorough person, I studied the reports side by side and they were the same exact report. Once you are tagged then you stay tagged. Do you know what it all means now?"

"I'm sorry, Captain, I don't," Hogan said. "This is all a little confusing."

"I'll make it clear and tell you what it means," Valencio said. "It means that the genetic tests we get to determine our ancestry are full of shit, Cadet Pilot Hogan. Completely full of shit. They just make that crap up so that we can feel connected to Earth. They want those born on the colony planets to feel as much like earthlings as those born on the home planet. The truth is, after a couple thousand years, we're all mutts. Doesn't matter what our names are, what our skin colors are, what our damned genetics tests say, we are grade A, prime mutts. All mixed up from centuries of breeding and spitting out little brats. Do you know why I'm telling you this, Cadet Pilot Hogan?"

"No, sir, I do not," Hogan replied.

"Because you may think you're Irish, but you aren't," Valencio said. "Just like I'm not Navajo. But do you know what you are that doesn't need to be tested or proven by some bullshit report?"

"No, sir."

"You are a cadet pilot in training," Valencio said. "You are sitting in a motherfucking fighter skiff with impotent plasma canons on each wing and dummy missiles under your ass. That I can prove by just looking at you. So, it doesn't matter what you signed up for, it doesn't matter what a fucking test said, it doesn't matter if you believe you are Irish or a cruiser navigator or the fucking commandant of Perpetuity. All that matters is the fact you are sitting in that fucking cockpit and you have a fucking job to do!"

"Yes, sir," Hogan replied. "I apologize for my mistake, sir."

"Good," Valencio said. "Am I going to have any other problems with you, Hogan?"

"No, sir."

"That's what I like to hear," Valencio said. "Now, as for the rest of you, we are staying out here until each sixteen can keep a tight formation and understands the basics of the different flight patterns. Once I am satisfied you can do that, and I know things on the Perpetuity are calmed down, then we will return to the flight deck and I may let you get a hot and some sleep. If you cannot satisfy me then we will stay in our skiffs until you do. That means no hots, no sleep, no shit breaks, nothing. You fly until you die. Am I understood?"

There was a general silence.

"AM I FUCKING UNDERSTOOD?"

"Yes, Captain!" the squadron shouted.

"Then get back into your sixteens and spread out! I want thirty meters between sixteens, single file! Once you sorry excuses for fighter pilots get that accomplished then maybe I'll let you fire your fake weapons! Do it NOW!"

Valencio tensed as all of the fighter skiffs moved at once, but after a few close calls they managed to get into their sixteens and into a single file formation.

"Zenobia?" Valencio asked over the command comm channel. "You take the first half. Richtoff? You take the last half. Split them up into two groups and paint yourselves. I want red and white. Put the debris field between your groups. Once you are ready then we talk them through the basics. Half speed at first then we work them up to full speed. Once we know they won't kill each other or crash into any debris then we start over and let them go."

"This is going to be an all-nighter, isn't it?" Zenobia asked.

"It is. You have an issue with that?" Valencio asked.

"Nope," Zenobia replied. "I'm just on my fucking period. Gonna get messy in this fucking cockpit."

"War is messy," Valencio laughed. "And I am sorry about that. But the way North is up my butt, I have to come back with something solid or he'll get me reassigned. I may hate the Perpetuity, but fuck if I'm going back out into the shit. I've seen enough of that."

"Amen," Zenobia said.

"Are we done talking?" Richtoff asked. "I'd like to get to work."

"You bleedin' too, Richtoff?" Zenobia laughed.

"Just out my ears from having to listen to you whine, Zenobia," Richtoff replied.

"Oh! That was good! I didn't know you had it in ya, Richtoff!" Zenobia guffawed.

"That's enough," Valencio said. "Split those useless rookies up and let's get to it."

Twenty-Three

Perspiration soaked through the armpits of North's uniform as he sat at Terlinger's desk and waited for the connection to go through with Central Space Command. The CSC logo swirled in the air in front of him, twisting and turning in on itself, over and over, until North thought he was going to be sick. After a few nauseating seconds, the logo disappeared and was replaced by the battle-scarred face of a less than pleased General Colletta Birmingham.

"Major North," Birmingham frowned. "I have already been briefed on what has happened on the Perpetuity, so all you need to do is tell me what you have discovered so far."

"Nothing, General," North replied. "We have no solid evidence that the attack was anything but an isolated event. I have suspicions, but nothing concrete as of yet."

"Nothing?" Birmingham asked. "How can that be, Major? What have you been doing all this time?"

"Getting set up to take over Perpetuity," North said. "Corporal Ngyuen has assisted me with proper command codes. I'll step in until you can send a replacement for Commandant Terlinger."

"No need," Birmingham said. "You will remain in place for now. I want your head of security to take over the investigation. What is his name?"

"Sergeant-at-Arms Coop Metzger, General," North answered.

"Yes, have Sergeant Metzger conduct the investigation into the attack," Birmingham said. "That's his job anyway. I need you to focus on the recruits and getting the CSC the numbers we need. Our timeline doesn't change because some DG radical blew himself up."

"I'm sorry, General, but I don't know if I can hit the cadet numbers you gave Commandant Terlinger," North said. "It was going to be hard before all of this happened. Now? Close to impossible. We lost quite a few thousand recruits, not to mention some key personnel. I'll need more staff and more recruits to fill your numbers."

"Recruits are already on the way, Major," Birmingham said. "We have emptied every ghetto on Earth, as well as all the garbage colonies in the lesser systems in order to fill the quota needed. You can expect another six waves of fifty thousand over the next two days."

North leaned back in his chair as he felt tightness in his chest. He tried not to let the discomfort show, but he could tell by the narrowing of the general's eyes that she easily saw his physical reaction to the news.

"This is the tipping point, Major," Birmingham said. "We cannot lose ground now. The CSC needs a steady stream of troops going out to the front. We are going to reclaim lost systems and then take new ones. No matter the cost. The Estelians will try to resist, but our intel says they do not have the numbers needed to counter our attack. They have the superior position within the galaxy, but that will end shortly."

North's throat was almost as tight as his chest felt, but he managed to force himself to speak.

"General, I am not sure how I can get that many recruits trained in a week," North said. "I don't even know if we have the resources to feed them all. I'll have to retrofit some sim bays into barracks just to house them all."

"They do not need to be housed, Major," Birmingham said. "They need to be trained. Resources are coming in with the next batch of recruits. All injectables. Pharma, food, and hydration. You line them up, shoot them up, and teach them how to fire a scorcher. That is now your job. They shit in their pants, they piss in their pants, they do not sleep. They can drop dead on the spot, for all I care. Better that you break the weak ones now than having them break in battle. I want the numbers ready by the end of the week. Are we understood?"

"Loud and clear, General," North said. "I'll let the staff know immediately."

"Don't bother," Birmingham said. "The CSC is now instituting the first protocol. All communications will be direct via individual interface chip. The staff of Perpetuity is getting this information as we speak. Those not used to direct communications may have a hard time adjusting. Please weed out those that cannot handle the downloads. Report them to the CSC and their duties will automatically be reassigned to those more capable."

"Direct download?" North asked. "General, that could be very dangerous with the amount of pharma these people will be given. The safeguards will be in place to protect cerebral integrity, yes? If cadets are in the middle of a sim and get direct downloads, it could fry them. At the very least it'll put them out of commission for a few hours, which I cannot afford to have happen."

"Major, I have the utmost confidence in you," Birmingham said. "I know you will make sure that doesn't happen. If the CSC can't get the numbers it needs from new cadets then it may have to resort to bringing older personnel back up to the front to fill those numbers. I do not think either of us wants to see that happen, do we?"

"No, General, we do not," North sighed. "I'll oversee the transition. You'll get your numbers and I'll handle my staff."

"Good," Birmingham said. "Then I'll leave you to it. My assistant already tells me that Sergeant-at-Arms Metzger is interrogating suspects as we speak. I'll send him a message of my approval. I know you'll show the same initiative with the recruits. One week, Major. One week."

The general's face blinked out and was replaced by the CSC logo again. North swiped his hand across the desk and the logo disappeared.

"Corporal!" North shouted.

Ngyuen appeared immediately at the office hatch.

"Yes, Major?" she asked.

"We're you standing out there listening?" North asked.

"No, Major," Ngyuen said. "It's the new protocol. My chip alerted me that your call with General Birmingham had ended, so I expected you to need me."

"Great," North sighed again. "Where's Metzger right now?"

"He is on Security Level Four," Ngyuen replied. "He has a do not disturb request on his comm, sir. I have been told that he is with a suspect."

"A suspect? He found someone and didn't alert me?" North asked.

"He has been handed full authority with finding any infiltrators, sir," Ngyuen said. "The information given to the staff said as much. Was the CSC information incorrect?"

"You've already received a chip communication?" North asked.

"We all have, sir," Ngyuen said. "Haven't you?"

"No. No, I haven't," North said.

"Well...that's interesting," Ngyuen said, her entire demeanor changing. "I'll alert Doctor Jagath immediately. Your chip may have been damaged somehow. Perhaps in the attack earlier."

"I don't have time to see Doctor Jagath," North said. "I've got to get down to the recruit bay and make sure we are ready for more intake. The commandant has to make a speech and that is now my duty, I guess."

"That is already being handled, sir," Ngyuen said. "I have sent a copy of the intake speech to all pertinent personnel. The speeches will happen, sir, just not by you. The personnel are on full alert and ready for the influx of recruits coming our way. It would be better if you see Doctor Jagath to have your chip checked, sir. You won't be at the efficiency level the Perpetuity needs if you cannot receive the communications from CSC."

"Fine," North said. "Tell Jagath I am on my way. I'm going to stop by my quarters first though."

"I would suggest you see the doctor before you take any pharma, sir. It may interfere with the examination," Ngyuen said. "If that is what you intended to do when you arrived in your quarters. I don't mean to presume."

"Well, you did," North said. "I'm not going to pharma up, Corporal. I am going to clean up. I stink with sweat and blood and everything. I'm going to put on a clean uniform and then go see Jagath. Tell him fifteen minutes."

"Yes, sir," Ngyuen said. "And what shall I do about Lieutenant Linklater?"

"What about Linklater?" North asked.

"He has been calling for you, sir," Ngyuen said. "He is in the server tower. Says he has something to show you as soon as you can get away."

"That's not going to happen until next week," North said. "Tell him to deal with whatever it is on his own unless it is going to slow down training. Is it?"

"Sir?"

"Is it going to slow down training?" North asked.

"I do not know, sir," Ngyuen said. "The lieutenant wouldn't give me any specifics. But, I do not think so or I would have been alerted. The new communications protocols have me connected to the simulation training numbers. They are on track for our previous goals and are now being ramped up for our new goals. If the lieutenant's issue affected the simulations then the numbers would be off."

"Fine, whatever," North said. "Tell Jagath I am on the way and tell Linklater that he is on his own."

North stood and stretched. He walked to the hatch and stepped past Ngyuen as the corporal moved out of his way. The major was almost out of the reception room hatch and into the corridor before he realized something.

"Wait, why was Linklater calling you and not me?" North asked.

"I have had all direct communications to you rerouted to me, sir," Ngyuen said. "CSC orders to keep you on track. It is not a hardwired order, though, so you can override and handle your own communications if you'd like."

"I would like," North said. "And don't ever do that again. You tell me next time the CSC gives an order like that."

"I wouldn't have to tell you, sir, if you go see Doctor Jagath and get your chip repaired," Ngyuen said. "If that is the issue."

"What the hell does that mean?" North snapped.

"Nothing, sir," Ngyuen said. "I just know how much stress you are under."

"Were you in Terlinger's shit this much too, Corporal?" North asked.

"Of course, sir," Ngyuen said. "It's my job to be in the commandant's shit. I wouldn't be a very good assistant if I wasn't."

North studied Ngyuen for a few seconds then nodded.

"Fine," North said. "Just be prepared for me to bite your head off now and again."

"It comes with the territory, sir," Ngyuen said. She cocked her head and grinned. "Doctor Jagath is expecting you in fifteen minutes. He asks that you not be late since he is busy still with the wounded from the attack."

"I'll be on time," North said. "Hold down the fort while I'm gone."

"I will, sir," Ngyuen said. "You can count on me."

Twenty-Four

The stun baton sparked as Metzger dragged the tip across the table. A battered recruit sat manacled, his head lolling, one eye swollen shut, and blood dripping from between his lips. The recruit watched the stun baton with his non-swollen eye until it reached the end of the table and Metzger started dragging it back in the opposite direction. When the stun baton was directly in front of the recruit, the bloodied young man looked up and winced.

"Please," the recruit muttered. "No more. Please."

"Doesn't have to be anymore," Metzger said. "I just need you to tell me who else is on this station."

"I don't know," the recruit whined. "I've already said I'm not an Estelian. I was born on Earth!"

"Then why won't your chip register as valid?" Metzger asked, tapping the tip of the stun baton on the table slowly.

Tap…tap…tap…tap…

"My chip is defective," the recruit replied, bloody drool dripping off his chin and onto the table. "Has been for awhile."

Metzger rubbed the tip of the stun baton in the spot of drool then placed the tip under the recruit's chin and pushed his head up.

"The CSC doesn't recruit defectives," Metzger said.

"They do now," the recruit said. "I'm from the Green Quadrant, Amazon Sector, Sao Paulo region. I ain't had a working chip since I was a kid. The one the academy gave me when I graduated was like fourth hand and half rusted when they put it in. Got me my rations and bed, but never did work well enough for me to get a job. I told you all of this!"

"Don't get pissy, kid," Metzger said, tapping the baton against the young man's throat. "I know you told me all of this. That's the problem. I don't want to hear the same words over and over. I want to hear new words. You're going to start giving me new words or I fry your voice box. Just burn that Adam's apple right out of your throat. Sure, you can get a synthetic replacement, but won't be your voice no more. Just some computer voice manufactured by some robot fuck in Yellow Quadrant. Ha! If you're lucky! You'll probably get an aftermarket job made on Trafflek or from the Velf System. You want to sound like a Velfian? Those colonists are messed up."

"Please, Sergeant, I don't know any other words," the young man pleaded. He flinched as Metzger pressed the baton harder against his throat. "Please! I'm a ghetto kid that got scooped up by the CSC while I was napping with my girl!"

"Why the fuck were you napping?" Metzger said. "Hard working men and women are dying out there and you are napping? I should cook your gizzard just for being a lazy piece of shit."

"I was napping because you can't sleep all night where I come from," the young man replied. "You'll get jumped and harvested."

"Bullshit," Metzger said as he switched on the stun baton.

The recruit screamed and shook as the voltage slammed through his neck. The scream quickly changed tone as Metzger kept pushing, jamming the baton as far into the young man's throat as he could without choking him to death. Metzger smiled as the recruit's skin started to sizzle and turn red then a crusty black.

The young man's scream ended in a hoarse croak and a final whine before he passed out and collapsed forward onto the table, his head making a hollow thunk on the rough metal surface.

The hatch to the interrogation room opened and a guard looked in.

"Want another?" the woman, Corporal Keisha Bunk, asked.

"Yeah," Metzger smiled. "But bring the fucker in before you take this one out. I want him to see what he has to look forward to."

"Will do," Bunk nodded. "How long we keeping this up?"

"As long as it fucking takes!" Metzger snapped. "What the fuck kind of question is that? You think the DGs take breaks? You think the sons of bitches that are hiding on the Perpetuity are going to call time fucking out?"

"I was just wondering if you wanted me to load up some pharma," Bunk replied, not even phased by Metzger's outburst, well used to them. "Supply dropped off a fresh crate. Me and Pinnti was about to get right. I can bring you a couple."

"Yeah, bring me one," Metzger said then smiled. "No, bring me a dozen."

"A dozen? You wanna die?" Bunk grinned. "That much pharma will make your heart explode out your ass. Watched my uncle do six at once and he was bleeding from his pores for two days. Ain't pretty."

"I know it ain't pretty," Metzger said. "That's why they ain't for me."

Bunk looked at the collapsed recruit then over her shoulder and out into the corridor where several more suspects were shackled to the floor.

"I get ya," Bunk smiled. "I'll get the pharma while Pinnti brings in the next victim."

"Good," Metzger said. "I need to have some answers by the morning and a hard pharma push may be the only way." He tapped the back of his head. "CSC's gotta get what CSC wants."

Twenty-Five

The vents above North's head sucked up the cleaning steam then reversed and blasted him with hot, dry air. He stood there, his head nodding as he struggled to stay awake, well past time for another dose of pharma. He wanted nothing more than to grab an injector and get right, but Ngyuen's words kept running over and over in his head.

No, that wasn't it. It wasn't her words so much as her demeanor. North couldn't quite put his finger on it. Maybe if he had some pharma…

"No," he growled into the mirror as he grabbed his uniform and slipped it on. "No pharma. Not unless I have to."

He picked up his soiled uniform and began to toss it into the laundry chute when something fell out and clinked on the metal floor. North bent down and picked up Terlinger's medal. He stared at it for a couple seconds then tucked it into a pocket of his new uniform. He turned and the room about him took a serious sideways dive. North put out his hand and braced himself against the wall. A few deep, deep breaths and the sideways feeling dissipated. He double checked himself in the mirror then strode to his hatch and out of his quarters.

Station personnel rushed past him. There were perfunctory nods, but very few salutes or acknowledgements of his rank and authority. North found that strange, but also knew it probably had more to do with the added stress of the CSC's expectations than anything to do with him personally. Not to mention the issue of Commandant Terlinger having just passed. The man had been a growly bastard, but he was respected on the station.

The lift opened up in front of North and he had to blink a few times to figure out why he was standing there.

"Getting on, sir?" a woman asked. "Sir?"

"What? Oh, sorry, Private. Yes, thank you," North smiled as he stepped onto the lift.

"Are you going down to the recruit bay, sir?" the private asked. "I am heading that direction as well to help with the individual scans. All hands on deck, right?"

She looked up at North, a broad smile on her face.

"Sir? Are you alright?" the private asked, her smile fading.

"What? Oh, yes. My apologies. Just a lot on my mind, Private," North said. "The CSC has sure handed me a shit sandwich. Just trying to figure out which end I take a bite from first."

"Oh...okay," the private said. "So, the recruit bay?"

"What? Uh, no," North said. "I'm going to the medical bay. Chip is acting up. Corporal Ngyuen won't let it drop, so I guess I have an appointment with Doctor Jagath." North stopped talking and glanced at the private. "Not sure why I gave you all that information. Probably more than you wanted to know."

The private just gave a weak smile in response then pressed her wrist and pretended to scan a generic report on the demographic makeup of the latest batch of incoming recruits. After a couple of seconds, the lift stopped and the private gave a short salute then hurried off.

North watched her go and rubbed at the bridge of his nose as the lift doors closed again.

"Medical bay," North said.

"State the level, please," a computerized voice responded.

"Whichever one Doctor Jagath is on," North said.

"Medical Bay Nine, Level Five," the voice said.

North steadied himself as the lift ascended. He pressed his wrist and waited for an image to come up.

"Interface, please," he said when nothing happened.

No image appeared.

"Interface, please," North snapped.

Still no image.

"Son of a bitch," North growled. "Cancel request. I'm going to the server tower."

"Doctor Jagath is not in the server tower, Major North," the voice stated.

"No shit," North replied. "I'm changing my mind. Take me to the server tower."

"Doctor Jagath is not in the server tower, Major North," the voice stated once more.

"Right, got that, thanks," North snapped. "I'm not going to see Doctor Jag-."

"You have an appointment with Doctor Jagath," the voice said. "Doctor Jagath is expecting you, Major North."

"Doctor Jagath is just going to have to wait," North said. "I'm going to go find Lieutenant Linklater first. Reroute the lift, please."

The voice did not answer.

"Hello? Reroute the lift, damnit!" North shouted.

"Corporal Ngyuen has authorized medical appointment rescheduling," the voice said. "Rerouting lift to server tower."

"Are you shitting me?" North growled. He pressed his wrist then growled louder when nothing happened. "Fucking Ngyuen. Approve my schedule. Approve me going to the server tower. Fuck that fucking bitch!"

The lift doors opened just as his last words came out and a group of techs all took a couple of steps back at the venom they encountered.

"What the fuck are you looking at?" North asked.

They did not respond.

"Fucking interface is on the fritz," North growled as he stepped from the lift and pushed through the group of techs. "Damn chip is out."

"Fucking doubleganger," a tech muttered.

North whirled on the man and grabbed him by the neck. "What was that?"

"Nothing," the tech choked.

"Right," North said and tossed the tech aside.

A couple of the other techs gasped, but covered their mouths quickly. North glared at them then looked down the corridor.

"Which way to the server tower?" North asked. "Damn, what fucking level am I on?"

"That way, sir," a tech said, pointing to the left. "Two junctions down."

"Good. Thanks," North said.

The techs hurried into the lift as North stalked off. Just as the doors to the lift closed, North heard the words "report to Metzger." North spun about, but the lift doors had already closed and the techs were gone.

"Fuck them," he muttered.

Two junctions later and he was staring at the hatch to the server tower. He placed his wrist in front of the panel, but nothing happened. Luckily it was an older panel, so he pressed it manually and the hatch opened instantly. But there was no lift. Instead, the hatchway was crisscrossed with holograms stating "Caution! Caution! Open space! Caution!"

"I can see that," North said as he peered into the server tower and saw the empty space before him.

He grabbed onto the handles on each side of the hatch and leaned in, looking down first then up. Far above him he could see the bottom of the lift.

"Hey!" North shouted. "Link? You up there?"

"Major?" a voice asked behind North, causing the major to jump and almost lose his hold on the safety handles. "You looking for Lieutenant Linklater?"

North turned on the voice and came face to face with Hal Wendt.

"Do I know you?" North asked as a stabbing pain shot from the middle of his forehead, up over his scalp, and lodged right at the base of his neck. "Oh…shit…"

Wendt dropped the packs he was holding and grabbed North's uniform just as the man started to fall backwards. He pulled the major in to the corridor and helped him to sit down on the floor next to the hatch.

"Whoa there, Major," Wendt said. "Whoa. Take a load off, sir. You almost took a tumble that you wouldn't have liked."

"What's your name?" North whispered.

"Wendt, sir," Wendt replied. "You know that. We play poker each month."

"Wendt? Right, right. Poker," North smiled then frowned then smiled then frowned. "Fuck. My head is killing me." North reached out and gripped Wendt's uniform. "You have any pharma on you? Any injectors?"

"No, sir, sorry," Wendt said. "None on me." He grabbed up one of the packs and opened it then pulled out a small tube. "I have some hydration, though. That may be what you need. I heard down at the mess that you were there when that DG blew himself up. You're probably in shock, sir. The bruises on your face don't look like they are helping, either."

"Are you a fucking doctor?" North snapped.

"Well, no, sir, but-."

"Then shut your fucking mouth," North said, his hands gripping Wendt's uniform even tighter. "You shut your damned mouth, do you hear?"

"Yes, sir. Sorry, sir," Wendt said and let the pack and hydration tube go so he could try to get North's fingers from his uniform. "Sir? Do you mind?"

"What the hell, North?" Linklater asked as he swung out of the hatch and into the corridor. "You trying to kiss Wendt or something?"

"Link?" North asked, turning his attention to the lieutenant.

"Yeah, it's me," Linklater said, giving Wendt a worried glance. "I heard your lame ass calling me. I guess Ngyuen finally told you I've been calling."

"I was supposed to go see Jagath, but I came to see you," North said. "Not sure why. It all hurts way too much. Should it hurt? I just need some pharma. You got any, Link?"

"Well, this is a bit dramatic," Linklater said. He looked to Wendt. "He been like this the whole time."

"Yeah," Wendt nodded as he got North's fingers from his uniform and took a couple steps back. "Says his head is killing him."

"Really?" Linklater replied. "Give me your interface scanner."

"Shouldn't we get him to a medical bay?" Wendt asked. "I don't think this is tech related."

"Only one way to find out," Linklater snapped. "Give me your interface scanner."

Wendt shrugged and pulled his scanner from his belt and handed it over. Linklater knelt down next to North and placed the scanner to the base of North's skull.

"Hey," North mumbled. "Fuck you, Estelian trash."

"Really?" Linklater sighed. "Shut the fuck up and let me do my job, North."

The scanner beeped shrilly and Linklater frowned.

"What the hell?" Linklater said as he handed the scanner over to Wendt. "You seeing what I'm seeing?"

Wendt took the scanner and his eyes widened. "He's got a jam. No outside transmission showing, though."

"So it's on him," Linklater said. "Great. Just what I need. Like the servers aren't enough, now I got to scan his whole body."

"I still think we should get him to a medical bay," Wendt said.

"You know why you aren't an officer, Wendt?" Linklater asked as he pulled a different scanner from his belt and started running it up and down North's body. "Because you aren't a duplicitous prick. I am. I know when something ain't right."

Linklater's scanner beeped and he stopped, hovering over one of North's pockets.

"What have we got here?" Linklater asked then reached into North's pocket. He pulled out Terlinger's medal. "Weird."

He scanned the medal then stuffed it into his own pocket.

"Was that it?" Wendt asked.

"No," Linklater said. "Not sure what it is."

"Looks like a medal," Wendt said.

"Yeah, it looks like it," Linklater said. "But it's not."

"So, it isn't the jammer?" Wendt asked.

"I just said it wasn't," Linklater snapped. "Keep up, Wendt."

Linklater scanned down to North's toes then started back up. When he got all the way to North's forehead the scanner beeped again.

"Hold him," Linklater said as he set the scanner aside.

"What?" Wendt asked. "Why?"

"Because I found it," Linklater said. "Just hold him."

Wendt held North by the shoulders as Linklater pressed his thumbs against North's forehead.

"Ow! Fuck!" North shouted as blood started to pour from a small slit in his skin. "What the hell, Link?"

"Shut up and be still," Linklater said.

North was not still. His whole body began to shake and shudder as Linklater pressed harder. Then North started to scream.

"Got it!" Linklater said. "Subcutaneous motherfucker. How the hell did that get in there?"

Linklater held a small piece of metal between his thumb and forefinger then tossed it quickly to the ground as it sparked and sent a small wisp of smoke up into the air.

"Oh, man, that feels better," North said. "My head doesn't hurt as much." North turned and focused on Linklater. "Don't have a craving for pharma anymore, either."

"Bullshit," Linklater said. "I know you."

"Okay, but the craving doesn't make me want to kick your ass for an injector," North said. "What the fuck just happened?"

"I squeezed a jammer out of your forehead," Linklater said. "How's your chip feel?"

North realized he was getting direct downloads and paused before answering.

"Jesus," North said as he stood up. "How long have we been on alert?"

"What?"Wendt asked. "We're not on alert."

"We sure as hell should be!" North snapped. "I just received an alert of Estelian warships just passing Neptune and coming our way fast!"

North stood up, swayed a little, then shook it off.

"I need to get to the bridge," North said. He pressed his wrist and an image of Ngyuen came up.

"I see you have your chip back online, sir," Ngyuen said. "Despite not seeing Doctor Jagath. I assume you are calling because of the alert."

"You think?" North said. "Why the hell hasn't a station wide alert gone up?"

"CSC orders, sir," Ngyuen said. "Training is to continue on schedule. They will be handling the Estelian threat, sir. Quads have been dispatched from Titan Base. Cruisers and destroyers on are standby. They do not expect the Estelian warships to get far."

"Meet me on the bridge, Corporal," North said. "We need to sound general quarters."

"That would directly counter the CSC's directives, sir," Ngyuen said. "But I will meet you on the bridge. Should I get General Birmingham on line?"

"Not until I get there," North said. "But let Metzger know what is happening. I want security ready."

"Yes, sir," Ngyuen said. "I will see to that right away."

North pressed his wrist and Ngyuen's image vanished. He looked down at the blackened speck of metal on the floor.

"Find out where that came from," North said to Linklater.

"I'll add it to my list of shit to do," Linklater said. "Which is getting longer and longer. Oh, here." He pulled Terlinger's medal out of his pocket and handed it to North. "Something special?"

"I don't know," North said. "Maybe. Hey, do me a favor." He looked at Wendt with suspicion.

"He's good," Linklater said. "What's the favor?"

"Don't mention that jammer to anyone, alright?" North requested. "I want to sort a few things out first."

"Blabbing about this thing wasn't on my list," Linklater said. "But I do need to speak to you about what is."

"Not the time," North said. "I'll get with you once I have a handle on the Estelian situation."

"There're really Estelian warships heading our way?" Wendt asked.

"Yes, but that's not general knowledge until I make the announcement," North said. "Keep that under wraps as well."

"Yeah, sure," Wendt nodded.

North started to jog away then stopped and turned. "Hey, Link?"

"What?"

"Thanks for fixing my head," North said.

"Someone has to," Linklater said. "And come see me the second you can get away. This is serious."

"Will do," North nodded then took off running towards the lift.

Twenty-Six

"Looking better!" Valencio called out. "But still not even close to good!"

She flew her fighter skiff around a sixteen, causing several cadet pilots to panic and almost lose control.

"See that? That's what I mean!" Valencio shouted. "A small distraction and you get all wobbly!"

"Hey, Captain?" London asked over the comm. "Have you heard anything from the Perpetuity?"

"No," Valencio said. "I'm on intracomm, remember? You're supposed to be monitoring communications."

"Yeah, I am," London said. "I thought I caught some chatter about Estelian warships then the chatter stopped. Just wondering if you got an override communication from the station that I wasn't privy to."

"Just tell me what's going on, London," Valencio ordered. "I don't have time for this conversation."

"I told you. Estelian warships," London said. "The chatter cut off before I could get specifics."

"That's all you have for me? Estelian warships?" Valencio asked. "That was probably flight control jabbering and a supervisor told them to can it."

"I don't think so," London replied. "It sounded a lot more urgent than that."

"Then call in for clarification," Valencio said.

"I have and they won't confirm or deny," London replied.

"They what?" Valencio asked. "What do you mean they won't confirm or deny? They have to do one or the other."

"I'm just telling you what I was told," London said. "They refuse to confirm or deny that I heard what I heard."

"They're messing with you," Zenobia interrupted.

"Pay attention to your cadet pilots, Demon," Valencio said. "I have this."

"I'm just saying I think they are messing with London, is all," Zenobia responded. "It's because of that thing with Hurley's lady friend in the mess."

"Jesus, that was months ago," London said. "And that chick was nailing anything that looked at her. I was hardly the only offender."

"Just saying," Zenobia said.

"Do we have to have this conversation?" Richtoff asked. "I am trying to instruct some highly incompetent cadet pilots."

"Richtoff is right," Valencio said. "Can the crap and get back to work. London? Patch me through to the Perpetuity. I'll get to the bottom of this."

"You got it, boss," London replied. "Your comm is open."

"Flight control? This is Captain Valencio," Valencio called. "I am hearing rumors of possible Estelian warships. Is this correct?"

"Sorry, Captain," a woman responded. "But we cannot confirm nor deny that rumor. All information regarding Estelian warships will have to come from Major North."

"Then put me through to Major North," Valencio ordered. She switched the comm to intra. "Demon? Take my cadets. I'm not letting flight control off until I get to the bottom of this."

"Roger," Zenobia said. "Come on, morons! Move your asses over to me! NOW!"

Valencio watched as her sixteens flew off in ragged formation and over to Zenobia's groupings.

"Flight control? You still there?" Valencio asked.

"Yes, Captain," the same woman replied. "We cannot patch you through to Major North at this time. We have been told he is occupied currently."

"Occupied? With what?" Valencio asked.

"Not our place to know or our place to say," the woman answered.

"Then give me a long range scan reading," Valencio said. "You can't deny me that. Not while I'm running flight drills in the vacuum."

There was a pause. "I'll have to check with my supervisor."

"What is your rank?" Valencio asked.

"Corporal, sir," the woman replied.

"And I'm a captain," Valencio said. "Is your supervisor ranked above me?"

"No, sir," the woman replied.

"Then give me long range scan readings," Valencio snapped. "That is an order, Corporal! Are we clear?"

"Yes, sir," the woman said. "Sending long range scan readings to you now. I apologize for the hesitation, Captain. I was under general orders to keep things buttoned up."

"Understood, Corporal," Valencio said as she waited for the scan readings to appear on her screen. "I'll be sure and mention that if I am questioned about how I received these scans. I can certainly... What the hell?"

"May I go now, Captain?" the woman asked, her voice displaying severe anxiety as raised voices could be heard off comm. "I have other duties to attend to."

"Yes, of course," Valencio said. "Thank you for the scans."

Valencio focused her attention on what was scrolling across her screen. She tapped at the interface and the scroll transformed from raw data and into a three-dimensional representation of what was coming towards Perpetuity and Earth.

"My god..." Valencio whispered. "They've already gotten past the Pluto blockade and Neptune outpost. How have they gotten so far so fast?"

Valencio watched the Estelian warships in the image begin to multiply as the data continued rendering. She counted at least eight full-size battleships with several smaller ships in flanking positions.

"London? I just sent you the scans," Valencio said. She tried to keep her voice from shaking, but she could not say she was one hundred percent successful. "London? Do you see this?"

"Hold on," London said. "I'm transferring the data to my... Jesus, Buddha, and Vishnu..."

"So, you are seeing it?" Valencio asked.

"I don't know what I'm seeing," London said. "That's not just some warships, that's a full blown, fucking armada!"

"Eight, no, ten battleships with what? A dozen cruisers and destroyers?" Valencio asked. "That's my count. A dozen cruisers and destroyers."

"Ten battleships, yes," London said. "Eight cruisers and seven destroyers."

"What? Where are you seeing those numbers?" Valencio gasped.

"Rotate one-eighty," London exclaimed. "They're using the battleships' size to block our scans. You can catch bits and pieces of the other destroyers hiding amongst the battleships."

"Twenty five warships," Valencio sighed. "Pluto and Neptune gone. That leaves Titan Base, the Asteroid Belt stations, and the Mars colonies to stop them."

"Looks like Titan Base has launched quads," London said. "I'm catching punch blips all over the place. I'm guessing contact in fifteen minutes."

"Those pilots better not punch in too close," Valencio said. "They're going to be sick as dogs when they get there. I hate punching."

"No one likes punching," London said. "But, no choice now, really."

"Take over long range scans, London," Valencio ordered. "I want real time stats and I don't want to deal with Perpetuity again. There's something wrong back there."

"I hear that," London said. "You can count on me, boss."

Twenty-Seven

Retching sounds were all that filled the comm as the six squadrons of RT-90 quad-winged fightercrafts punched out of interspace, stopping a close five hundred kilometers from the Estelian armada. Once the retching slowed, the six squadrons separated from each other, with each squadron consisting of eighty quad fighters, divided into their own attack sixteens.

The quad fighters were the elite attack vehicles of the CSC. Flown by a single pilot that utilized an AI copilot instead of a human one, the quads were armed with two plasma cannons, six disruptor missiles, and four strafing guns per wing, giving them enough firepower to rival some of the smaller CSC and Estelian cutters.

As the squadrons spread out, the approaching Estelian warships followed suit, moving out of their close formation and into a wide arc, giving them a fuller firing field.

"Hercules squadron, we are taking the left flank," Captain Luella MacAbee called out. "Ares squadron is on our six. Hermes squadron takes right flank with Zeus squadron on their six. Hera squadron is head on with Artemis squadron hanging back for support. We clear on this, people?"

"Clear," Captain Vincent Joyner, Ares squadron leader, replied.

"Got it," Captain Steph DuLaque replied as her quad banked right, leading her Hermes squadron on its flanking attack.

"Clear," Captain Walker Wilson said. He hit his thrusters and led his Zeus squadron into their following position behind Hermes.

"Ready to headbutt these DGs!" Captain Chet Munanga, Hera squadron leader, exclaimed.

"Holding tight," Captain Ellen Garcia said. "Artemis squadron will hang back and pick up the slack where we're needed."

"Ain't gonna be no slack from my side," DuLaque said. "Hermes will do its job and slap some doublegangers down!"

"You sure about that, DuLaque?" Garcia laughed. "You forgetting how I saved your ass back in the Gallent system? Plenty of slack there for me to pick up."

"Can't count that, Garcia!" DuLaque replied. "Those DGs punched in right on top of us!"

"Excuses, excuses," Garcia laughed.

"Enough shit talk," MacAbee said. "Let's get to work."

The sixteens within each squadron moved as one, a seamless choreography of quads breaking from the main body and into their battle positions. As the squadrons spread out and readied themselves, the Estelian Armada came to a full stop.

"Mac? You see this?" Munanga asked. "They're making it way too easy for me to come at them."

"I see it," MacAbee replied. "Sensors show their weapons ready, but thrusters are powering down."

"They want to be sitting ducks?" Munanga asked.

"I don't know," MacAbee responded. "Eyes sharp, people. Looks like they are setting a trap."

"What kind of trap?" Joyner asked. "There aren't any other warships on the scanners. Can't really set a trap without something to fill it."

"Just move into positions and wait for my call to attack," MacAbee ordered. "Move ass and watch your scanners."

"Roger."

"On it."

"Almost in position."

"Locked and loaded."

"You seeing this?" Garcia asked. "Hey! Do you guys see what I'm seeing? Check your fucking scanners!"

"Those are punch waves," MacAbee said. "Somethings coming through right behind us!"

"How the fuck can they do that?" Wilson asked. "What the fuck, Mac? They can't punch in behind us!"

"Titan Base! Titan Base this is MacAbee!" MacAbee called over the comm. "Titan Base, come in!"

There was a squelch of static then a faint voice. "Captain...base...attack."

"We are in attack positions," MacAbee replied. "But we have punch signals coming in from behind. What's going on back there? Why aren't interspatial locks in place?"

"Cap...gangers...destroyed," the voice replied.

"Yes, we are going to fucking destroy the doublegangers!" MacAbee shouted. "But why are we getting punch wave readings? Are more CSC ships coming in?"

"No...Titan...attack...sabotage," the voice said. "Half...destroyed...heavy casualties...defenses offline...locks down..."

"Repeat that last part, Titan!" MacAbee yelled. "Did you say interspatial locks are down? Titan? Can you hear me, Titan?"

"Affirmative...locks down...base lost," the voice responded. "Evacuation impossible...your own...luck..."

A loud explosion could be heard then the comm squelched and went dead.

"Motherfucker..." MacAbee whispered.

"Jesus shitting the bed," Wilson said. "We're on our own, aren't we?"

"Looks like it," MacAbee replied. "Squadron leaders, we are on our own. If Titan Base is down then we are all that stands between here and the asteroid belt. Those folks better keep the interspatial locks in place or these bastards will be able to punch halfway into the system."

"What about the wave signals behind us?" DuLaque asked.

"Nothing we can do until we see solid opponents," MacAbee replied. "Stay on target and focus on the armada. Whatever is punching through will have to be dealt with later."

"Let's thin the big boys' numbers before they can try," Joyner said. "We're with you, Mac."

"All squadrons in position?" MacAbee asked. When she received acknowledgement from each squadron leader, she crossed herself, kissed her ring finger, patted her control console five times then flipped off the armada in front of her. "Take it to them, people! CSC or die!"

"CSC OR DIE!"

Twenty-Eight

Hera squadron raced headlong at the Estelian armada. The eighty quads broke into their sixteens, turning one target into five. Hera sixteens One and Five pulled up, their quads angling up and over the armada while sixteens Three and Four dipped down, going for the armada's belly. Hera sixteen Two kept their direct course, never wavering from the head on attack.

"Snap in with your AIs, pilots," Munanga ordered from Hera sixteen One. "We'll need all the advantages we can get. If your AI tells you to fire or dive then you fucking listen and do it. No hesitations. Lightning reflexes and sure shots. No missing. Missing will get you killed."

Munanaga kept his eyes locked on the three battleships that grew closer and closer as he angled his quad's arc back down towards the Estelian warships. He relied on his physical senses, confident that his AI would alert him to anything picked up by the scanners. He felt a calm come over him as he flicked the safety off his weapons array and placed his thumb over the disruptor missile controls.

"Enemy defensive systems at full," his AI announced in his earpiece. "Adjusting targeting to weak points in Estelian shielding. Please fire missiles in three, two, one."

Munanga pressed his thumb down and four disruptor missiles shot from his wings, their thrusters sending them towards the closest battleship at a speed that almost was too fast for his eyes to track. He watched the projectiles fly at their target, a sly grin on his face.

"Second wave ready?" he asked his AI. "Can't let them get comfortable."

"Waiting for data from initial attack," the AI replied.

Munanga caught sight of dozens more missiles flying past as the rest of sixteens One and Four's quads fired as well. Over a hundred disruptor missiles shot towards the Estelian battleships, all concentrated at the same targets. Munanga counted in his head as he waited for contact and detonation.

"Come on, babies," Munanga said. "Make daddy proud."

One second after those words were spoken the missiles impacted with the battleships' shields. His helmet visor tinted almost to black as the explosions threatened to blind him. When the last explosion died out, Munanga's sly smile turned to an alarmed grimace.

"What the shit?" he cried out. "Where'd they go?"

The three battleships the two Hera sixteens had been aiming at were gone. Not a hint of them having been in front of the quads at all.

"I need readings stat!" Munanga yelled over the comm. "Anyone else seeing a big fucking blank spot in front of them!"

Voices from his squadron replied and confirmed that the targets were no longer there. Munanga tapped at his scanners, replaying the readings from just seconds before. His jaw went slack as he realized that the battleships hadn't been there for some time.

"AI? What the hell just happened? I saw those battleships with my own eyes!" Munanga shouted. "How the fuck could we fire at nothing?"

"I am sorry, Captain," the AI replied. "All readings indicated that targets were directly ahead. Further study of the data will be needed."

"We don't have time for further study! Find me those ships!" Munanga yelled as he pulled his quad up and banked to the right.

His sixteen and sixteen Four did the same and followed the captain as he chose two new targets.

"Battleship and destroyer," Munanga said. "We hit those fucks with everything we have."

"Negative, Captain," the AI said. "Readings similar to the previous targets detected. This could be the same scenario we just encountered."

"Only one way to find out," Munanga said. "Give them hell, Hera!" More disruptor missiles were released, but Munanga didn't wait for the results of the impacts. "Close in on the cruisers on your three! Plasma cannons concentrated on their bridges! Let's knock some holes in those defenses!"

Explosions erupted behind Munanga's quad as the second wave of missiles detonated. He was not surprised when his AI spoke.

"Negative impacts," the AI said. "No ships detected."

"Then how the hell are the missiles detonating?" Munanga asked. "They have to hit something to blow!"

"Answer not available," the AI said. "More study needed."

"You think faster than the Makers! How do you not have answers?" Munanga yelled. "Get me some fucking answers!"

He opened up on the two cruisers in front of him with his plasma cannons. The bright blasts were aimed directly at the cruisers' bridges and began to pummel their defensive shields. He grinned as he watched the shields light up bright blue then turn to purple as the plasma started to weaken the defenses. Then his grin faltered as he saw the cruisers shimmer, shimmer, and disappear.

"You have got to be joking," Munanga growled. "What the hell is going on?"

Twenty-Nine

DuLaque's AI relayed Munanga's shouts as a background stream of information, but the captain ignored her comrade's frustrations as she concentrated on taking Hermes squadron towards the armada's right flank.

"We're going for a full swing!" DuLaque ordered. "Sixteens One through Five line up! We stay tight until my go ahead then spread out and take it to 'em!"

The leaders of each sixteen acknowledged her orders and Hermes squadron got into position with each sixteen lining up in an almost single file formation. DuLaque took point, her quad racing towards the armada at a speed that bordered on reckless. Her shoulders were hunched as her hands were plunged into the control panel, one hand manipulating the flight stick and the other working the accelerator.

"Pulling back on the thrusters would be advised," her AI warned. "Point of no return imminent in eight seconds."

DuLaque counted six then powered her thrusters down and whipped the quad hard to the left.

"Now, Hermes!" DuLaque yelled into the comm as she activated her weapons and opened fire on the cruisers and destroyers in her sights. "Give them everything you've got!"

The sixteens that made up Hermes squadron spread out, lining themselves up in a wide and ever expanding arc that came close to covering the entire right flank of the Estelian armada. Missiles flew, plasma bolts burst forward, and strafing rounds barked as Hermes squadron followed their leader's orders and sent everything they had at the warships.

Flashes of impacts with the ships' shields lit up the vacuum, becoming so bright that many of the quad pilots had to squint into the attack even with their helmet visors at full tint. The quads pressed the attack by easing their thrusters forward, closing the distance between them and the Estelians.

"Watch for the counter," DuLaque warned. "No way these DGs are just going to let us smack them around without trying to smack back."

"Missiles depleted," DuLaque's AI announced. "Plasma cannons at half. Strafing guns online and ready for use."

"Double the power in the cannons," DuLaque said. "I want each bolt to hurt even more."

"Acknowledged," the AI replied. "Plasma cannon power doubled. Depletion will occur in half the time now. Would you like an emergency reserve?"

"Yeah," DuLaque said. "Save me ten percent. Gotta have something to fight my way out with if things go south."

DuLaque could hear some of her pilots call out as they fired their last missiles and switched to plasma cannons while others switched from plasma cannons to missiles. The quads' strafing guns were near limitless, so no one announced any issues or changes with those weapons.

"What am I looking at?" DuLaque asked her AI. "Any damage to the DGs' ships?"

"Impossible to ascertain at this time, Captain," the AI replied. "The attack is too concentrated to scan past the Estelians' shields."

"Give me a report as soon as you have one," DuLaque said.

"Of course, Captain," the AI responded. "As soon as-."

DuLaque didn't hear the rest of her AI's comment as she yanked hard on the flight stick, sending her quad spinning to the left as a wave of missiles came flying at her. She continued the spin, keeping her quad moving as missile after missile followed her.

"How the hell did those get through?" DuLaque yelled as she pushed her thrusters to full, ending the wing over wing spin and instead taking her quad into a spiraling nose dive. "AI? How did the DGs get missiles through their shields and past our fire?"

"Their method is uncertain," the AI replied. "Calculating scenarios now."

Screams could be heard over the comm as Hermes squadron was quickly ripped apart by the oncoming missiles. Voices were cut off by the brief sounds of explosions as quad after quad was destroyed. DuLaque pushed those sounds from her head as she struggled to maintain control of her quad and avoid the ever encroaching missiles.

"Reverse strafing guns!" DuLaque ordered. "Give me some tail fire while I try to get us clear of these things!"

"Strafing guns reversed," the AI replied. "Targeting missiles now."

DuLaque's quad rocked to the left as a missile detonated on her right side, the concussion nearly causing her to lose control. She held the flight stick with all of her strength, her knuckles cracking from the strain, even though it made no difference to the highly calibrated sensors. Her instincts told her to hang on so she hung on.

Another explosion sent her veering right then several more directly behind her caused her quad to flip end over end for half a kilometer before she could regain control.

"Clear of missiles," the AI announced. "Strafing guns offline."

"Why'd you take them offline?" DuLaque asked as she swung her quad around to face the armada.

"I did not," the AI replied. "The mechanisms have overheated. Waiting for cool down procedure to finish before bringing them back online."

"Good call," DuLaque said. "Where are we with plasma cannons?"

"They are still available," the AI said. "Thirty percent left before hitting ten percent reserve."

DuLaque started to respond then stopped as she watched the carnage before her. Missile after missile collided with her squadron, ripping quads apart with abandon. The vacuum was no longer filled with the attack on the armada's shields, but filled with the brief explosions of half of Hermes squadrons' quads.

Her eyes scanned the area and she saw what was left of her people trying to regroup into ragtag sixteens, but each time they grouped together they were instantly torn apart by missile fire.

"Spread out!" she ordered. "Give them smaller targets! Evasive maneuvers now!"

Her call was almost too late as she watched an entire sixteen obliterated before her eyes before her pilots split up and went their separate ways. Estelian missiles tried to follow, but they were taken out by strafing guns as each quad employed the same rear defense that DuLaque had.

With the explosions considerably less, DuLaque could focus back on the armada and the warships she should have been attacking.

Except there were no warships. Her targets were gone.

"This isn't possible," she said. "AI? Tell me I am wrong."

"I cannot tell you that, Captain," the AI replied. "I am unsure as to what you are referencing."

"The armada," DuLaque replied. "Where is it? How could they fire on us if they aren't there?"

"I am uncertain as to your meaning, Captain," the AI said. "All scanners indicate that the Estelian armada is directly in front of this quad."

"No, it is not," DuLaque insisted. "I am looking right at where it should be and I am telling you there is nothing there."

"The data from the scanners would presume otherwise," the AI said.

"Then check for some type of cloaking tech!" DuLaque yelled. "Because I can't see a fucking thing from where I'm sitting!"

Thirty

The entire scene was chaos.

That was all Captain MacAbee could think of as she watched Hercules squadron get decimated. Cannons from the Estelian armada carpeted the vacuum with wave after wave of plasmatic death. Entire sixteens were vaporized as the quads were ripped apart at the molecular level.

"No," she whispered. "How...?"

"Captain?" her AI asked. "How what?"

"What am I looking at?" MacAbee asked. "They don't have that many cannons. How are they firing with that many cannons?"

"Scanners indicate that the Estelian armada is no longer in our proximity," the AI said. "All ships have entered interspace and punched to an unknown location."

"What? No, that's not true," MacAbee said. "I can see the armada right there. They are shredding my squadron! Check your fucking scanners again!"

"The data has been checked and verified," the AI responded. "No Estelian warships engaging with Hercules squadron."

"Bullshit!" MacAbee shouted. "Fucking bullshit! Look! Look at that!"

"Scanners are at full, Captain," the AI said. "All readings show departure punch waves consistent with the amount and size of the Estelian armada. Their warships are no longer in this region."

"Punch waves? We would have seen that," MacAbee said. "There would have been aftershocks. Give me a timeline on their departure."

The AI did not respond.

"Did you hear me? Give me a timeline!" MacAbee ordered again.

"Timelines are inconsistent with data, Captain," the AI said.

"What do you mean by timelines?" MacAbee asked. "Is there more than one timeline?"

"Multiple departure times have been detected," the AI replied. "This has created several timelines to track."

"When does the first one start?" MacAbee asked.

"Three seconds prior to engagement with the armada," the AI said.

"They left before we attacked?" MacAbee asked, her mind reeling. "But how are they fighting back?"

The AI didn't respond.

MacAbee watched as the quads from Hercules squadron that were able to run from the Estelian onslaught came at her, ready to regroup for the next phase of the battle.

"AI? Give me a long range channel to the Asteroid Belt stations," MacAbee said. "We have to call this in immediately."

"Communications link has been attempted with the Asteroid Belt stations, Captain," the AI said. "But there is no response."

"Shit," MacAbee said. "More sabotage?"

"Unknown," the AI said. "There is no pingback from the communications attempt. This would indicate the signal is being blocked. If the Asteroid Belt stations are not destroyed then they are being prevented from receiving transmissions."

"To do that then the Estelians would have to be behind us," MacAbee said.

Then the pieces began to fit together.

"Mother of God," she whispered. "They've learned how to navigate interspace without killing the crew! AI! Open channel to all squadrons!"

"Channel open," the AI said.

"All squadrons! This is Captain MacAbee! Disengage from the armada you see and turn around!" MacAbee called out. "They aren't where we think they are! They're directly behind us!"

Thirty-One

"Directly behind us?" Garcia asked as she banked her quad hard and turned it around. "How is that possible, Mac?"

"I don't know," MacAbee replied over the comm. "But it explains why we picked up punch waves on our rear. The Estelians have figured out how to stay in interspace while still attacking. The armada we see in front of us is a remnant, not the real thing. They keep punching back and forth!"

"But their crews? That'd kill them," Garcia said. "Even Estelians can't handle that kind of stress."

"Well, they are," MacAbee stated. "Ignore the science and focus on the fight."

"Got it," Garcia said as her quad slowed and she stared out at an empty vacuum. "If we focus on the fight then we need to lock onto the punch waves and attack those."

"Good call, Garcia," MacAbee said. "Artemis squadron is closest, so you have the lead on this. I'll rally what's left of the other squadrons and be at your position shortly."

"Roger that," Garcia said, her eyes studying the vastness of the solar system before her.

Somewhere out there, far, far off, was Earth and billions of people counting on the quads to keep the Estelian armada from getting any closer. Or at the very least, cutting the numbers down enough that the Asteroid Belt stations, and Mars colonies, could deploy sufficient defensive measures. If the Asteroid Belt stations and Mars colonies couldn't handle the armada then there was the Perpetuity, at least; that last line of defense that stood just past Earth's moon.

"AI, lock on the punch waves previously detected," Garcia said. "Give me a full count."

A second passed before the AI responded. "Waveforms are intermittent. Twenty-five punch waves detected after careful analysis."

"Lock a disruptor onto the nearest, most consistent wave," Garcia ordered. "Prepare to fire."

"Calculating," the AI said.

"Really? You had to tell me that?" Garcia grunted. "Going to have run diagnostics on your CPU if you can't just crunch the numbers like normal."

"This scenario is outside the norm," the AI said. "Careful consideration must be taken when factoring in the strength and distance of the wave coupled with the timing of its appearance."

"How about its disappearance?" Garcia asked, suddenly struck with an idea. "Can you time the missile to strike just before the punch wave disappears?"

"That is possible," the AI replied. "But it could yield a different result. Instead of impacting when the warship is on this side of interspace, the missile could impact with the warship and detonate within interspace itself."

"Now you're talking," Garcia smiled. "Let's do that."

"You would like the missile to detonate within interspace?" the AI asked. "Technically that is not possible as nothing truly exists within interspace."

"Well, we all know that's not true since we travel through that shit all the time," Garcia said. "My still queasy stomach tells me that. And like Captain MacAbee said, forget the science and focus on the fight. Can you make the calculation or not?"

"Calculating," the AI said.

"Oh, for fuck's sake," Garcia sighed. "Just fire the fucking missile."

One second, two seconds, three seconds passed before one of Garcia's disruptor missiles went flying out into the vacuum. The captain watched it shoot off, its thruster a blue glow against the blackness of space.

"Uh, Captain?" one of Garcia's squadron pilots asked. "Did you just fire a missile at nothing? Are you seeing something we're not?"

"Hold tight, Denver," Garcia said. "Just watch the disruptor do its thing."

There were a few other inquiries, but Garcia quieted her squadron with a harsh growl. The comm went silent just as the disruptor missile seemed to hit its target. Then it was gone.

"Now we wait," Garcia said. "I kind of have a theory that if we-HOLY FUCK!"

The vacuum before Artemis squadron tore open as Estelian warship after Estelian warship began to appear, many of them listing to one side and smoking as explosions rocked the vessels. Two destroyers turned towards each other and collided, their hulls ripping apart, sending debris and Estelians floating into the vacuum.

"Take it to them, Artemis!" Garcia shouted as she pushed her thrusters to full and aimed her quad right at the broken armada. "If we hit them fast enough then they won't be able to regroup or escape!"

"Data indicates the disruptor missile impacted a cruiser, causing a chain reaction of explosions within the interspace," the AI said. "That is theoretically not possible according to the laws of physics."

"Then someone needs to come up with new laws because it is obviously possible!" Garcia shouted, aiming her plasma cannons at the bridge of a battleship that rolled towards her. "Mac? Mac, are you seeing this?"

"I'm seeing it, Garcia!" MacAbee replied. "Incredible! We are coming up behind you. I have three full squadrons with me."

"Three? That's all that made it?" Garcia asked as she fired her cannons at the battleship then dove quickly as pieces of the vessel broke off and spun out at her. "Who's still with us?"

"Wilson here."

"DuLaque here."

Garcia waited for the other three captains to call in, but none did.

"Shit," she swore as she pulled up and shot past a hunk of metal twice the size of her quad. "We got fucked."

"We got fucked hard," MacAbee said. "But we're about to do the fucking."

"I hear that," Garcia said.

She rolled her quad to the left and then back to the right as several plasma blasts came at her. An alarm sounded in her cockpit, but it was silenced quickly as the AI took over and handled any damage done.

"Anything I need to worry about?" Garcia asked.

"Starboard thruster is at seventy-five percent," the AI said. "Adjusting power of port thruster to compensate. Both thrusters now at seventy-five percent. Please keep that in mind when initiating maneuvers."

"You know I will," Garcia said.

She brought her quad around and went back at the battleship for another attack run. A huge hole in the starboard hull of the ship spewed flame and fiery debris. Garcia aimed her quad for the hole, pushing her thrusters to their limit.

"Captain, you are being too aggressive with the quad," the AI warned. "My compensation for the reduced power in the starboard thruster does not mean the thruster is one hundred percent stable. I would suggest powering back and using more caution."

"Time for caution is long gone, AI," Garcia said, leaning forward in her cockpit, her eyes locked onto the gaping hole in the Estelian warship. "Caution is for pussies."

She fired two missiles and pulled up hard. Another alarm rang out and Garcia tried to ignore it. But her quad began to sputter slightly and she knew it wasn't something she could blow off.

"Talk to me, AI!" Garcia ordered. "What's happening?"

"Integrity in wing four has been compromised," the AI said. "It does not appear it will stay attached much longer."

"Junk it," Garcia said. "Then junk wing three. We're going two-winged now."

"Maneuverability will be severely compromised," the AI said. "As will weapons capability."

"Then we deal with what we have," Garcia said. She was about to speak when her entire quad shuddered and she found herself in an out of control spin. "AI!"

"The battleship you attacked has exploded, Captain," the AI said. "It's engines went critical at the same time as the explosion, multiplying the force by a thousand. The damage to the armada, as well as CSC quads, is considerable."

"Mac? You still there?" Garcia called out as she struggled to right her quad. "Mac?"

"Here, Garcia," MacAbee replied. "What the holy fuck did you do?"

"I put a firecracker in a hornets nest," Garcia said.

"I grew up on Skaern, Garcia," MacAbee responded. "I have no fucking clue what that means."

"Skaern? Think of it like I shoved my thumb into a Gosstog's asshole," Garcia grunted, still trying to regain control of her quad. "Then I punched it in the nuts."

"Not the brightest thing to do," MacAbee said. "You took out a few of your people, Garcia."

"I know," Garcia said. "Wasn't the plan. My AI says the battleship's engines went critical just as my missiles exploded. It turned into an exponential shitstorm. I'll take full responsibility when this hell is over and I'm brought before a CSC tribunal."

"We have to live first," MacAbee said. "We'll deal with the tribunal later."

"Gotcha," Garcia said. Sweat dripped into her eyes and she tried to blink it away. "AI! Why haven't you junked wings four and three yet?"

"Detachment protocols will not respond," the AI said. "I am attempting to reroute systems to the locking mechanisms."

"Hurry it the fuck up!" Garcia shouted. "I keep spinning any longer and I'm going to barf all over this cockpit!"

The quad did keep spinning, rolling, tumbling through the vacuum. Garcia caught glimpses of Estelian destroyers, battleships, cruisers, then CSC quads. All ships there then gone, there then gone, over and over, around and around.

A loud thunk echoed through the cockpit and the quad gave a hard lurch to the right. The rolling slowed, but did not completely stop. A second thunk echoed through the cockpit and the quad suddenly responded to Garcia's will.

"There we go," Garcia said as she regained control. "Thanks, AI. Those wings were about to-."

The view in front of her cockpit was suddenly blocked as one of the jettisoned wings came right at her. Alarms rang out and she shoved the flight stick down as hard as she could, sending the quad into a dive. The broken wing flew over her and she glanced up and back as she raced past. Then she saw what was about to happen and tried to pull up, but couldn't.

The tip of the severed wing dug into the top of the quad, tearing a six foot long, two foot wide gash all the way back to the thrusters. Alarms rang out and lights began to flash all through Garcia's cockpit. Then silence as everything went dark.

"AI?" Garcia called out. "AI, can you read me?"

Nothing.

"Mac? Wilson? DuLaque?"

Nothing.

"Shit," she said as she looked about the pitch black cockpit. "Shit, shit, shit."

She patted herself down, hunting through her flight suit for a halogen. She found one in her breast pocket and switched it on then shone it about the cockpit. After a brief examination she came to one conclusion.

"Totally fucked," she muttered.

Her fist punched her control panel over and over then she took a deep breath and got to work.

"One system at a time," she said as she popped open a panel next to her right elbow and pulled out a portable diagnostic scanner and small tool kit. "One system at a time."

She pushed away the thought of how long it would take to try each system. She wouldn't even let the thought of how much air she had left enter her mind.

"One system at a time," she repeated over and over as she went to work.

Thirty-Two

"Garcia? Garcia, come in," MacAbee called. "Garcia, come in. I repeat, come in."

"I don't have a visual," DuLaque said over the comm.

"Neither do I," Wilson said. "I thought I saw her quad go tumbling off, but then she was gone."

"Dammit," MacAbee said. "That leaves us. DuLaque? You take what's left of Hermes and Artemis and spread out one click to my right. Wilson? You have Zeus and Hera. You're on my left. I'll take Ares with what's left of my Hercules. We are going in fast and furious. Unload what you have then punch it back to the rendezvous point off Titan Base."

"But Titan Base is gone," DuLaque said.

"We don't know that," MacAbee replied. "Just because we lost contact doesn't mean it's gone. We take out as much of this armada as we can until we're empty then get the fuck gone. Understood?"

"Understood," DuLaque replied.

"Roger that," Wilson said.

"Then take it to them, people," MacAbee said. "No pulling back, no fucking mercy."

The quads split into their squadrons, took aim at the damaged armada, and went in for the attack.

MacAbee watched as an Estelian cruiser exploded right in front of her, turning the vacuum into a shrapnel filled hell. She dove and banked right then pulled up and turned a hard left. MacAbee hit her thrusters hard and swung her tail out in order to get away from a massive piece of paneling that rocketed towards her.

She cleared the paneling, but found herself facing a wave of plasma bolts. Dive, right, climb, left, roll, roll, dive, dive, roll, climb, right, right, level. Fire.

An Estelian destroyer was broadside to her quad, its plasma cannons firing non-stop. MacAbee opened up with her strafing guns as her quad swerved and dodged the oncoming bolts. She dipped and rolled, keeping the Estelian's targeting computers continually guessing. Her strafing guns never stopped, even when she wasn't aimed directly at the destroyer. Round after round flew through the vacuum, peppering the armada at random.

"Save some of that for an actual target," DuLaque said.

"Thanks for the advice," MacAbee replied. "Now fuck off."

"Fucking off," DuLaque said.

MacAbee pulled up and came at the destroyer from underneath. The plasma guns on the bottom hull targeted her quad, but she was able to take out half before they could get a bead on her. Then the plasma bolts came and MacAbee found herself without any room to maneuver.

"Wing one hit," her AI said. "Wing two hit."

"Salvageable?" she asked.

"No," the AI replied.

"Toss 'em," MacAbee ordered. "Divert power to remaining thrusters."

"Ejecting damaged wings, diverting power to remaining thrusters," the AI said.

A bolt came at MacAbee's cockpit and she rolled the quad to avoid it. But her roll took her right into the path of four more bolts. Alarms rang out everywhere and MacAbee felt her flight suit pressurize and seal around her body.

"Life support compromised," the AI said. "Unable to repair damage. Recommend ejection."

"I don't think so," MacAbee said, her eyes locked onto the belly of the destroyer. "I'm useless if I eject."

"Captain, the quad is damaged beyond repair," the AI said. "Your effectiveness is already depleted. It is best you save yourself."

"No," MacAbee said. "Divert all power to one thruster. Push it to critical."

"That would result in the full destruction of this quad," the AI said. "My protocols will not allow that."

"Pilot override," MacAbee said as she tried to keep some semblance of control over her broken quad. "Push thruster to critical, AI. That is an order."

MacAbee sent the quad directly at the hull of the destroyer. She felt everything start to fall apart around her as the vacuum took its toll on the unpressurized vehicle.

"All power diverted to single thruster," the AI said.

"Good," MacAbee said as she opened fire on the destroyer with everything she had left.

Then she pushed the accelerator to maximum.

The cockpit was so damaged that she could barely make out the destroyer anymore around the cracks and fissures. She saw a new wave of plasma bolts come right for her, but a quick calculation told her she would be at her target before they reached her.

"CSC or die!" she yelled just as her quad slammed into the belly of the destroyer, ripping right through its hull and into the substructure. "Fuck y-."

Thirty-Three

The destroyer to DuLaque's right exploded in a massive fireball that was quickly consumed by the vacuum, leaving only sparks and scorched debris to fill the space.

"Mac?" DuLaque shouted. "Mac? You still with us?"

No answer.

"Shit," DuLaque said. "Goddamn it, Mac."

The captain checked her scanners and was surprised to see only three battleships, four destroyers, and two cruisers left in the armada. Whatever Garcia had done it had decimated the Estelian forces.

"Hermes and Artemis," DuLaque called out. "We have the most numbers. Concentrate all fire on the three battleships. Come in fast from above then dip under and rake their bellies."

She heard several acknowledgements, but not as many as she would have liked.

"No time to get weak, people," DuLaque said. "We're here to stop these DGs, not give them a scolding and then tuck tail and go home. No one said this was a survivable mission. So get your heads straight and understand that if you live today it's probably because you didn't fight hard enough."

There were a few choice words directed at her, but none of the quads fell out of formation as she led the squadrons towards the three Estelian battleships.

Plasma blasts came at her and she accelerated, pushing her quad faster as she climbed above the attack. Voices from the quads behind her cried out as the squadrons began to take hits. Screams were cut short and curses were flung, yet no one begged for mercy or panicked and fled. Artemis and Hermes stayed on course, stayed on mission, and took the attack to the battleships.

"Concentrate on the communications arrays just below the bridges," DuLaque ordered. "Keep them from coordinating with each other. We're going to divide and conquer here, people."

She smiled to herself as she heard a little of MacAbee in her tone.

DuLaque continued to push her quad, staying just ahead of the Estelian plasma cannons' targeting. It was a tight race, but she kept her course and took her quad to the apex of its climb then shoved the flight stick as hard as she could and went into a dive that pushed her whole body back into her seat. Even in the zero gravity environment of the vacuum, her life support systems could still create G-forces that nearly took her breath away.

She flicked her thumb and sent the last of her missiles down at the battleship's bridge and the communications array just below it. Her eyes tracked the disruptors' paths and she barely had time to pull up out of her dive before several explosions erupted along the Estelian warship's hull. Her entire quad rocked violently from the concussions and she reluctantly pulled back on the throttle in order to maintain control.

But, with the slower speed she became vulnerable to the few Estelian plasma cannons that were operational and had her in range. Alarms rang out in her cockpit as she felt her quad shudder then begin to sputter and finally die. She pushed the throttle to full, but there was no response.

"AI? I need a status-."

Her words were cut off as the entire back end of her quad was ripped apart by plasma bolts. Then the quad was gone, nothing but chunks and pieces of metal with fragments of its pilot interspersed between.

Thirty-Four

"Empty!"

"I'm out!"

"Last missile deployed!"

"Just lost power to my plasma cannons!"

"I can't pull up! I can't pull up!"

Wilson watched in horror as quad after quad fell before the remaining Estelian warships. Some were able to do damage while some just floated in the vacuum, impotent targets just waiting to be picked off. The captain emptied his strafing guns at a passing cruiser then slammed his fist into his control panel as his AI informed him that all weapons systems were depleted.

"How many quads still have power?" Wilson asked his AI. "Give me numbers now!"

"Forty-one quads have power," the AI replied. "The remainder are adrift."

"Good to know," Wilson said. "Listen up, people! Our guns are empty, but our mission is far from over. We may not have disruptor missiles, but we still have something that can pack a punch. Our quads. I know you don't want to hear this, but if we are going to give Earth a fighting chance, we have to make a stand here. If another Estelian armada comes in behind this one then we can kiss the home world goodbye. The entire safety of our species depends on what we do next."

Wilson punched in coordinates and then sent them to what was left of the CSC squadrons.

"These are the remaining warships," Wilson said. "I have tagged your quads with preferred targets. Split up and take aim. Command override is in place, so you shouldn't have any resistance from your AIs. Point your quads at your target and push your thrusters into the red. I want your quads to go critical when they impact. Are we clear?"

There was an unanimous response.

"Good," Wilson said. "Now, let's put these fucking DGs in their graves!"

The captain was about to hit his throttle when proximity warnings blared in his cockpit.

"AI? What am I looking at?" Wilson asked.

"Three squadrons of Estelian quads have entered the system," his AI replied. "They have punched out of interspace above, below and behind our squadrons. We are boxed in."

"Motherfucker," Wilson growled. "Squadrons? I'm sure your AIs just alerted you to what's happening. We have no time for hesitation. Full throttles now! Take it to these sons of bitches!"

Wilson accelerated as hard and fast as he could, aiming his quad directly for the bridge of one of the Estelian battleships. He could hear the war cries of his fellow pilots then those cries lost as the Estelian squadrons began to fire and close ranks around the CSC quads.

A thousand meters out, eight hundred meters, five hundred, three, two.

Wilson's quad erupted in short lived flames as he was ripped apart by the concentrated plasma bolts of the three Estelian quads that converged on him.

The last thing he saw was the approaching hull of the battleship. His last thought was that his sacrifice was worth it. He would never know if that was true.

Thirty-Five

The image of General Birmingham filled half of North's view, the other half being a scanner rendering of the battle at the far side of the solar system.

"General, I understand the need to keep training on schedule, but don't you think that an approaching Estelian armada is slightly more important?" North barked. "Scanners are showing that our squadrons got their asses handed to them. There is no response from Titan Base, including the cruisers and destroyers stationed there, and we all know that the Asteroid Belt stations and Mars colonies are not equipped to go to war. Not even the Mars platforms. Not on a scale this large."

"Which is precisely why we need you to keep training the cadets," General Birmingham barked back. "How will we win this war against the doublegangers if we do not have the manpower to do so?"

"Ma'am, manpower will mean nothing if we lose the entire solar system!" North shouted. "You are ramping up for a full ground assault, but the DGs are coming at us with a fucking armada! The war right now is not being waged on planets, but in our own backyard!"

"I am well aware of where the war is being waged, Major," Birmingham growled. "I am also aware that your tone is getting seriously close to sedition."

"To what? Ma'am, I only have the CSC's best interest at heart," North countered. "I am trying to—"

"Then be quiet and do your job, Major," Birmingham interrupted. "Run the Perpetuity like I have ordered you and let me handle the warfare. You train the cadets, I send the cadets into battle. There is no room for discussion on this."

"Then at least let me shift the focus from ground troops to fighter skiffs," North said. "I can revert the simulation bays to flight training instantly. We have enough training skiffs on the flight decks to add at least three squadrons to the fight."

"No, Major, that will not be needed," Birmingham said. "Reinforcements are on the way as we speak. They should punch in before the Estelian forces reach the Asteroid Belt stations."

"Sir?" a tech said from North's right. "Major North? I am picking up multiple punch waves from the battle site."

"More warships?" North asked.

"No, sir, looks like Estelian quad squadrons," the tech replied. "Several of them."

"Quads?" North asked. "Shit."

"I know what you are thinking, Major," Birmingham said. "And this development does not change anything. You proceed as ordered or you will be removed from your duties. I can replace you by just snapping my fingers, Major North. Do not test me on this. I have tolerated your objections only because I know you are the best man to run the Perpetuity. Do not force me to change my mind."

North watched the scanner images and shook his head as the signals indicating CSC quads began to blink out rapidly until there were none left. He took a deep breath then looked at the general.

"I'll keep the schedule on track, ma'am," North said. "You can count on me."

"Good, Major," Birmingham grimaced. "You leave the defense of this system to me. The CSC will not let the Earth fall to the Estelian threat. We will prevail because we always prevail."

"Of course, General," North said then saluted. "CSC or die."

"CSC or die," Birmingham said then her image blinked out, leaving North to stare at the long-range scanners and the Estelian warships left.

"What are we looking at?" North asked.

"Sir?" the tech replied.

"Give me a count on the Estelian warships," North said. "I want to know what's coming at us."

"Yes, sir," the tech said. "It appears they have two battleships, three destroyers, two cruisers, and three squadrons of quads."

"That's a lot of firepower heading this way," North said. "I want simulation bays twenty-seven through thirty-eight to start running fighter skiff training sims immediately."

"Sir, but the general said not to do that," the tech said. "I heard her give you a direct order."

"Now I am giving you a direct order, Private," North snapped. "Which order are you going to obey? The one from a woman that is millions of kilometers from this station or the one standing right over you? I'd advise choosing wisely."

"Sir, with all due respect, I cannot ignore what I heard," the tech said. "A direct order from you does not supersede what the general said. All simulation bays are supposed to be for ground troops only."

"Your patriotism is admirable," North said. "But misplaced. I've been out there in the thick of it, Private, have you?"

"Well, no, sir," the tech admitted. "I came straight from Earth to the Perpetuity. I'm a local."

"So then you have no idea what this war is really like," North stated. "And trust me, it isn't always what the CSC wants you to think it is. It's messy and brutal and way more complicated than any newscast you may have heard. In war, you have to make tough choices, choices that aren't in your best interest, but in the best interest of the entire human race."

"I'm just a tech, sir," the tech said. "I leave those decisions to officers like you."

"And this officer is ordering you to switch out the simulation bays," North said. "So knock it the fuck off and do what I say!"

The tech stood and saluted North then stepped away from his console.

"I respectfully decline, sir," the tech said. "I understand if you need to take disciplinary action against me."

North started to speak then closed his mouth as he noticed all eyes were on him. The rows of techs that sat at their consoles on the Perpetuity's bridge all stared at the major with looks ranging from surprise to outright contempt. North did a quick count and realized the contemptuous looks outnumbered the rest by a large margin.

He did not have the support he had hoped for.

"Disciplinary action is not necessary," North said. "I withdraw my previous order. Carry on."

"Yes, sir," the tech said and sighed with relief as he sat back down at his console.

North focused on the rest of the techs, staring them down until each went back to work and put their attentions back on their jobs instead of him. With a final glance at the scanner image of the Estelian armada, North turned quickly and strode from the bridge.

He made it out into the corridor and was almost to the lift when four security guards stepped in front of him.

"Sergeant-at-Arms Metzger has requested your presence, sir," one of the guards said. "If you will accompany us, please."

"Good for him," North smirked. "But he could have just called. Let Metzger know I'm busy at the moment and will come see him as soon as I can."

"I am sorry, sir, but Sergeant Metzger gave us strict orders not to return without you," the guard said, her hand going to the stun baton on her hip. "He was very clear on that."

North narrowed his eyes then met the gazes of each of the other guards. He could tell instantly that they were all pharmaed to the gills and ready to put him down without a second thought.

"I am going to hand Metzger his ass when I get there," North said as he held his hands up and shrugged. "You all understand that, right?"

"Yes, sir," the guard said. "It is expected. But that is between you and Sergeant Metzger. We are only here to escort you to him."

"Yeah, you said that," North said. "Just hold on a second. I need to call this in to my assistant."

"You can call as we walk, sir," the guard said.

"Can I?" North grumbled. "Thank you, Corporal. How kind of you."

North pressed his wrist as he was surrounded by the guards and led to the lift.

"Yes, Major?" Ngyuen asked as the woman's image appeared over North's wrist.

"Where the hell are you, Corporal?" North asked. "You were supposed to meet me on the bridge."

"Yes, well, I was called to the medical bay to speak with Dr. Jagath," Ngyuen said. "I am actually on my way to you right now."

"Don't bother," North said. "I've been summoned by Metzger and am being escorted down to the security levels."

"I'm sorry, sir, did you say you are being escorted to the security levels?" Ngyuen asked.

"That's exactly what I said," North replied.

"Who is escorting you, sir?" Ngyuen asked.

"Four of Metzger's people," North said. "Which I thought were my people, but apparently I was under the wrong impression as to who is in charge on this station."

"Which security level?" Ngyuen asked, her face tight with alarm.

"Which security level?" North asked one of the guards.

"That is need to know, sir," the guard replied.

North stared at her for a second then shook his head and looked back at the image of Ngyuen. "You catch that?"

"I did, sir, and I have to say it is quite troubling," Ngyuen replied. "I'll report this to CSC immediately."

"Don't," North said. "I have a feeling you won't get anywhere with them. I may have overstepped with General Birmingham."

"Overstepped?" Ngyuen asked then shook her head. "I'll come to the security levels and find you, sir. We will get this sorted out."

Ngyuen's image blinked out and North grinned at the guard closest to him.

"Hear that?" North asked. "My assistant just told me we'd get it sorted out. My assistant. She's a corporal and I am a major. Not to mention, I'm also acting commandant on this training station. But, hey, she's going to find me to get it all sorted out."

The guard didn't respond. North just shook his head as they stepped in front of the lift.

"Quite a fucking day," North said as the lift doors opened and he was escorted inside.

Thirty-Six

The wrench slipped from between Linklater's fingers and clattered against the ladder then began to tumble into open space as it fell down the long shaft of the server tower.

"Cocksucking fucker dick fuck shit fucker cock!" Linklater yelled as he slammed his hand against the ladder over and over.

"Feel better?" Wendt asked as he looked up at Linklater. "For what it's worth, you missed my head. Thanks for that."

"I totally fucked my hand up," Linklater said as he flexed his fingers and winced. "Ladders are hard."

"You're exhausted and frustrated," Wendt said. "I get that. You aren't used to the grunt work we do in maintenance. You're more used to pressing buttons and waving your hand in front of consoles. You deal with images and simulations. I deal with nuts and bolts and grease and heavy shit."

"Go fuck yourself, Wendt," Linklater said. "I did my time in the shafts and vents of plenty of stations and bases. I know my way around hard work, thank you very fucking much."

"So what's the problem?" Wendt asked. "That was just a wrench. I have a dozen more like it in the pack on my back."

"The problem is we have possible Estelians on this station, the simulations are glitching, North won't take five fucking seconds to listen to me, and we're having to ladder it down dozens of levels to chase some data line that goes from a bank of destroyed mystery servers to Makers know where!"

"Is that all?" Wendt chuckled. "I was in the middle of getting me some when you had me pulled away. That sweet thing is not going to wait for me forever. The women are fickle on the Perpetuity, trust me. They either get their rocks off when they want or they move on to some other guy or girl."

"You're only saying that because we're alone," Linklater said. "You sure as fuck wouldn't be saying that in the mess hall."

"No, I sure as fuck would not be," Wendt replied. "Doesn't change the fact it's true. Badass ladies demand some badass lovin'."

I start to lose my reputation as a badass lover and this station is gonna get pretty lonely for me. That's all I'm saying."

"Jesus, how do you get any work done, stud?" Linklater scoffed.

"I manage," Wendt said. He stopped descending the ladder and frowned at the server bank in front of him. "Hold up. This isn't right."

"What? Are we there?" Linklater asked.

"Yeah," Wendt said. "But I'm not sure where. These servers are just backups. They are on hold unless needed."

"So? We're looking for where the data was being sent," Linklater said. "It would make sense it was being sent to backup servers."

"Except that these are dead," Wendt replied. "Take a look. These aren't even lit for standby. No power, nothing."

"Then they aren't the right servers," Linklater said. "Keep going. I don't want to hang out on this ladder all day."

"No, these are the right servers," Wendt said. "I know it. I pinged a signal through that cable and it went to here then it stopped. Even if these servers were just relays, they'd still show power."

Wendt unslung his pack and clipped it to the ladder then he tightened his belt and clipped that to the ladder as well.

"Get comfortable," Wendt said as he undid his pack and pulled out a power driver. "I'm going to see what the fuck is up."

"Get comfortable?" Linklater asked. "How the hell am I supposed to do that?"

"Clip in and hang tight," Wendt said.

"Clip in? With what?" Linklater frowned. "I'm not maintenance."

Wendt looked up at Linklater and shook his head. "See? Soft."

He rummaged around in his pack and pulled out a ring of carabiners then held it up to Linklater.

"Take these and clip in," Wendt said. "Be ready to hold whatever I hand you. I'll net up most of this stuff, but there could be things I need right away."

"I'm your assistant now?" Linklater asked as he clipped himself to the ladder. "How the hell did that happen?"

"You're in my world now, Lieutenant," Wendt said as he placed the driver against a bolt in the first server. "We'll get done a lot faster if I take lead on this."

"I was doing just fine when we were up in the lift," Linklater said.

"That's because those servers were crushed," Wendt said as he removed a bolt and tucked it into his breast pocket. "That was a salvage job. This is a little more technical."

"Do you have any idea how many systems I'm proficient with?" Linklater snapped. "I built half the protocols for the simulation bays myself. I know my way around this server tower."

"Yet you had no idea what those crushed servers were," Wendt said, removing another bolt then another. "And you didn't know these servers were dead."

"Neither did you!" Linklater almost yelled.

"But it's not my job to know," Wendt grinned. "It's my job to fix. It's your job to know."

"You're an asshole, Wendt," Linklater said.

"If you say so, sir," Wendt chuckled as he removed the last bolt and pried the face plate off the server. He stared at the empty space for a couple seconds before he tossed the plate aside. Allowing it to clatter its way down to the bottom of the shaft.

"What the hell did you do that for?" Linklater asked. "We're going to need to put that back on."

"Probably not," Wendt said. "There's no server."

"What? Let me see," Linklater said. He started to climb down then got hung up by the carabiners clipping him to the ladder. "Son of a bitch."

After a few moments of cursing and unclipping, Linklater was able to get down the few rungs in order to see inside the empty server. Wendt just swung aside, keeping one foot and one hand on the ladder. He nodded as Linklater shook his head in confusion.

"That's a lot of space back there," Linklater said, pointing to a small box that their mystery cable was plugged into. "Where the hell does it go?"

"I have no idea," Wendt said. "But there's only one way to find out."

"Give me a driver," Linklater said. "I'll start on the other face plates."

There was a clunk and clang from far above in the shaft. The two men looked up, squinting into the darkness that was only broken by the twinkling of lights from the thousands of servers in the tower.

"Was that the lift?" Wendt asked.

"Can't be," Linklater said. "I put it on lockdown and called it in to Dornan. It would take Major North's command to override that."

"Maybe it is Major North," Wendt suggested. "You did tell him to come back and talk to you."

"Shit, you're right," Linklater said. There was another clang. "I'll try to reach him."

Linklater pressed at his wrist as Wendt began working on a second faceplate.

"North?" There was no response. "Major North, come in." Still no response. "Son of a bitch."

"Try Ngyuen," Wendt said.

"Corporal Ngyuen?" Linklater called. "Corporal Ngyuen, this is Lieutenant Linklater. Corporal Ngyuen? Corporal Ngyuen! Come in, you twat!"

Wendt removed two more faceplates then looked over at Linklater.

"Try anyone," he suggested.

"Dornan?" Linklater announced. "Dornan, come in."

There was a hesitation then Corporal Dornan's image flickered to life above Linklater's arm.

"Lieutenant?" Dornan asked, looking confused. "I was told you were unavailable."

"What? Who the hell told you that?" Linklater asked.

"Security," Dornan said. "I received a message you were unavailable and that all requests that needed officer authorization should go directly to Corporal Ngyuen for Major North's approval."

Linklater looked over at Wendt as the man removed three more faceplates, his driver whirring so fast that a distinct smell of burning ozone filled the shaft. Wendt glanced at Linklater briefly and shrugged then went back to his task of pulling off faux server faceplates.

"I don't know what the hell is going on, but right now I don't care," Linklater said. "I have been trying to reach Major North to see if he is in the server tower. Can you access the personnel tracker and tell me who is in the lift? We're working on some servers and don't need that lift coming down on our heads."

"You should have put it in lockdown," Dornan replied.

"I did, Dornan," Linklater snapped. "I'm not a moron."

"Then the only person that could override that is Major North," Dornan said.

"He's a genius," Wendt said.

"Was that Wendt? Tell the sergeant he can suck it," Dornan said.

"Just shut up and check the system," Linklater growled. "Tell whoever is up there to get the hell out and put the lift back on lockdown."

"Okay, okay, hold on," Dornan said.

"Jesus, you could sleep in here," Wendt said as he got more faceplates off, creating an opening wide enough for a person to wiggle through. He stuck his head in and looked down then looked up. "It's this whole level. There's basic framing, but no actual guts to any of these servers. Hold on. What's that?"

"Hey, Lieutenant? I'm not showing anyone in the lift," Dornan said. "It's empty."

There was a loud clank and the distinct sound of metal on metal then a loud screech. Linklater and Wendt both looked up into the shaft.

"That's not good," Wendt said.

"Dornan, there is someone in the lift!" Linklater yelled. "Tell them to get the fuck off it and stop messing around!"

"There is no one on the lift," Dornan insisted.

The screech happened again then a thunk that was not only heard, but could be felt. The ladder started to vibrate, then shake, then full on shudder.

"It's coming down," Wendt said. "It's coming down fast!" Wendt unclipped himself from the ladder, took off his pack, and tossed it into the empty space behind the faux servers. "Lieutenant! Come on! Get in here!"

Linklater watched Wendt scramble inside the empty space then looked down at Dornan's image above his wrist. "Dornan? Shut down the server tower lift."

"I'm already trying," Dornan replied. "Even I can hear that thing rumbling down at you."

"Then what's the problem?" Linklater asked.

"The lift is in lockdown," Dornan said. "I can't override your command!"

"Eight four three one one delta alpha one one three!" Linklater shouted. "That will override!"

"It's not working! Now it's just showing me that the lift is offline!" Dornan yelled.

"LIEUTENANT!" Wendt shouted and grabbed at Linklater's arm. "Get your fucking ass in here!"

"This is insanity!" Linklater yelled. "Dornan, I swear to God that if you don't get this lift shutdown, then the next time I see—"

Linklater's head rocked to the side as Wendt's fist connected with his jaw. Stars danced before his eyes and he tried to shout something but the words wouldn't quite form. He felt hands fumbling at his belt then he was roughly pulled inside the server tower wall. His arm caught on something sharp and he felt pain then warm blood start to trickle down his left bicep.

"I...I..." Linklater stuttered.

"Shut up and get back," Wendt hissed as he pulled Linklater as far away from the shaft as possible. "You're going to want to..."

But Wendt's words were lost as the shaft was filled with a high-pitched screeching and then the thunderous noise of the lift rushing past the opening at a speed it was not designed to move at.

"Shit," Linklater said just before a massive crash filled the tower causing both men to clamp their hands over their ears. "SHIT!"

There was a loud whump and the acrid smell of smoke began to waft up to the opening. Linklater coughed hard and then even harder as the smoke grew thicker.

"Someone set something on fire in the lift!" Wendt yelled as he coughed as well. "We're going to asphyxiate!"

"We can -*cough cough*- climb back -*cough cough*- out the shaft," Linklater said.

"We won't make -*cough cough*- it," Wendt wheezed.

Linklater looked about the empty space and then saw their mystery cable above them. It snaked around a couple of struts then was lost from sight inside a conduit in the wall.

"That -*cough cough*- goes somewhere," Linklater said. "Maybe we -*coughcoughcough*—"

"Yeah -*coughcoughcough*-," Wendt nodded as he handed Linklater a driver and started working at the bolts in the wall in front of them.

The drivers whirred furiously while the two men coughed and hacked, their throats growing raw and rough, their eyes watering and noses dripping. The acrid smoke was a thick black and it started to make it almost impossible to see in the space despite the multiple halogens that Wendt turned on and slapped against the wall.

"Here," Wendt gasped as part of the paneling on the wall gave way. "Pull."

Linklater and Wendt dug their fingers in the small space Wendt had made. They pulled with what little strength they had and managed to bend the paneling down enough to step into. Wendt picked up one of the halogens and handed it to Linklater then grabbed one for himself.

The two stepped into a low-ceilinged corridor that was barely wide enough for them to walk in. Their shoulders rubbed against the dust coated walls as they hurried down the corridor, trying to put as much space as they possibly could between them and the toxic shaft.

"There," Wendt said as they got to the end of the corridor and stepped into a space that was a perfect square. "A hatch."

Linklater nodded, his arm across his face to block the smoke that followed them. He grabbed onto the wheel in the middle of the hatch and tried to turn it, but it wouldn't budge.

"Hold on," Wendt said as he dug around in his pack. "This will -*cough cough*- help."

He aimed a spray can at the wheel and pressed the button on top. A stream of white foam hit the wheel where it connected to the hatch as Linklater kept trying to turn. Suddenly, the wheel spun so fast that it slipped from Linklater's hands and he had to jump back to keep the hatch from smacking into him as it opened wide.

"In," Wendt said, shoving Linklater in the small of the back. "Go!"

The two men stepped inside and Wendt yanked the hatch closed then spun the wheel, locking it into place.

"Okay," Linklater said as he shown the halogen around at the small room. "Wasn't expecting to see this."

The room was only about four meters by four meters with a short ceiling about two and a half meters high. Along one wall was a small cot and a couple of crates of supplies. Right next to that was a desk where the mystery cable snaked down and ended, connecting to a control console.

"That's a comm system," Wendt said.

"Yes, it is," Linklater agreed.

The console actively blinked with lights, indicating it was transmitting and receiving.

"The data wasn't going to server backups," Wendt said. "It's being broadcast somewhere."

"Fuck me," Linklater sighed. "This is not how I thought my day would go."

Thirty-Seven

It was painfully obvious to North that the stains on the table were not from someone's lunch. Not from a condiment or spilled drink. His eyes studied the surface of the table, moving past the main body of the stain to the splatter pattern that told him exactly what had been happening in the interrogation room.

The hatch opened and Metzger strode in, his eyes wild and his skin a sickly yellow. He licked his lips over and over then grabbed a chair, swung it around and sat down with his arms over the back, facing North.

"Major," Metzger nodded. "I'm glad you came willingly."

"Didn't have much of a choice," North said. "Your guards made that very clear." North spread his hands out, palms up, on the table in a placating gesture. "Listen, Coop, we've known each other a long time. We've worked together on the Perpetuity for a few years now. Hell, we even ran into each other out in the systems on more than one occasion before our call to duty lead us here. I know you're a good man, and I know the lure of pharma, believe me, but you can't just—"

"Shut the fuck up, Bartram," Metzger snapped. "I don't need a lecture."

"Bartram? Sergeant, do I need to remind you that you are addressing an officer?" North asked, his eyes narrowing. He straightened his back and folded his arms across his chest. "I don't know what the hell you are up to, but you're digging yourself a pretty deep hole, Sergeant Metzger."

"From Coop to Sergeant Metzger just like that," Metzger said, snapping his fingers. "Sure, we've worked together for a long time, but that doesn't mean I don't think you're a self-important, holier than thou prick. You think I don't know what you say about me behind my back, *Bartram*?"

"What? What do I say about you?" North asked. He studied Metzger's eyes, seeing how dilated the pupils were, and realized he was stuck in a closed room with a very dangerous animal. "If I said anything that could be considered disparaging, it wasn't meant to be. Yeah, you can be rough around the edges, but you get your job done. And in all the time I've been here, I haven't ever found fault in the way you do your job."

"BULLSHIT!" Metzger yelled as he slammed his hands down on the back of the chair. "Bullshit, bullshit, bullshit!"

North waited for Metzger to calm down, not wanting to open his mouth and accidentally provoke the man further. It took Metzger a second to get his breathing slowed. He glanced down at his hands and frowned.

"Bruised them up hitting the chair," Metzger said, sounding like it was meant more as internal dialogue and not for North's ears. "Gonna make it hard to hold my scorcher when the time comes."

North stayed quiet.

"Oh, not so smug now, are you Bartram?" Metzger sneered. "Is the major scared of a little ol' sergeant?"

North just smiled his most appeasing smile, but did not take the bait.

"You know why you're here, Bartram?" Metzger asked. "Because I received a call from General Birmingham that you may not be so keen on taking orders from the CSC anymore. She wanted me to keep an eye on you and make sure you toe the line. I told her she could count on me."

"So you had your people grab me and throw me in here?" North asked. "That's a little more than keeping an eye on me, Coop."

"No. No, you don't," Metzger said, wagging a finger back and forth. "No Coop for you, Bartram. You had that chance, but you shit on it when you went back to Sergeant Metzger. You can call me Sergeant-at-Arms. I'll call you Bartram because you're in my domain now, but you call me anything other than Sergeant-at-Arms and we will have a problem. And more problems are not what you need, Bartram. No, sir, they are not what you need at all."

"What do I need then?" North asked.

"You need to tell me what you have been up to," Metzger said. "You see, Bartram, when the general told me that maybe you couldn't be trusted, a few things started to click into place. That recruit blowing himself up in the bay, you being the last person to see the commandant alive, that dust up you had in the commandant's office with the 'cloaked' attacker, you fighting with the general over the comm, and then trying to get a tech to switch out the simulation bays. Not to mention your little pharma habit. We all know about that."

"Those are a lot of pieces," North said. "But I don't see how they fit other than they're just part of the same crazy shit everyone else on this station has been dealing with."

"So you don't deny the pharma habit?" Metzger grinned.

"I don't have a habit, no," North said. "I may come to rely on pharma more than I should, but that's due to the stress and workload of my job, not because I have any addiction. The CSC encourages all officers to keep up to level even if that means an extra boost now and again."

"An extra boost now and again?" Metzger laughed. "Is that what you're calling it?"

"I actually haven't had any pharma in a couple hours," North said. "Been too busy today."

"I bet you have. I bet you have," Metzger said. He reached into his pocket and pulled out three injectors then slapped them onto the table. "But now you're not so busy. I bet you'd love to get right, wouldn't you? Have a little taste and clear the cobwebs."

North stared at the injectors. He could feel his body respond to the idea of a little pharma boost. His mouth began to salivate and his pulse increased. A lump formed in his throat and he had to swallow a few times to dislodge it. His skin prickled then went slightly clammy as he broke out into a cold sweat. It took all his willpower not to reach across the table and snatch up an injector.

"Oh, you want it," Metzger said. "Jesus, man, look at you! You're shaking like a dog that's pissed on the floor and is waiting to get hit! Holy shit do you have it bad!"

"I'm fine," North said, his shaky voice betraying him. "Don't need anything now except a square hot and some sleep."

"Yeah, right, sure that's all you need," Metzger chuckled. He picked up one of the injectors and placed it to his wrist. "Well, if you ain't gonna have some then I hate to see it go to waste."

"Coop, I think you've had enough," North said.

"What did you fucking call me?" Metzger yelled as he tossed the injector aside and lunged across the table. "What did you just call me?"

Metzger grabbed North by the collar and yanked him close to his face. North could smell the fetid after burn of pharma that wafted from Metzger's pores and, if he hadn't been convinced the man was a hundred kilometers past stable, he knew it then. It had been a long time since he'd witnessed a pharma binge like the one Metzger was on. Not since his infantry days out in the systems.

"I warned you, Bartram," Metzger said. "I said, if you called me anything except for Sergeant-at-Arms, that you were going to have a problem. Now you have a problem."

Metzger shoved North back and the major tumbled backwards out of his chair. He lay there on the floor, his eyes watching Metzger closely, not making any sudden moves that would incite the sergeant further.

"Bunk!" Metzger yelled as he sat back down. "Bunk!"

The hatch to the interrogation room opened and Bunk peeked her head in.

"Yeah, Sergeant?" Bunk asked then her eyes saw the injector on the floor as it sat in a small pool of pharma, cracked and broken. "Ah, man, what the fuck? Did the junkie do that? What a waste. Good thing we have that crate of—"

"Shut the fuck up, Bunk," Metzger snapped. "Just go get me my stick."

"Your stick?" Bunk asked, puzzled.

"My stun baton, you dumbshit," Metzger said. "Jesus, you'd think that pharma would make you just slightly smarter."

"Why didn't you just say stun baton?" Bunk asked. "That would have been easier. Who has a stick on this station? Sticks are on planets and shit, Sergeant."

"Bunk," Metzger said quietly.

Bunk stiffened and frowned. "Right. Sorry. I'll get you your stun baton. You want another injector too?"

"Yeah," Metzger said as he picked one up off the table. "Better make it two more. I'm feeling low."

North stayed right where he was as the hatch closed and Metzger activated the injector. His whole body stiffened then he slowly relaxed and smiled down at North.

"I can see why you love this stuff so much," Metzger said. "I was never much into riding this feeling, but now that I'm all clear on what's going on I can see the benefits."

"Clear on what's going on?" North asked cautiously.

"Yeah, Bartram," Metzger said, setting the spent injector down on the table. He picked up the other one and twirled it in his fingers, spinning it faster and faster as he talked. "It's so clear now. So clear how you've been secretly bringing in doublegangers. You let them file in with the recruits, hidden amongst thousands of scared faces so that no one can see the lies in their eyes."

Metzger snorted and slapped his leg.

"Lies in their eyes," he laughed. "That's a good rhyme. Lies in their eyes."

"You don't honestly think I'm working for the Estelians, do you?" North asked, suddenly a lot worried than he was before.

When Metzger came in all jacked up, North thought he was just dealing with a man that had snapped under pressure. But with the revelation that Metzger thought he was an Estelian collaborator, he knew he was in way too deep to just talk his way out.

"Oh, I know you aren't working for the DGs," Metzger laughed, the injector spinning, spinning, spinning. "You *are* a DG. It's so *obvious*."

Metzger pulled Terlinger's medal from his pocket.

"This," Metzger said. "Why'd you steal this from the commandant?" He tucked it away. "Don't matter. You'd just lie."

North's mouth went completely dry. It was considerably worse than just being a collaborator. Anyone suspected of being an actual Estelian could be executed without prejudice. No trial, no tribunal.

"Test me," North said quickly. "Get a scanner and test me. You'll see I'm not a fucking doubleganger. It's an easy test, Sergeant-at-Arms Metzger. Just have Bunk bring you a scanner and you'll see...that... Shit."

"Uh-oh," Metzger smirked. "Did you just realize that maybe I've had the scanners recalibrated after that suicidal fuck killed all those recruits and murdered the commandant? Yeah, I did exactly that. Made sure every scanner was in working order and wouldn't be acting up. I bet that screwed up your plans, didn't it? Thought you could get away with tampering all the scanners, didn't you?"

"I didn't tamper with anything," North said. "It's just that my chip has been acting up lately. Even if you scan me you may not get a clean reading."

"Is that so?" Metzger asked. "So you aren't hearing the orders coming in from CSC right now then?"

"Orders? No, I'm not," North said. "Listen, like I said, you may not get a clean reading, but if you just—"

"Oh, I know I won't get a clean reading," Metzger said. "I won't get a clean reading because you're a damned doubleganger. You're a murdering, disgusting, lower than shit doubleganger. I shouldn't have had Bunk bring me my stick, I should have had her bring my scorcher so I could put you out of your misery right now."

North waited a second then asked, "Why don't you?"

"What's that?" Metzger asked.

"Why don't you shoot me?" North pushed. "Why not take your scorcher and blow my head right off? What's stopping you?"

"Not what the general wants," Metzger said.

"Is that what she told you? She ordered you not to kill me?" North asked.

"No, she didn't, but Ngyuen relayed the message to me," Metzger said. "Interrogate, but don't terminate. Interrogate, but don't terminate. Damn! That's almost as good as lies in their eyes!"

"Ngyuen told you not to kill me?" North asked.

"Yeah, she's been a huge help with the questioning of the suspects," Metzger said. "Some of those sad little DGs didn't even know they were admitting anything, but Ngyuen helped me break the code, get past their lies and bullshit to see what they were really saying."

"Ngyuen has been helping you," North whispered.

"What's that?" Metzger asked.

"That Ngyuen can really be a huge help, that's for sure," North said.

"Not much help to you, though," Metzger said. "I mean she'll help me figure out what you have really been saying in here once we play the recordings back, but ain't a thing she can do to get you out of the mess you made. Shit, Bartram, after all we've been through, I almost feel sorry for you." He stopped spinning the injector. "I should let you have this since it could be the last bit of pharma you ever see. Wherever the CSC takes you won't have the good stuff like this."

"You should have it," North said. "Take that taste on my behalf."

"I should, shouldn't I?" Metzger nodded. "Yeah, why waste it on your DG ass? Scum like you doesn't deserve good pharma."

Metzger stared down at the injector for a few seconds then put it to his wrist and activated it. Again, his body went stiff. North didn't hesitate. He took that moment to make his move.

He was up and diving at Metzger before the sergeant even knew what was going on. North cleared the top of the table easily, his arms wrapping around Metzger's torso as his shoulder slammed into the sergeant's chest. Metzger huffed loudly and started to sputter in surprise as the two men fell to the floor.

Metzger cried out as the back of his head hit the floor, but the amount of pharma in him kept the pain at bay. North could see that instantly and again he did not hesitate as he brought a forearm down across Metzger's throat then slammed his fist into the side of the man's head over and over.

His eyes wild and bloodshot, Metzger tried to push North off of him, but the lack of oxygen took its toll. He clawed at North, spittle flying from his lips as he choked and gagged. Then slowly his strength ebbed and he just laid there, North's weight pressing down on him.

"Coop?" North asked as Metzger's eyes closed. Cautiously, North eased up on the pressure to Metzger's throat. "Coop?"

North placed his fingers to Metzger's neck and was glad there was still a pulse. He needed the man out of commission, not dead.

"Sorry, Coop," North said as he patted Metzger down, hunting for anything useful, but the man was too careful, even in his pharmaed state, and he'd left anything that could be used as a weapon outside of the interrogation room.

Just as North stood up, the hatch to the room started to open and North sprang into action. He reached out and grabbed Bunk by the arm as the woman stepped inside. Her eyes went wide as she saw Metzger's unconscious body. She tried to cry out as North's grip yanked her through the hatch and right at his waiting fist.

"He—!" Bunk started to scream, but the word was cut off by North's knuckles shattering her front teeth.

"Fuck," North shouted as he let Bunk go then slammed his elbow into the spot right between the guard's eyes.

He shook his hand, sending droplets of blood flying everywhere from the gouges Bunk's teeth had made across his fist. Bunk stood there in front of North for a second then her legs gave out and she crumpled to the floor, half of her draped across Metzger.

North pulled the stun baton from Bunk's hand, started to flee the room, then turned and snagged the injectors from Bunk's other hand. He stuffed the pharma into a pocket, activated the stun baton, and rushed through the hatch into the corridor beyond.

Two surprised guards just stared at him, as if they couldn't comprehend what was happening. North could see they were just as pharmaed as Metzger and Bunk, so he dialed the stun baton as high as it would go and readied himself.

"As acting commandant of the Perpetuity, I order both of you to stand down," North announced. "Lay your weapons on the floor and we can resolve this peacefully."

North almost rolled his eyes as he saw the indecision on the guards' faces. They didn't know whether to listen to the major or to go at him. They also seemed confused whether they should use their stun batons or their scorchers they had slung across their backs. Their arms sort of twitched back and forth as their pharmaed minds short circuited.

"Just put your weapons down and back away," North said, taking one cautious step after the other towards the guards. "That's an order, gentlemen. You don't want to end up on the front lines. You have a nice gig here on the Perpetuity. Comply with my orders and you'll stay here."

But with North's next step, the guards seemed to come to and they both went for their scorchers.

"Shit," North said, diving and rolling across the floor at the guards.

He closed the distance and swung out with the stun baton, connecting with the first guard's knee. The blow alone would have crippled the man, but it was the thousands of volts of electricity pulsing through him that took the guard down. He collapsed in a heap of twitching muscle and flailing limbs.

North spun about on his knee and slammed the stun baton against the thigh of the second guard just as the man had brought his scorcher around. The weapon barked and a plasma bolt singed the side of North's face, but the major ignored the pain and jammed the stun baton into the guard's gut. North rolled to the side and let the man fall on top of his comrade then jumped to his feet and slammed a boot into the back of the man's head, just in case.

"Should have listened," North said as he tucked the stun baton into his belt.

He grabbed up both men's' scorchers, slung them across his back then knelt and removed their pistols and stun batons. He found their cuffs and secured their hands behind their backs then stood up and looked down the corridor one way then the other.

He knew he couldn't really hide on the Perpetuity, not with his chip and wrist interface. If he wasn't locked out of the system, he could implement a security lockdown and at least clear the corridors of nonessential personnel. But he had a sinking feeling that his new privileges as acting commandant had been removed.

North picked a direction and jogged down the corridor to the first lift doors he could find. He pressed his wrist to the panel and sighed with relief when the doors slid apart. He hurried in then realized he had no idea where to go. Where could he hide? Who could he trust?

What the fuck was going on?

"Locate Lieutenant Linklater," he called out as the lift doors closed. "Take me to him."

"Lieutenant Linklater cannot be located," a computerized voice replied. "Please request another destination."

"Shit," North muttered. "Uh, main level of the server tower. Take me there."

"Server tower main level," the voice said. "Acknowledged, Major North."

North unslung one of the scorchers and checked the ammunition level. It was fully loaded, but he wasn't exactly sure if that was a good thing. He aimed the barrel at the lift doors and secured the butt of the plasma rifle against his shoulder. North had no intention of harming anyone. Not if he could help it. But he also had no intention of getting caught again.

He had to find out what the hell was happening on the Perpetuity, that was his number one priority, and if some folks got hurt in the process then that was just how war was.

Thirty-Eight

The fighter skiffs floated in the vacuum, a bunch of immobile dots across the massive canvas of space.

"There's nothing coherent coming from the Perpetuity," London said over the comm. "Half the people I speak with are pharmaed out of their gourds and the other half are covering their asses and refusing to give me any information."

"Captain? Are you getting anywhere?" Zenobia called out. "Is Major North responding?"

"I can't get him on the comm," Valencio replied as she flew her skiff between the waiting cadet pilots' vehicles. "I'm getting the same run around as London. I had Ngyuen on the line for a second, but she refused to answer any questions then she cut me off."

"You're her superior!" Richtoff snapped. "That woman can't cut off a captain! You should report her and bring her up on charges!"

"I'll get right on that, Richtoff," Valencio said.

"What do we do now?" London asked. "We have Estelian warships heading this way. They're one punch from reaching the Asteroid Belt stations. If they take those out then it's only Mars between us and them."

"We head back to the Perpetuity?" Zenobia asked. "Park these rookies on the flight deck and wait and see?"

"Give me a second," Valencio said. "Let me think."

"Not much to think about, Captain," Richtoff said. "There're only three of us out here trained to fly combat."

"You're forgetting me," London said.

"No, I'm not," Richtoff replied. "You're a cargo jock, not a fighter pilot."

"Well, that's just a dick thing to say," London responded. "I've been in as much shit as you have, Richtoff. This cargo skiff isn't just a mule, you know. It does have two plasma cannons."

"Good for it," Richtoff said. "Doesn't make it effective against Estelian warships, though. They'll blow you out of the vacuum before you can pull the trigger."

"Shut up, both of you," Valencio ordered. "Demon?"

"Yeah, Captain?" Zenobia answered.

"Are there still supply rocks out past the debris field? Or did Commandant Terlinger decommission those?" Valencio asked. "I know he was going to, but North never let me know if he did."

"Uh...why are you asking me, Captain?" Zenobia responded. "North didn't inform me either."

"Because you take joy flights out past the debris field all the time," Valencio said. "You're good at hiding your logs, but I'm better at finding them."

"Shit," Zenobia said. "I just have to get out of that can every once in a while."

"I know why you do it, Demon," Valencio said. "And I obviously have no problem with it or you'd have been busted a long while ago. I just need to know if those supply rocks are still floating out there."

"Yeah, they are," Zenobia replied.

"They have fuel cells?" Valencio said. "Enough for all of the skiffs?"

"Not that many, no," Zenobia said. "Maybe enough for half. Why?"

"Boss? Please tell me you aren't thinking about doing what I think you are thinking about doing?" London asked.

"That's a lot more thinking than you normally do, London," Richtoff said.

"Stop busting my balls, Richtoff," London said. "Boss?"

"I am thinking about doing it," Valencio said. "Did you bring enough fuel cells to make up the difference?"

"I did," London said. "But only enough to get the skiffs out there. We won't have enough to get back if we need to."

"We can refuel at one of the orbiting platforms around Mars," Valencio said. "That'll give us enough to get out to the Asteroid Belt stations."

"Whoa, whoa, whoa!" Zenobia called. "Did you just say Asteroid Belt stations?"

"I did," Valencio replied.

"Fuck yeah!" Zenobia cheered. "We're gonna take it to them, aren't we? Fly right in their faces and shut their lame ass attack down!"

"That's the plan," Valencio said.

"Oh, I am so down for that!" Zenobia yelled. "This is great!"

"I am not in agreement," Richtoff chimed in. "These rookies will be dead the second we punch out of interspace. The Estelians will tear them apart."

"That's if they even survive the punches," London said. "None of these cadets have ever punched in a fighter skiff. It's not like being on a transport and punching."

"I know," Valencio said.

"And if they do survive the punches without puking their guts out for ten hours," Richtoff said. "These skiffs have zero shielding. One round from a strafing gun and it is all over."

"I know," Valencio said. "I don't expect any of the rookies to fight. I doubt any of us will fight."

"They won't? We won't?" Zenobia asked, obviously disappointed. "This isn't sounding so fun anymore, Captain."

"Not supposed to be fun, Demon," Valencio said. "It's supposed to be war."

"What's the plan then, boss?" London asked.

"We get to the supply rocks first," Valencio replied. "We load up on all the fuel cells there then punch out to the Mars platforms."

"I'll call ahead and let Mars know we're coming," London said.

"Don't," Valencio replied. "Let's keep this amongst us for now. I don't want anyone tipping off the Perpetuity."

"Not like anyone's paying attention on the station," London responded. "Mars may appreciate knowing there's still some folks out here that haven't lost their fucking minds."

"Maybe," Valencio said. "Or Mars may be just as bad."

"Oh," London said. "I didn't think of that."

"Fuel cells first then Mars," Valencio said. "We stay cautious."

Thirty-Nine

Two cadets stood facing each other, their scorchers barking plasma bolts. Being training rounds, the bolts only produced minor shocks to their systems, not catastrophic bodily damage like true rounds would. Even still, the shocks should have dropped them to their knees after a couple of direct hits.

Yet both cadets stood there, taking the pain, their mouths open and throats bellowing rage-filled epithets at each other. When the scorchers dinged, the cadets glanced down at their empty weapons, flipped them over so they could grip them by the barrels, then charged right for each other.

The first cadet swung high, while the second cadet swung low. The second cadet's scorcher hit the first cadet right in the thighs, knocking the young woman off her feet and into the inches of mud that the simulation bay had coated the entire scenario with. The second cadet lifted his empty scorcher up over his head then brought it down with such force that when it connected with the first cadet's face, it not only caved in the woman's head, but cracked right through and ended up stuck a quarter meter into the ground.

The cadet grunted as he tried to free the scorcher, yanking and pulling with all of his strength. The weapon began to wiggle free, but the cadet never had the chance to lift it again as his spine was severed from a knife blade to the back. He cried out as he lost all feeling below his waist then collapsed on top of the corpse at his feet.

"You think you can fight, you worthless fuckstick of a maggoty piece of shit infested meat chunk?" Master Sergeant Lawrence Kim screamed. "Do you, you fucking stain on humanity's taint?"

The cadet tried to roll over to face the master sergeant, but he couldn't get the leverage. He just swiped at the man that stood over him with a hand that grew weaker and weaker with each pass.

"Oh! You think you can take me!" Kim laughed. "You think you can grab me and do what? Scratch my kneecaps off? Give me a leg cramp? You can't do fuck all, you failed abortion!"

Kim leapt into the air then brought both feet down onto the cadet's face, crushing his skull worse than what he cadet had done to his own victim. The master sergeant twisted his feet back and forth, pivoting at the hips and knees as he ground the cadet's pulverized head deep into the mud.

"Yeah, that's it. That's it right there," Kim said. "That's the feeling."

Satisfied, but not satiated, Kim looked up and scanned the area. He saw the thousands of cadets that filled the simulation bay all fighting each other. Most primarily clubbed at each other with their scorchers, while others resorted to more primitive tactics of biting, clawing, and scratching. Kim narrowed his eyes and gripped his combat knife tightly as he focused on a group of three cadets that were busy kicking and stomping another cadet.

"Now, that ain't fair," Kim snapped. "Three on one. Ain't fair at all."

Kim broke into a run, lashing out with his knife as he made his way to the three attackers. Cadets fell in his wake, their throats slashed, their faces cut, their hamstrings severed. When Kim reached the three cadets, he was coated in arterial spray.

"You think this is fair?" Kim shouted as he jammed the knife up to the handle in a cadet's eye socket. He yanked it free and slashed open a second cadet's belly, sending the man's guts spilling into the mud. "That seem fair? Does it?"

The third cadet tried to get his arms up to block Kim's attack, but he quickly found that it did no good as Kim hacked and hacked at the man, leaving only splintered nubs where hands and forearms should have been.

Kim stabbed the cadet in the throat then shoved his gurgling body out of the way to get to the cadet lying in the mud. The master sergeant bent down as the brutalized cadet tried to speak.

"What's that, you babbling hunk of jizz?" Kim barked. "You trying to say to tell your momma you love her? Fuck your momma! Fuck her right in her puckered asshole!"

Kim grabbed the cadet by the throat and squeezed until the young man's eyes bulged from his face and blood began to pour from his mouth and nose.

"You can tell your momma you love her yourself when you see her in Hell!" Kim roared.

He stood up, his chest heaving, and grinned at the world. Just before he licked the blood clean from his knife's blade. He was about to go after a pair of cadets that had stripped down to the waist and were busy stabbing each other in the chests with pieces of broken scorchers, but something else caught his eye.

"Pharma," he grunted as he caught sight of a cadet sitting off by herself, an injector in each hand. "Pharma!"

Half the cadets on the simulated battlefield stopped what they were doing and turned to look at the master sergeant. Then they turned to see what he was staring at.

"PHARMA!" the cadets roared as one.

The woman with the injectors in hand looked up and saw the thousands of enraged cadets all rushing towards her. She stood up from the mud and stuck one injector into her wrist and activated it then tossed that aside and did the same into the other wrist with her last injector. Her whole body shook as she flipped off the oncoming mob. She opened her mouth and let out a scream of pure triumph as she took off running towards the mob.

Woman and mob collided and the single cadet, freshly pharmaed, continued to scream her scream of triumph even as her body was ripped apart by a thousand hands.

Once the last scrap of the cadet was thrown aside, the mob turned on itself.

Master Sergeant Lawrence Kim stood in the middle of the mob, his face a rictus of glee as he killed anyone he could reach until he himself was taken down and killed by the very cadets he was there to train. If he had a rational thought left in his head just before the end, it would have been pride in the job he'd done, turning all the cadets into stone cold killers.

But rational thoughts were no longer part of Perpetuity.

Forty

"What have you got?" Linklater asked as he sat on the floor of the small room and watched Wendt tinker with the mystery communications system. "Anything at all?"

"Not yet," Wendt sighed. "So stop asking."

"You've been at this for hours," Linklater said. "Maybe it's time you stepped aside and let me take over."

"You don't know comm systems like I do," Wendt said. "You'll just mess it up and lose all of my progress."

"Progress? You've achieved progress?" Linklater laughed. "What progress?"

"Well, for starters, it's not transmitting any data," Wendt said. "I've checked it a few times and I can say with certainty that what we have here is an open pipeline. It's waiting to transmit data, but it hasn't been activated yet."

"So it's just holding?" Linklater asked. "Keeping a line open until data needs to be sent?"

"Yeah," Wendt nodded. "Whoever set this up wanted it ready at a moment's notice. Understandable since this isn't the most easily accessible location."

"They probably expected to be chased here," Linklater said. "This isn't a safe room, it's a tomb. The person gets here, transmits the data, is boxed in, and dies."

"Killed," Wendt said, looking over his shoulder at Linklater. "They don't just die, they get killed."

"Okay, so we have an open communications system, ready to transmit data at any second," Linklater said. "So what's the data? Those servers held something, but what?"

"They're destroyed, no way to know," Wendt said. "Whatever it was is lost now."

"Maybe not," Linklater said. "Move."

"What?" Wendt said. "I'm still working—"

"Move!" Linklater snapped. "It's my turn. You can handle the mechanics, but I'm better at the deep stuff. I want to get inside this thing and see if there is any residual data. Maybe we're thinking about this the wrong way."

"Fine. Whatever," Wendt said as he stood and stretched, raking his knuckles on the low ceiling. "Ow. Son of a bitch."

"Just sit on the floor and stay out of my way," Linklater said.

"Near death experiences usually bond people together," Wendt said. "It's just made you more grouchy."

"You're welcome to leave," Linklater said. "Open that hatch and step outside. Be sure and take a deep breath when you do."

"Eat shit, Linklater," Wendt said and held up a finger. "And fuck you with rank. Odds are I'm going to die in here, so I'm calling you Linklater. You call me Wendt."

"Last time I checked you weren't discharged by the CSC," Linklater said as he sat down in front of the communications system console. "Unless you want to be brought up in front of a court martial, you'd better keep calling me lieutenant or sir."

"Unless you want to suck my dick, you better get used to being called Linklater," Wendt said. "It's either that or shitface."

Linklater looked back at Wendt and glared, but the man didn't even wince.

"Fine," Linklater said. "Call me Linklater. But don't come crying to me when you're slapped in irons for insubordination after this is all done."

"Slapped in irons? What the hell are you talking about?" Wendt laughed. "You've been watching too many period vids. You think you're some damned sea captain now."

"Shut up and let me work," Linklater said.

"Go for it," Wendt said. "You aren't going to find anything that I haven't already found."

Linklater typed at the console for a minute and then grinned.

"I have something you didn't find already," Linklater said. "Fingerprints."

"Fingerprints?" Wendt asked. "Whose?"

"Terlinger's," Linklater said. "Terlinger's codes are all over this thing. Either he set it up or someone with access to his codes did."

"That's not too smart," Wendt said. "If it was discovered then he'd... Oh, right, no one expected to live if they got here."

"Exactly," Linklater said as he continued to work. "Just give me a few more minutes and I'll have this cracked."

Linklater tinkered with the system for a good thirty minutes before he threw up his hands in frustration.

"It doesn't want to talk to me!" Linklater said. "I've gone at it a hundred different ways and the system just sits there. It doesn't respond to any commands, it's like it's mocking me, just sending me around in loops."

"Wait...loops," Wendt said. "Move."

"No," Linklater said. "Just tell me what you want to do."

"No, move!" Wendt shouted, grabbing Linklater's shoulder.

"Let go of me, you little shit!" Linklater yelled, smacking Wendt's hand.

"Little shit? I could kick your ass sideways without breaking a sweat!" Wendt yelled. "Move!"

"No!" Linklater said as he stood up and shoved Wendt away. "I will fucking snap you in two!"

Wendt and Linklater stood there staring for a split second then they rushed towards each other. Linklater threw the first punch, catching Wendt across the jaw. But the blow barely slowed the sergeant. Wendt brought his elbow up and jabbed Linklater in the throat then tucked and threw his shoulder into Linklater's gut.

The lieutenant let out a harsh cough as the wind was knocked out of him. He tried to breathe, but his diaphragm was spasming too much. His fists pounded Wendt's back as the man lifted him up off the floor and then slammed him into the ground. Any air that was in Linklater's lungs was gone then.

"Just chill!" Wendt yelled. "Relax and you can breathe!"

Wendt rolled away from Linklater and leaned back against the wall, his body still tense and waiting.

Linklater was slowly able to suck in tiny amounts of air until the spasms in his diaphragm eased enough that he could take a full breath.

"Gonna...kill...you," Linklater said.

"And court martial me, yeah I get it," Wendt said. "But how about you listen to my theory first?"

"Fine," Linklater wheezed. "What...is it?"

"You said the system was sending you on loops," Wendt said. "But I don't think it is. I think the system itself is a loop. A continuous transmission that is being received back to this very console just to be transmitted back out again. That's why it looks like an open pipeline. It's an open loop, continually transmitting and receiving at the same time but appears to be doing neither."

Linklater blinked a few times then shook his head. "Asshole."

"What?" Wendt asked. "You think I'm wrong?"

"No...I think you're right," Linklater said as he pushed himself up and staggered to the console. "See if you can trap the signal."

"No, that would be bad," Wendt said. "If we interrupt it then it will all be lost. The data is here, it's just in the loop. Break the loop and we'll never know what was on those servers. It'll blip out of existence."

"Then how do we get to it?" Linklater said. "I've tried to get just a hint, but even my officer's backdoor keys don't work."

"Yeah, we need the real key," Wendt said. "We need something that will set the data free."

"You mean an actual physical key?" Linklater said.

"Yeah," Wendt replied. "I'm pretty sure there is a physical interface here where a key will fit." He pointed to a spot on the console. "Small, round, metal. About the size of a..."

"Medal," Linklater said. "Shit. That medal North had?"

"Yeah," Wendt frowned.

"Double shit," Linklater sighed. "We had it in our hands."

The two men looked at the hatch.

"We have to go back out there, don't we?" Wendt said.

"One of us does," Linklater replied.

"Flip a coin?" Wendt asked.

"I'll go," Linklater said.

"You will?" Wendt exclaimed excitedly then calmed down. "I mean, uh, you will?"

"I'm an officer," Linklater said. "I'll have better access to the station. Plus, North trusts me. If that medal he has is the key then it makes sense if I ask him for it."

They both just stared at the hatch and the dangers on the other side.

"So...you going?" Wendt asked.

"Yep," Linklater said.

Neither of them moved.

"Soon?" Wendt asked. "We don't have much time."

"I know," Linklater snapped. "I'm going, I'm going."

Linklater walked towards the hatch then stopped and turned around.

"I'm going to die out there," he said. "A plan may be a good idea."

"Don't have time for a plan," Wendt said.

"I open this hatch and all that smoke gets in here then you die too," Linklater said.

Wendt opened his mouth then closed it. He opened it again and again closed it. Then he nodded up and down.

"Yeah, we need a plan," he said.

Forty-One

The Perpetuity's corridors were chaos.

North ducked into a supply room, barely getting the hatch closed before a group of security guards pounded by, their scorchers up and ready. They were shouting orders back and forth as if each of them were in charge. It made no difference what they shouted, though, since all they did was keep running down the corridor, their sights set on some unknown goal.

North waited a full minute then cracked the hatch and stepped back into the corridor with a pistol drawn. He kept the scorchers cinched tight to his back, securing them for later use, knowing he needed speed and maneuverability at that moment, not fire power. He looked right then left, right into the fist of a frothing cadet. North stumbled back, but stayed on his feet. He lifted the pistol up, but it was knocked aside by a roundhouse kick that was obviously meant for his head, not his hand.

"Play to your strengths, cadet," North said as he raised his hands, palms out. "That is the first lesson of combat."

"My strength is I'm young," the cadet laughed, dancing around on his toes like a prize fighter. "You're just some old man that needs to be taken down so the new guys, the fresh faces can move up in the ranks."

North frowned and raised an eyebrow. "Are you fucking kidding me?"

He could tell by the size of the kid's pupils that the cadet was not fucking kidding him.

"Stand down and go sleep it off, cadet," North ordered. "You'll thank me in the morning."

"You'll thank me when you're dead!" the cadet shouted then lunged.

North dodged out of the way, throwing an elbow into the back of the cadet's neck as the young man rushed past. The cadet cried out, but didn't go down. He swung wildly as he twisted back towards North.

"Fucking DG!" the cadet yelled, "Fucking DG scum!"

"Seriously?" North asked as he ducked his head to the side then boxed the kid's ears.

The cadet stumbled back, shaking his head again and again, then roared and started to come at North.

"I don't have time for this," North said as he pulled his second pistol and put a round in the cadet's thigh. "I told you to go sleep it off. You didn't listen."

"You traitor!" the cadet yelled. "You'll hang for this!"

"I doubt it," North said as he bent over and retrieved the pistol the cadet had knocked out of his hand. He holstered it and gave a nod to the kid. "You're on some bad shit, kid. You'll be glad I didn't kill you for this."

North saw a group of cadets come around the corner of the corridor. Their eyes were just as wild as the cadet in front of him. North took a couple steps back then turned and started to jog in the opposite direction.

"Get that fuck!" the wounded cadet yelled. "He's a doubleganger! I saw it! I saw it!"

The group of cadets shouted something, but North couldn't tell if it was for him or the wounded cadet. They kept shouting until North reached the end of the corridor and started to turn the corner. Then the screams started up and as much as North didn't want to look, he hesitated and glanced back down the corridor.

The group of cadets had descended on the wounded cadet like rabid dogs. They pummeled and kicked him, ripping at his uniform, tearing it, and his body, to shreds. North stood frozen, the horror of the sight preventing him from moving any further.

"What the fuck?" he whispered.

As soon as the words left his mouth, all eyes from the murderous group turned to him. Even being several meters away, North could see that those eyes were nothing but black saucers floating in faces of rage. The cadets could have had blue eyes, green eyes, gold, hazel, brown, violet, it did not matter; all that could be seen were the completely dilated pupils.

North had a brief thought that with pupils that dilated, the cadets should have been blinded by the corridor's lighting, yet they didn't seem to even be slightly affected by it. It was a brief thought because a scream from around the corridor drew his attention instead.

"There!" a security guard yelled, his scorcher up. "It's him!"

"Fuck," North swore as he watched half a dozen guards sprinting towards him, the tips of their scorchers glowing red, telling him he had half a second before they discharged.

With no time to think, North went on instinct and chose the lesser of the dangers, even though it was far from ideal. Just as the guards began to fire, North turned and ran back towards the rabid cadets, a pistol in each hand. He fired into the group and dropped three of the cadets before they were on him.

North tucked and rolled, letting two cadets fly right over him as they went in for the attack. He kept rolling then came up into a crouch and fired at the cadets in front of him before pivoting and firing into the cadets that he'd avoided. The screams of the young filled North's ears, but he shut them out, knowing it was either them or him.

Jumping back up to his feet, North holstered a pistol and grabbed a still standing cadet around the neck. He swung the young woman around, so that he and she faced the end of the corridor and the security guards that had just reached it and were sprinting towards him.

Without regard for the cadets that North hadn't taken out, the security guards opened fire, their scorchers ripping through the chests and fresh faces of the young men and women. North stumbled back as a plasma bolt hit the woman he held square in the chest, but her body took all the damage, as he had expected it would, and he was left unharmed.

He opened fire on the security guards, his pistol sending round after round down the corridor. Three of the guards fell, holes appearing in their foreheads and between their eyes where flesh had been just seconds before. The rest of the guards dove to the ground, but they didn't stop firing. Plasma bolts impacted North's human shield, making him stumble back, messing with his aim so his next shots went wild.

North kept stumbling back then tossed the corpse he held aside and sprinted towards the other end of the corridor. It wasn't the direction he wanted to go, but his options had become seriously limited. He knew he could double back and get to the server tower another way.

A plasma bolt clipped his shoulder, but mainly singed his uniform, leaving only a superficial burn. But the impact threw him off and he stumbled just as he reached the corner, falling to his knees. The stumble saved his life as a mass of plasma bolts came at him from the corridor to his left.

North flattened himself on the ground and yanked one of his scorchers free. He opened fire on the new group of security guards, taking them all out below the knees. Shins and feet exploded in a mass of bone and flesh. The guards screamed and fell to the ground, their heads suddenly right in North's aim. He kept his finger pressed to the trigger until none of the guards moved, their heads nothing but smoking skulls and empty craters.

Scrambling to his feet, North made it around the corner just as the first group of guards got to their feet and gave chase. He could hear them yelling at him, ordering him to stop, calling him every vile name a traitor could be called. Even without seeing their eyes, North could hear that their voices were thick with the effects of pharma.

As he ran to the end of his corridor then took another corner, he knew his days of riding the pharma high were over. There was no way he could trust any injector to go into his arm. He didn't know what was wrong, how the station ended up so whacked out, but he did know that the new crates of pharma that the CSC sent had to be the reason. It was the why that he needed to figure out.

But first thing was first, he had to get to the server tower and Linklater.

Forty-Two

The fighter skiffs punched into orbit around Mars, their presence instantly detected. Valencio was not surprised when her comm exploded in her ear.

"Unidentified squadron!" a voice yelled. "You are not authorized to be in Mars orbit! Provide proper clearance or prepare to be fired upon!"

"Hold up!" Valencio yelled. "This is Captain Deena Valencio, Fighter Skiff Training Officer of the Training Station Perpetuity! Do not fire! I repeat, do not fire! I have a squadron of cadet pilots with me! Our skiffs are not armed!"

There was silence on the comm. Valencio angled her skiff so she could see the nearest orbiting platform, only a few kilometers away. Calling it a platform was a bit of a misnomer since it was actually a series of rotating discs stacked together on a single column. There was something about the platform that bothered Valencio, but she didn't have a chance to think it through too long before her comm squelched and a new voice came on.

"This is Colonel Hueng," a voice snapped. "I'm commanding officer of Mars Platform Eight. Please state your business, Captain Valencio. Your appearance was not expected and highly out of the ordinary, so your explanation had better be good."

"It is, sir," Valencio replied. "I have reason to believe that the Perpetuity may have been compromised."

"I have no indication of that," Hueng responded. "We are attempting to contact them right now, so know that if that is your excuse for punching a bunch of fighter skiffs into my vacuum space, the truth will be revealed shortly."

"Understood, sir," Valencio said. "I am sure your interaction with Perpetuity will back up my claim. You may not get any answers, but I am more than confident that enough questions will be raised for you to believe me."

"Why are you here, Captain?" Hueng asked. "Why not hold your position around Perpetuity and contact the CSC directly?"

"Our comm capabilities are limited, sir," Valencio said. "All direct communications with CSC would have had to be routed through the Perpetuity. These are training skiffs, and not combat ready vehicles."

"Is that so?" Hueng asked. "So your squadron is not armed?"

"Well, yes, sir," Valencio said. "I'd already stated that."

The thing about the platform still nagged at Valencio. Something was seriously off.

"Hey, boss?" London called out. "I think we should go."

"Hold tight, London," Valencio said. "Let me handle this."

"He's right, Captain," Zenobia chimed in. "I'm picking up power readings from the platform's weapons systems."

"Of course you are," Valencio said. "They already told us they would fire if we did not state our business. We expected this."

"That's not it, boss," London said. "I've been monitoring their comm. They haven't tried to reach the Perpetuity. Or if they have, it's on a sub-signal I can't lock onto. Both are reasons to get my asshole tingling."

"Too much information, London," Richtoff said. "Just tell us what you think."

"Boss, I think they are going to fire no matter what," London said. "This stinks like a trap."

"A trap? This is a CSC platform," Valencio said. "These are our allies."

"Not if they've been compromised like the Perpetuity," London said. "How'd the Estelians get past Pluto? Get past Neptune? What happened to Titan Base? How are they punching from place to place in this solar system without the locks stopping them, sir?"

"I don't know," Valencio said.

"You do," London said. "Those places were compromised too. Follow the line, Captain. Pluto all the way through the system. The Perpetuity was the last stop on the crazy train."

Valencio was about to respond when the nagging feeling solidified into a deadly revelation. Half the discs on the platform were dark. They should have been fully lit, the portholes and viewing windows leaking light from inside the platform, telling everyone around that it was full of busy personnel. But that wasn't the case. The discs were dark.

And dark in the vacuum usually meant dead.

"Fall back," Valencio said. "Get the skiffs out of firing range!"

But it was too late. Plasma cannons began to fire from the platform, sending bolts of death towards the fighter skiffs. And the rookie cadet pilots inside.

"Get back! Now!" Valencio roared as she banked her skiff to avoid three bolts that came at her. "Full reverse! Get your asses out of here!"

"Where to, Captain?" London yelled. "We have to refuel and get these cadets some firepower!"

Eight skiffs exploded then disintegrated before Valencio's eyes. She banked hard and hit her thrusters to push her skiff past the cloud of debris that was headed her way.

"Phobos," Valencio said. "We rendezvous at Phobos!"

"What? That useless rock?" Richtoff said. "There's nothing there, Captain!"

"Yeah, there is!" Valencio responded, ducking and dodging the barrage of plasma bolts flying at the training squadron. Three more skiffs were obliterated and Valencio pulled up hard, just clearing the wreckage. "But I don't have time to explain! Get as many of the cadet pilots as possible to follow you! Split up and head around the planet to Phobos!"

"I'll give you guys cover!" London shouted. "So move!"

Plasma bolts came flying from the cargo skiff as London activated the meager weapons system. Valencio watched as the bulky vehicle rushed forward, laying down enough fire to let a couple sixteens get away.

"That means you, Captain!" London yelled. "I'm not sticking around here all fucking day! Get to the moon and pull out whatever rabbit you have hiding up your sleeve!"

Valencio dove hard and fast, just barely avoiding a barrage of plasma bolts, she kept diving then pulled up and angled towards three sixteens of cadets that were just sitting there.

"The second we're clear, London!" Valencio shouted. "The very second we are clear, you are to get your ass to Phobos! I can't do what I need to do without you!"

"I'm touched, boss," London laughed. "I always thought I bugged the shit out of you."

"I need your cargo skiff, moron," Valencio said. "So try not to get it blown up!"

"Oh, well, that makes more sense," London said. "Don't worry about me. I'll be right behind you."

"You fucking better be," Valencio said and then she was gone with the traumatized sixteens following right behind her.

Forty-Three

Thirteen cadets. Raw recruits having just completed their first training simulation. They came rolling out of the simulation bay, covered in blood and guts, their weapons long since discarded, their hands and teeth all they needed to murder each other.

That was what faced North as he came around the corner and skidded to a stop, barely believing the sight before him. Men and women pummeled each other, their fists flying wildly, not caring where they hit as long as it did enough damage to maim, kill, destroy. Thumbs went for eyes, hands ripped off ears, feet caved in skulls. It was a bloody nightmare.

Then one stopped fighting, his head raised and twitching. Soon the others followed as if they could sense a new, fresh target in their midst. All heads turned towards North.

"A traitor," one of them mumbled through broken teeth and shredded lips. "You can smell it on him."

"You can see it in his eyes," another growled, a woman with half the skin on her face hanging down in flaps. "Liar's eyes."

"We hate liars," a third said. This one lifted his right arm to point at North, but instead of an accusatory finger, he pointed a bloody stump where his hand should have been.

"We hate traitors," a fourth snarled, tossing a severed hand aside.

"We kill liars," a fifth said. She was tall and muscular, her torso bare except for a combat harness. She looked unharmed and more like the one that had done the harming. She slowly pulled a knife from her combat harness and let the blade glint in the corridor light. "We kill traitors."

"I'm not fucking around, people," North said, aiming a scorcher at the group that was slowly walking towards him. "Come on. Be smart. Just back away and no one has to... Ah, fuck it."

He opened fire.

The plasma bolts tore into the mad group, ripping off limbs, opening bellies, decimating heads. Cadets fell to the floor, some screaming in pain, some long past that mortal affliction. North took careful, slow steps towards the group, making sure every shot he fired counted. All of the cadets fell, except for one.

Then North's scorcher clicked empty.

"Shit," he swore as he tossed it aside and pulled the other scorcher from his back.

The last cadet, the woman with the knife, grinned at him, showing blood red teeth flecked with human flesh. She raised her arm and threw the knife before North could get the scorcher up in time. The blade hit North's hand, knocking the scorcher aside, giving the woman time to close the distance between the two.

"Fucking traitor," the woman said as she swung a fist at North's head.

He dropped to a knee, grabbed up the knife that had slashed his hand, and jammed the blade into the woman's belly. He stood quickly and lifted the blade up, slicing the woman open from her navel to her sternum. Intestines and organs spilled out over his hand, but he ignored the disgusting mess as he grabbed the woman by the back of the head with his other hand, pressing her face to his.

"This is my station," North growled low. "Nobody calls me a fucking traitor on my station."

The woman coughed blood in North's face then her body went slack. North pulled his hands free and let her corpse collapse on top of the other dead cadets. He glanced down at the dead rookies, shaking his head at the pointless loss of life. A noise to his right made him turn and he saw another dozen cadets staring at him from the hatch to the simulation bay.

"You want to die too?" North asked.

The cadets roared and came at him, but he already had a pistol in his hand and ready. He fired off twelve shots, dropping each recruit with a hole in the head. North didn't bother looking at or thinking about those kills. He reloaded the pistol and held it to his side as he took off down the corridor, a steady stream of blood pouring from the wound in his hand.

North quickly realized he couldn't engage every group of cadets or guards that he stumbled upon and had ended up hiding and backtracking for most of his journey through the insane station.

Perpetuity had become Bedlam and the inmates were in charge. North passed a corridor and witnessed acts of pure evil he hadn't ever seen in combat. Cadet defiling cadet, guards defiling cadets, all laughing and screaming as they killed, raped, and ate one another.

North had to disengage, compartmentalize the horrors. He had a mission to complete, although he could not quite say what that mission was. Life for him on the Perpetuity became one step at a time, one corridor at a time, one blind corner at a time. Movement by movement as he made his way to the server tower, his mental armor thickening with each meter of ground he covered.

Then he was there. The main hatch to the server tower lift was right in front of him. He reached out and placed his wrist to the panel, but the hatch did not open.

"Unauthorized personnel," a voice rang out from a speaker above his head. "Unauthorized personnel detected. Security please report. Security please report. Unauthori—"

The voice stooped as North fired his pistol up into the speaker. Bits of metal and plastic rained down on him. He shook the debris from his face then looked at the panel by the hatch. That too was quickly obliterated as he turned his pistol on it and fired. Yet the hatch did not automatically open.

"Fuck," North said as he yanked at the panel and got the plate free.

He reached inside and started to pull at anything he could grab a hold of. He worked at it for a minute before he heard the hatch move.

"Perfect," he said as he pulled his hand from the panel and reached for the hatch.

The hatch came flying open and slammed into his chest, sending him stumbling back. North kept his footing and raised his pistol, waiting for the next attack, but no one came out of the hatchway.

North slowly began to circle around to the front of the hatch, his pistol covering the opening as he pulled a stun baton from his belt with his other hand. He noticed how much his hand was bleeding, seeing the knife wound as well as the shredded knuckles from when he'd smashed in Bunk's teeth. Not to mention his dislocated fingers. He knew the only reason he was keeping the pistol steady was because of the vast amounts of adrenaline pumping through him.

But without pharma, his body would not be able to keep the endocrine boost going. And it seemed that pharma was not exactly a safe bet at that moment. North didn't need more evidence of that fact. He only hoped he would get to Linklater before the inevitable system crash that his body was in for.

"Link!" North shouted as he moved towards the hatchway, quickly realizing that there was no lift waiting for him. "Link!"

The blow was hard and swift, nailing him right in his wounded hand. The pain was enough to push through the adrenaline surge and make him drop his pistol. North instinctively drew his hand to his chest and brought up his stun baton. He whirled around, but no one was with him in the corridor.

"You again?" he asked. There was no response. "I know you're there, you piece of—"

The wind was knocked from North's lungs as something hard hit him in the gut. He didn't know if it was a fist, a boot, a club or what. He didn't really care as he dropped to a knee and swung out blindly with his stun baton, catching nothing but air.

"Fucking...coward," North coughed. "Gotta hide...from me...to fight."

North swung the stun baton back and forth, back and forth, maintaining some space in front of him as he tried to scoot backwards and get the wall fully behind him. He sensed the next blow before it came, giving him time to duck and take the brunt to his shoulder and not the side of his head. But that was as good as it got for North as he found himself held around the neck by a shimmering forearm.

"Where is it?" the shimmer asked close to North's left ear. "Just hand it over and you get to live."

"Fuck...you," North choked.

"This can go easy for you, North," the shimmer said. "I don't want to kill you, but I will. Then I'll just search your body."

"Suck...my...dick," North said. "Search...that."

The pressure on North's throat increased, causing black spots to dance before his eyes. The blood in his head started to pound and it felt like it would explode out the top of his skull. North got his hand up and tried to pull the forearm away, but the shimmer just held tight.

"Come on, North," the shimmer said. "Just give it to me. I really don't want to do this."

"Then...don't," North gasped.

"I will," the shimmer said. "I swear to the Makers that I will."

"I...don't...know...what...you...want," North said.

"The key," the shimmer said. "I just need the key. Terlinger shouldn't have given it to you. That was a mistake. I aim to rectify that mistake."

"What...key?" North asked as his world started to dim. It was hard to hear the shimmer over the blood thumping in his ears. "I...don't have—"

"Hey!" a muffled voice called from the hatchway. "What the fuck are you doing, North?"

The pressure eased up on North's neck as his body was twisted towards the voice.

"Who the fuck are you?" the shimmer asked as a rag-covered person pulled itself out of the server tower hatch and into the corridor.

"Who said that?" the rag man asked. "North? What the hell is going on?"

The pressure eased even more and North took the opportunity to grab his stun baton and jam it back behind him. He activated it and almost wished he hadn't as the forearm spasmed around his throat and nearly ripped his head off. Then the choking stopped and the arm was gone. North pushed himself away and crouched on his hands and knees in the middle of the corridor, his lungs desperate for fresh air.

"Fucking...stay...away," North wheezed as he limply threatened the rag man with the stun baton. "I'll...fuck...you...up."

"Oh, shut your stupid mouth," the rag man said as he moved towards North. "You couldn't fuck up a drunk cadet right now. Get your ass up. I need your help."

North looked at the rag man then shook his head. "Link?"

"Yeah, who the fuck else did you think it was?" the rag man replied. Then he patted himself down. "Oh, right. Sorry."

Linklater unwrapped the rags from his head and tossed them aside. North glanced over and realized the rags were actually a wet and soot-stained uniform.

"What the hell was going on?" Linklater asked. "What was that?"

North glanced behind him, but didn't see even a hint of a shimmer.

"Baton should have shorted his shield," North said.

"Was that someone with a cloaking shield?" Linklater asked. "Holy shit. I never thought I'd see one of those in action. Who was it?"

"How the hell should I know?" North snapped as he held out a hand. "Help me up, will you?"

Linklater hurried over and helped North to his feet.

"Listen, North, you have something I need," Linklater said. "Something we all need. It may be the key, well it is the key, to what is all happening here."

"What is happening?" North asked.

Linklater started to reply then paused. "Uh...I don't know."

"Then how do you know I have the key?" North asked.

"Because you had a medal on you," Linklater said. "A medal you said Terlinger gave you."

North took a step back and raised the stun baton.

"What?" Linklater asked.

"Are you working with him?" North asked. "The shimmer? You are, aren't you? This is some tag team strategy, right? I wouldn't tell him so you come in next and try to get the info out of me?"

"Uh...no," Linklater said. "Paranoid, are we?"

"I've been fighting and killing guards and cadets for the last hour," North said. "And if I'm not the one doing it then they are doing it to each other. This station has gone to fucking hell, Link. I am far from paranoid, I'm just trying to survive."

"Cadets killing each other?" Linklater asked. "What the holy shit are you talking about?"

"Like you don't know," North glared.

"I don't, asshole!" Linklater shouted as he pointed at the server tower hatch. "I've been trapped in there since the last time I saw you! Someone tried to kill Wendt and me with the lift! Then they blew it up and sent some noxious gas through the shaft! Why the fuck do you think I had Wendt's uniform wrapped around my head? Because I like to sniff his crotch stink? Because the smell of piss is my favorite scent?"

"You really don't know?" North asked, his instincts kicking in. "You haven't seen any of it?"

"I haven't seen shit," Linklater said. "Except for you getting choked by nothing and then stunning that nothing."

North turned around slowly. "He could still be here."

"Who?" Linklater asked.

"I don't know," North said. He stopped turning and looked at Linklater. "What's so important about this key? Why did that guy want it and now you do?"

"Well, looky here," Metzger laughed as he came around the corner. "Why am I not surprised to find you little fuck buddies hanging out together? I always knew you were a fucking DG, Linklater. You just stunk like an Estelian." Metzger sniffed the air theatrically then wrinkled his nose. "Jesus, you actually do stink. Is that piss?"

"Fuck you, Metzger," Linklater said. "I do not have time for your shit. Now just turn around—"

"Uh, Link? Metzger is on pharma," North said. "A lot of it. Same shit that's making everyone batshit crazy."

"He doesn't look any more crazy than usual," Linklater said.

Metzger took aim with his scorcher and grinned. "That's because I'm not. Never been so clearheaded in my life. The orders coming to my chip tell me so. Blasting your face off is going to feel soooo good."

"Ah, fuck," North said and grabbed Linklater by the arm. "Run!"

North threw his stun baton at Metzger and took off down the corridor as fast as he could. Linklater was right on his tail when Metzger opened fire with his scorcher.

"Holy shit!" Linklater yelled. "He calls shooting at us clearheaded? Fuck him!"

They got to the next corner and sprinted around it. Right into four guards. North struck out with his fist and caught one guard in the face then kicked another in the groin, sending both to the floor. He grabbed the barrel of a third's scorcher and turned it to the side just as it discharged, sending a plasma bolt into the fourth guard. North hammered his fist into the scorcher guard's throat, crushing the woman's windpipe and yanked the scorcher free, turned it on her and fired. Then he fired down at the two collapsed guards and looked over his shoulder at Linklater.

"Fucking A," Linklater said. "You killed them."

"Of course I did," North said, nodding at the guards. "Grab their scorchers."

North turned around and aimed at the corner of the corridor. As soon as Metzger started to come around, North fired the scorcher, melting a chunk of the corner's wall.

"Close, North!" Metzger yelled as he jumped back. "Really close! Looks like you have more blood on your hands, asshole! You shouldn't have killed my guards! I'm keeping a list of everything you're going to get hanged for! If I let the CSC have you! Probably going to rip you apart myself, though! Looking forward to that!"

"Go," North said as he backed away, carefully stepping over the guards' corpses. He kept the scorcher trained on the corner. "Link?"

"Yeah, yeah, I'm going," Linklater said as he stood up with three scorchers hanging over his shoulder. "Uh, where to?"

"Right now? Away," North said, firing a plasma blast at the corner as Metzger tried to peek around. "Just go."

Linklater turned and started running. North fired at the corner until the scorcher was empty then bent down and picked up two pistols from the guards, turned, and took off after Linklater.

When he caught up, he asked, "Uh, why do you smell like piss?"

"Uric acid," Linklater said. "Helped to neutralize whatever was in the smoke."

"Oh," North replied.

"No, seriously," Linklater said.

"Right. Sure," North said.

"Oh, fuck off," Linklater growled.

Forty-Four

It took one last kick for the hatch to break free and float off away from the nearly totaled quad. Garcia pulled herself free of the cockpit and out onto the shredded and scorched frame of the fighter, expecting at any second to be blasted out of the vacuum by a plasma bolt. She gripped the edge of the hatch, the magnets in her flight suit's gloves keeping her from floating off into the less than open space. Behind her visor, her mouth hung open as she surveyed the scene.

Wreckage was everywhere, Estelian and CSC. Partial quads bumped into each other then ricocheted out into the vacuum. Chunks of Estelian destroyers, battleships, and cruisers collided with the partial quads, turning them into shrapnel that exploded and flew in all directions. Garcia ducked back inside her quad's cockpit as a rain of metal flew past. She stayed down for a few minutes, only daring to pull herself back up after the last bit of metal floated past.

"Jesus," she whispered as she looked out at the massive debris field.

She remained cautious, sitting on top of her quad, as she studied what was left of the battle. She hoped to see some sign of life, some movement amongst the graveyard of spacecrafts. But there was nothing, just the husks of mangled warships and the shells of dead quads.

Occasionally, she caught a glimpse of a flight suit, but never an intact one. She turned her head as fast as possible to avoid seeing the frozen and frigid remains that the suits held. She was very grateful for the tinted visors the helmets had since she wasn't sure she could handle looking into the dead eyes of a fellow pilot.

She sat like that for a couple of hours, just watching it all swirl around her. It was like a nightmare ballet of death; a graveyard dance of the bones of enemies. It was another hour before her suit started to beep, bringing her out of her morbid reverie.

Garcia tapped at her wrist and was shocked to see she had about thirty minutes of air left before she became just another lifeless marker of the battle in the vacuum.

"No," she said to herself. "I lived. I keep going."

She scanned the debris and looked for a quad that could be intact enough to have an air supply left. There was one that was at least a kilometer off, pinballing back and forth between the hunks of a destroyer that surrounded it. Garcia calculated the trajectory and realized there was no way she could get there with just one push. Too much interference from other pieces that floated back and forth in her path.

Looking left then right, Garcia searched the debris field for a different route, then saw it. Half a quad was about to float by her, maybe ten meters away. Its trajectory would take it past a tangle of scorched struts that looked to have come from a cruiser. That tangle was moving at a downward angle towards a blasted Estelian quad that was more hole than fighter. The blasted quad was moving at a different angle back towards the quad that Garcia wanted to get to.

The timing was going to be rough, but she knew if she aimed right, she could hop from one piece of junk to the next and the next until she got to her destination.

"Let's just hope this works," Garcia said as she bunched her legs and got ready to jump. "No one to save my ass if it doesn't."

With a quick prayer to the Makers, Garcia lunged out into the vacuum, her arms tucked to her side as she tried to make as small a target as possible. There was still so much junk and shrapnel whizzing by her that she knew she had just as much of a chance of getting sliced in half by a severed quad wing than she had of actually making it to her target. The half-quad she was aiming for got closer and closer and she reached out for it at the last minute just as it was about to rush by.

She hesitated, catching the half-quad as it passed, instead of meeting it head on, in order to avoid changing the thing's trajectory. Everything in the vacuum was about the laws of motion. Equal and opposite reaction. Inertia and momentum. Garcia wanted to break as little of those laws as possible.

Her gloves clamped onto the half-quad's hull, dragging her with it as it sped by. But even that small impact caused the half-quad to veer slightly off course. Its trajectory took it directly towards the sparking tail section of an Estelian cruiser. Garcia considered jumping to the tail section and finding a new route, but as she got closer she saw that the hunk of warship was spinning too fast, with too many jagged pieces of metal sticking out that would just love to slice right through her flight suit. Her suit's material could handle the vacuum, but not the damage the tail section could cause.

Garcia had to think fast since the half-quad was almost to the tail section. She looked about, desperate for a new route, then saw the spiraling wreckage of a destroyer's thruster. It was large, hollow, and smooth, with nothing sticking out that could impale her. But it was moving very fast, almost faster than Garcia thought she could move.

The shadow of the tail section loomed over her and she pushed fear and uncertainty from her mind. She disengaged from the half-quad and leapt back into the vacuum. She stretched her arms out, knowing she would need every inch of her body to catch the mangled thruster shell. It was a risk, one that almost took her left arm as she pulled it quickly away from a twirling cockpit hatch, but risk was all she had.

The thruster got closer and closer and Garcia smiled as she realized she'd be able to slide right inside without an issue. The shell would give her some protection from the debris that threatened to cut her apart. It would also allow her to survey the area for her next move in relative safety. Not that she had much time to survey, as her suit reminded her with a series of shrill beeps.

She looked at her wrist and blanched as she saw she only had fifteen minutes of oxygen left. Fifteen minutes. She was so busy studying her air levels that she didn't see what was flying at her until it was too late.

Her body doubled over as the corpse of one of her fellow pilots slammed into her midsection. She tried to get herself free and push off, hoping she could still keep moving towards the thruster, but the corpse had too much junk wrapped around it, catching her in a net of snapped cables and broken wires.

Garcia wanted to scream. She wanted to yell and pound her fists on the corpse, but she kept her calm, knowing that panic would just lead to using up her oxygen that much faster. She carefully extricated herself from the tangle of wires and cables and then shoved away, watching as the corpse floated off into the vacuum to join the rest of her dead comrades.

Then she was bouncing off something big. She tried to turn herself around, but she was spinning wildly in the vacuum, her body flying end over end around the deadly debris that seemed to envelope her. Then the panic did come and she yelled as her view was up and down, up and down, up and down, over and over and over.

She passed more corpses, more mangled quads, more parts and pieces of warships. With every second, she expected to be sliced and diced by the multitude of deadly hunks and chunks that surrounded her. Then it ended as abruptly as it had begun.

Her body became still and her gloves and boots clamped onto the solid metal she found herself on. As her suit beeped, Garcia looked around and saw she was up against the hull of a fairly intact Estelian cruiser. In fact, it looked almost unharmed, except for a few choice plasma blast scorch marks and the fact that it only had one of its three thrusters intact.

Which made Garcia wonder when the Estelian attack would come. She was close to an external airlock hatch and she crept towards it, her eyes locked on the entrance, waiting for it to open and an Estelian scorcher to be pointed out at her.

But the scorcher never appeared.

She got to the airlock hatch and looked in through the small porthole. The airlock itself looked undamaged, although there were no lights on inside. Garcia studied the manual opening mechanism next to the hatch and was surprised that it looked like it worked exactly like the CSC mechanisms. She grabbed the handle, turned it 180 degrees then slammed it back down.

And waited.

Nothing happened.

That meant there was no power to the hatch. She would have to open it the hard way. Garcia grabbed the airlock handle again and yanked it upright. Then pushed it back down. Back up and then back down. Over and over she repeated the motion until the hatch began to move, slowly being opened by her constant pumping of the handle.

Her suit let out a long beep that refused to stop. She glanced down at her wrist and saw she had one minute left. She took a deep breath and kept pumping until the hatch was open enough she could wedge her fingers in between it and the ship's hull. She braced her feet and pulled, forcing the hatch open enough that she could slip inside.

The long beep ended abruptly and Garcia knew she was out of time and out of air. All she had was the air in her lungs. She tried to get the airlock closed, but her arms began to feel heavy and she couldn't get the thing to move. She clamped her boots to the airlock's floor and looked about the tight space, desperate for something that would let her live, if only for a few minutes more.

She saw it instantly.

Bolted to the wall was a med kit. She knew inside the med kit, if it was anything like a CSC med kit, would be a small canister of pure oxygen. She unbolted the kit and tore it open, almost crying with relief when she saw the canister.

But that didn't mean she was out of the woods. The canister of oxygen had a small face mask on it, designed to go over a person's head that didn't have a flight helmet on. Or that was stuck in the vacuum. In order to get the oxygen from the canister to her lungs, she would have to get the canister into her suit somehow.

Garcia's vision started to dim and she decided to try the first idea that came to mind. She pulled out a utility knife from a pouch on her belt and made a tiny slit in her flight suit. The pressure change gave her a blinding headache and she almost passed out, but she hung on long enough to work the face mask of the canister in through the slit. She cranked the knob on the canister and her suit started to fill with sweet, precious oxygen.

As it was designed, the flight suit automatically sealed itself around the slit, trapping the face mask inside, making an airtight seal between Garcia's suit and the canister. She took a few deep breaths, which made her head swim from the pure oxygen, and looked about the airlock.

Right in front of her was a porthole that looked into the Estelian warship. She glanced through and saw a small control station and a hatch she assumed led to a hallway. She knew if she was going to get inside, and if the warship was still pressurized, she'd have to close the hatch behind her. She had no idea how much oxygen was in the canister, but she hoped it was enough to get the job done.

She found the internal handle that would act the same way as the one on the hull of the ship. She repeated the up and down pumping until the hatch was almost closed then she grabbed the wheel in the middle and yanked as hard as she could. It took all of her strength, but she managed to get it shut and spun the wheel, locking the airlock tight against the vacuum.

Garcia spun about and hoped that the rest of the ship was locked tight against the vacuum.

She walked to the internal airlock hatch and grabbed its handle. She pulled out, spun it 180 degrees and slammed it back down. Completely expecting the same results as before, she was shocked to see the hatch open on its own. That meant there was still some power somewhere, but just not going to the outer hatches. Or just not going to the one hatch.

Cautiously, very aware she was in enemy territory and unarmed except for her utility knife, Garcia opened the hatch and stepped into the control station. She closed the hatch behind her, spun the wheel to lock it and then waited.

She waited and waited until her suit began to beep again. Its sensors must have noticed the supply coming from the oxygen canister was dwindling. Garcia had no choice but to move from the control room and into the rest of the ship if she wanted to live.

She said a quick prayer and went to the hatch into the main part of the ship. She pressed the control panel next to the hatch and it popped open at her, although haltingly and not as fast as she was used to a hatch opening. She stuck her head out into the corridor beyond and waited again.

Nothing.

No sound, no sign of any Estelians.

She stepped into the corridor. The hatch closed behind her with a loud thud and she jumped then spun about in a circle, waiting for the Estelian guards to come for her.

No guards.

Her suit beeped one last time then Garcia began to feel lightheaded. Whether there were Estelians on the way to kill or capture her no longer mattered. She would be dead in seconds without air.

More prayers, although very quick ones, and she unclasped her helmet and lifted it off her head. She squeezed her eyes shut and opened her mouth, letting out the stale breath she held. Then she took a deep breath and waited to die.

She did not die.

Air had never tasted so good.

Garcia opened her eyes, expecting a firing squad of Estelians to be standing in front of her, but the corridor was still empty. She stood there, listening, waiting, fearing.

"Can't just stand here forever," she said, her voice echoing down the corridor. "Gonna have to say hi to the DGs at some point."

She started to walk down the corridor then realized she still had an oxygen canister sticking out of her suit. Garcia set her helmet down then wiggled out of her flight suit. She kicked her suit to the side of the corridor then spotted something she knew would come in handy.

Picking up her helmet, she smashed it into the glass case holding a fire axe. She pulled out the bright red weapon and hefted it by the handle, feeling its weight, studying its sharp edge that could easily slice through metal.

"Okay. I can do this," she said as she walked down the corridor. "Bring it, you doubleganger fucks."

Forty-Five

"What are we waiting for, Captain?" Richtoff asked as the squadron of fighter skiffs waited in the vacuum just above one of Mars's two moons. "I see nothing but a stupid rock down there."

"There's more than that," Valencio said. "Trust me. But we can't get to it until London gets here."

"What if he doesn't?" Zenobia asked. "Is there a backup plan?"

"I'm working on one," Valencio said. "But it won't be fun."

"How long do you think until the Estelians punch in?" Zenobia asked. "If they've already taken down the Asteroid Belt stations then they should be here any second."

"You just answered your own question, Demon," Valencio replied. "If you already know the answer then don't bug me. I'm trying to concentrate."

"Just talking out loud, Captain," Zenobia said. "Helps me ignore the pure horror of this bullshit."

"We'll make it," Richtoff stated. "We're damn good pilots."

"But what about the cadet pilots?" Zenobia asked. "You think they have a shot?"

"They have a shot," Valencio said. "Just not a good one."

Proximity alarms rang out in Valencio's cockpit and she looked down at her scanners then out the hatch at the red planet before her. A small dot came zipping from orbit, aimed right at the training squadron. Valencio really wished she had an armed weapons system instead of a mock one. The dot was too far away to tell if it was London or not.

"Defensive positions," Valencio ordered over the open channel. "Group your sixteens in a tight V."

"I think the defensive positions these cadets take should be to tuck their heads between their knees and kiss their asses goodbye," Zenobia laughed.

"Channel is still open," Richtoff snapped.

"I know," Zenobia replied.

"London? Come in. Is that you?" Valencio asked, switching her comm back to private. "London, fucking answer me!"

"It's me, boss," London replied, his cargo skiff getting closer and closer. There was some obvious damage, but the craft looked like it would hold together. "Remind me that being a hero sucks Gropp balls."

"You ever seen a Gropp?" Valencio asked.

"Yeah, I have," London replied. "Those balls are the scaliest things I've ever had the misfortune of viewing. And huge! How do those buggers walk?"

"Shut up about Gropp balls," Valencio said. "I need you to land on Phobos with me. We're going to load up on fuel cells and arm these skiffs."

"Whoa, what?" London asked as his cargo skiff came to halt alongside Valencio's fighter. "Arm the training skiffs? With what?"

"Plasma and missiles," Valencio said. "I told you there was something on Phobos. Well, more like something in Phobos. Just land with me and you'll see."

Valencio banked her skiff and aimed directly for the surface of the small moon. London brought his cargo skiff around and followed right behind.

"Demon? Line up the sixteens," Valencio ordered. "Then pick the most capable cadet pilots we have and get them ready for vacuum duty. We'll need as many hands as possible to load up the skiffs."

"You want these bumbling dorks to get out of their skiffs and into the vacuum?" Zenobia laughed. "We'll probably end up watching half of them float away to die from their own stupidity."

"A risk we'll have to take," Valencio said. "Just make it happen. London will be back with supplies shortly."

Valencio aimed the nose of her skiff directly at a large crater on the surface of Phobos. She counted off the distance until she knew she was close enough to make the maneuver required.

"Depot override protocol scepter one niner eight four," Valencio said. "I repeat, depot override protocol scepter one niner eight four."

"Depot override protocol scepter one niner eight four acknowledged," a computerized voice replied over the comm. "Please identify yourself."

"This is Captain Deena Valencio of the Training Station Perpetuity," Valencio replied. "Enemy warships are en route and munitions are needed."

"Thank you for identifying yourself, Captain Deena Valencio of the Training Station Perpetuity," the computerized voice responded. "Enemy warships are not detected. Verifying voice patterns for deception. Deception not noted. Override granted. Welcome to Phobos, Captain Valencio."

The crater before Valencio's skiff began to split in half, with the bottom retracting into the sides, revealing a wide open landing bay. Valencio cut her thrusters and coasted towards the landing dock then pulled up on her flight stick at the last second, gave her thrusters a slight bump, and brought the skiff in for a landing on the far side of the bay.

"You get the middle, London," Valencio said. "Put your skiff down and make sure you are suited up. This has to be done in zero G without atmosphere."

"There's no life support?" London asked.

"There is if we shut and lock down the landing bay," Valencio said. "But we don't have time to do that. We'll be working in flight suits."

"Son of a bitch," London said. "I didn't know manual labor would be involved. I'd have just let that platform blast me out of the vacuum. I hate manual labor."

"Shut up and land," Valencio said.

London landed his cargo skiff as Valencio opened her hatch and pulled herself out of her skiff. She jumped down to the cargo bay floor and activated her magnetic boots, securing her feet to the metal deck so she wouldn't drift off into space.

The cargo skiff's main hatch opened, revealing an empty space with only London standing in it. He walked down the ramp that automatically extended to the landing bay's deck, his own boots magnetized to the surface.

"Where's the gear?" London asked.

"Bolted to the walls," Valencio said. "I'm going to undo each package and toss them to you. Get ready to catch."

London stopped at the bottom of the ramp and held up his hands. "Whoa, boss, I suck at catch. I'm a flyer, not an athlete.

There's a reason I sit on my ass and fly glorified boxes for a living."

"You can catch," Valencio said, making her way to the group of long crates bolted securely to the landing bay's wall. "You're going to have to. Otherwise I have to close the bay and get out the forklifts. I do not want to do that, London, are we clear?"

"Catching it is," London said as he clapped his hands together. "Bring it on."

Valencio grabbed a drive wrench from the wall then undid the bolts holding the crates. Normally she would have secured the bolts, but she just let them float off away from her, the shiny metal fasteners spinning end over end. With the bolts off, Valencio pulled the braces from the crates and let those drift away as well. She grabbed the first crate, gripped it tight, turned, and shoved it towards London.

The warrant officer crouched at the bottom of the ramp and waited for the crate to get to him as it floated in the zero gravity environment. The impact knocked him back a step, but he stayed upright. He turned and walked the crate up into the cargo skiff, set it down quickly, laughing as it bounced and tried to float up against the ceiling. He stomped it in place with a boot then turned and clapped his hands again.

"This ain't so bad," London said. "Keep them coming."

"Don't get cocky," Valencio said. "Those are the missile crates. You may want to be a bit more careful when setting them down."

London looked at the crate he'd just handled roughly and nodded. "Message received loud and clear."

"Good," Valencio said. "Here comes the next one. We fill up your skiff and then you get up to the squadron. Demon and her cadet pilots can load the fighters. We repeat until we are full. Got it?"

"Then what, boss?" London asked. "We fight an Estelian armada with training skiffs? Even at full capacity, and piloted by veterans, these skiffs won't last long. But they aren't piloted by veterans. It's going to be chaos. They'll more than likely shoot each other. Or us."

"I'm not going for a coordinated attack, London," Valencio said. "I know the limitations of what we are working with. I'm hoping to have directed, destructive chaos. If we can slow the armada down then that may give the Perpetuity some time."

"Time for what?" London asked. "I hate to break it to you, boss, but I don't think the Perpetuity needs time. I think it needs sanity. If it's anything like that Mars platform then we are going to die to protect a bunch of folks that have lost their minds."

"We do our jobs and we die with honor," Valencio said. "Not much more we can ask for."

"I'd like to ask to live, please!" London exclaimed. "Can that be noted officially? I'd really rather I lived with honor than died with honor. Just saying."

Forty-Six

North jammed the pistol up under the cadet's chin and pulled the trigger. A spray of blood, bone, and brains covered his face as he tossed the body to the side then aimed at the next cadet that was rushing towards him. North pulled the trigger, but the pistol clicked empty as it emitted a small whine and powered down.

"Fuck," North said as he threw the pistol at the cadet, nailing the young woman between the eyes. She stumbled back, but didn't lose her footing and just came at North even faster. "Double fuck."

The young woman reached North and threw a left hook. North blocked it with his right arm and cracked her across the face with his left fist. The cadet's head rocked to the side, but she recovered and threw a hard kick at North's groin. Blocking it with both hands in a cross, North lunged forward and slammed his forehead against the woman's face, crushing her nose.

That time the cadet did get knocked off balance and North dropped to the floor and swept her legs out from under her. As she fell, he grabbed her neck and helped gravity slam her to the floor. The back of her head exploded against the metal, sending shards of skull shooting this way and that with chunks of brain spilling everywhere.

"North!" Linklater yelled as he tried to use a fire extinguisher to fend off two cadets coming at him. "North!"

"Hey!" North yelled as he jumped up and rushed the cadets. "Over here!"

One of the cadets turned in time to see North's boot flying at his jaw. He cried out as the bottom half of his face was nearly torn free, sending him spinning down to the floor. North stomped hard, crushing the young man's windpipe then threw his shoulder into the side of the second cadet, sending both of them to the corridor floor.

North found two very strong hands around his neck as he tried to roll free of the cadet.

"Extinguisher," North choked as he boxed the cadet's ears to no avail. "Link…"

"Right!" Linklater yelled as he brought the fire extinguisher down on the back of the cadet's head.

North shoved the cadet off of him then sent an elbow into the young man's temple. The cadet's dilated eyes rolled up into his head as the life left his body.

"Makers," Linklater said. "They wouldn't stop."

"More coming," North said as the sound of quite a few boots on metal echoed down the corridor.

"Where are we heading?" Linklater said.

"To get the medal," North said. "Metzger took it off me. It's either in security or on Metzger still. We find that then get you back into your server tower shaft."

"Looking forward to that," Linklater said. "Remind me to grab a spare uniform."

"Why?" North asked.

"Well, long story, but there's a good reason," Linklater started. "You know that uniform—"

He didn't finish as a plasma bolt hit the wall right by his head.

"Hey, boys!" Metzger yelled. "There ya are! Miss me?"

"Does he have to be such an ass?" Linklater grumbled as he and North took off running again.

"Where ya going, boys?" Metzger called after them, firing his scorcher over and over. "You can't run! I'm dialed into your chips! I can track you anywhere on this station! I just got held up by some crazy cadets! Man, has this station gone to shit or what?"

"I really don't like how stable he sounds," Linklater said. "Why isn't he a crazy fuck like everyone else?"

"I don't know," North said. "I watched him shoot enough pharma to kill an elephant."

"You'd have to bring one back from extinction first," Linklater said.

"Yeah, that's how much pharma he took," North said as they ducked around a corner, glad not to see rabid cadets waiting for them. "I think he could bring one back from extinction with his mind, he's so fucking high."

The two men sprinted down the corridor, relieved at the small break from the constant violence. No cadets meant no slowing down. No slowing down meant they could keep from getting their asses shot off by Metzger. Although, North wasn't sure how long that could last.

"He's steering us away from the lifts," North said. "We have to get to one so we can get to the security levels."

"That's sort of like walking into the lion's den," Linklater said.

"Now who's talking about extinct wildlife?" North said. "But if you want that medal then the lion's den is where we have to go. Because it's either there or it's on Metzger."

They turned another corner and skidded to a stop.

At least three dozen bloody and battered cadets stood in the hall, their eyes wide and pupils dilated. At their feet were another dozen cadets, all brutally beaten to a pulp. Blood and chunks of flesh were strewn everywhere.

"Nope," Linklater said. "Not going that way."

North slapped at his belt, but he had emptied his last pistol already.

"Not unarmed, we aren't," North said. "Come on. Back this way."

They spun around and then stopped again. Coming down the last corridor was Metzger, a wicked smile on his face and a glowing scorcher to his shoulder.

"Now where?" Linklater asked.

North looked from the group of homicidal cadets to an open hatch only a few feet from the bloody mob. He frowned then grabbed Linklater by the arm.

"Come on," North said. "I think I know how to take care of Metzger."

"Good," Linklater said. "But do we have to get closer to the crazies?"

"Yes," North said. "A lot closer."

The mob of cadets turned their attention from their victims and looked at North and Linklater, their soulless eyes boring holes in the two officers.

"North? What's the plan?" Linklater asked. North yanked him out of the corridor and into the open hatch. "No! Wait! This is not a good idea!"

The hatchway was coated in blood and bodily fluids. The fluids led to a second hatch where North placed his wrist to a panel beside it. The hatch didn't open.

"Shit!" North shouted. "My fucking interface is still locked!"

The hatch suddenly opened and three crazed cadets came rushing out. North jumped to the side and shoved Linklater away from him as he stuck out his leg. The first cadet tripped over it and went sprawling with the other two crashing down on top of him. North leapt on them, cramming his forearm into the backs of the heads of the top two as he stripped them of their scorchers. He tossed a scorcher to Linklater then jumped up and shoved the lieutenant through the open hatch just as the mob from the corridor came through the first hatchway at them.

"Go!" North yelled. "Inside!"

They hurried through and the hatch closed behind them. Linklater looked down at his scorcher then over at North.

"This is a training rifle!" Linklater yelled. "What good is a training rifle going to do?"

North looked out at the simulation in progress and the horrors being committed by the mad cadets that fought everywhere. He flipped the scorcher around and gripped it by the barrel then gave it a hard swing.

"They make good clubs," North said. "Come on."

"Where? Into that?" Linklater nearly shrieked. "This is a shitty plan, North!"

"Only one I have," North said. "Metzger will be coming for us. We can maybe get a chance to ambush him and take him down."

"Or we get killed by these insane fuckers!" Linklater said as several eyes turned towards them.

"No, we won't," North smiled. "You recognize where we are?"

"I do not give two shits where we are," Linklater said.

"Look around, Link!" North yelled. "Look at the sim! Where is this?"

Linklater studied the landscape then nodded. "Yeah, I know where we are. I was still working on this sim. It shouldn't even be running."

"Well, I'm guessing your techs aren't in their right minds either. One of them probably activated it," North said. "Come on.

We need to get to the forests around the lake country. It'll give us cover and more than likely these idiots haven't gotten there yet. If Metzger gets through here alive then we'll be ready for him."

"I fucking hope so," Linklater said. "Only problem is we have to get through here alive as well."

"We will," North said. "We have an advantage."

"Oh, what's that?" Linklater asked as several cadets started to stomp their way towards them.

"We aren't crazy," North said as he hefted the scorcher and ran straight for the oncoming cadets.

"You sure about that?" Linklater asked just before he followed. "AAAAAAAH!!!"

Forty-Seven

The silence of the Estelian warship was almost more terrifying than the constant anticipation that someone would jump out at her with a scorcher and end her life right there in enemy territory. Garcia gripped the fire axe with all of her strength as she struggled to keep the weapon from slipping out of her sweaty palms.

Not that the ship was completely silent. There were the constant echoes from various bits of debris colliding with the hull of the ship. Every time a thunk or clang would reach Garcia, she expected a squad of Estelians to come rushing out of a hatch at her. By the end of the second hour of searching the ship for signs of life, Garcia was close to screaming, her nerves were so frayed.

"Hello?" Garcia shouted, done with stealth. Not that she had been considerably stealthy since she'd pretty much walked down the middle of each corridor she came to. "Hey! I'm right here, you DG assholes! No more hide and seek! Come on out and face me, you damned doublegangers!"

Garcia paused in the middle of the corridor, ready for the violent response she knew was going to come. But it never did. She adjusted the grip on her axe again and again, holding it over her shoulder until her muscles started to protest. After counting to two hundred without any repercussions for her shouting, Garcia relaxed slightly, letting the axe fall to her side.

She swung the axe back and forth as she decided that her time haunting the corridors of the eerily empty ship was over with. Garcia found the next hatch and looked at the panel next to it.

"Recreation Room Six," the panel read.

Garcia cocked her head, her eyes studying the words again and again. Then she looked down the hall, leaning back from the hatch and read the words stenciled by the corner.

"Level Twenty-Three, Crew," the words read.

Garcia had been on a lot of CSC cruisers, destroyers, and battleships. She knew the layout of those warships like the back of her hand. It was more than surprising that not only could she read the words on the panel, and stenciled down at the corner of the corridor, but that they matched the same layout as a cruiser she had served on when she was fresh out of training.

"Recreation room, eh?" she wondered. "If you have four game tables, five couches, three vid screens, and a refreshment dispensary tucked into the corner then I'm going to shit."

She reached out and pressed her wrist to the panel, not expecting the hatch to open at all.

It did.

With a clang and a loud squeak, the hatch opened inward. Garcia hesitated then shoved the hatch all the way open with the head of the axe. She looked one way down the corridor, looked back the other way, and took a deep breath. She stepped through the hatchway and into the recreation room.

Four game tables, five couches, three vid screens, and a refreshment dispensary tucked into the corner.

"Fuck me," she whispered.

One of the vid screens came to life while the other two just flickered weakly.

"Please select a program," a voice from the vid screen said, making Garcia jump and swing her axe around. "Please select a program."

Garcia calmed down and approached the vid screen, her eyes studying the menu of program choices that slowly scrolled from the bottom of the screen up. She recognized the titles. They were entertainment programs that she had watched a hundred times. Next to their names were the words "Newly Uploaded".

"Newly uploaded a few years ago, maybe," Garcia said. "I guess DGs are pirating old CSC programs now."

"Please select a program," the voice said again.

"Dream Hunters, Season Two," Garcia said.

The screen went to black then the opening credits of a silly children's animated show began to play.

"Mute," Garcia said as the ridiculously cheery theme song started up. The song went silent, but the images of dancing children with plasma nets chasing images over sleeping children's heads kept playing. Garcia watched for a couple minutes, shaking her head back and forth. "I loved this show."

She tore her attention away from the screen and walked around the room, her hand trailing along the game tables, her fingers coming away covered in dust. Her stomach growled and she looked at the refreshment station longingly. She had no idea if it worked or if it even had any food stocked, but she walked over to it anyway.

"What the hell do you need this for?" she asked as she stared at the interface screen on the front of the station. "DGs don't eat like we do."

That was one thing she knew from training, that DGs don't eat like humans. They may take on human appearance, but they didn't require the same nourishment a human body did. There were rumors that they lived off the life forces of the people they captured, draining them until the prisoners died and they could assume their forms, but something about the refreshment station bugged Garcia.

It took her a minute to notice what it was that bugged her. Scuff marks. Lots of scuff marks against the dispenser chutes where food and drink would come out if an order was placed.

Garcia ran her fingers along the spots worn smooth and then pulled back as she felt the station humming under her touch. She reached for the interface screen, pulled back, then pressed the icon indicating "drink."

A sub menu came up listing every liquid refreshment she could possibly want, except for alcohol. That had to be obtained in the ship's officers' club or the cantinas for the enlisted personnel.

Garcia chose a simple cup of water and jumped back as the cup dropped from one of the chutes and was quickly filled. She grabbed it, sniffed it, then set it aside. She chose another drink, a fruit juice she was familiar with that originated in the Boone system. Another cup dropped and was filled. Garcia sniffed that and set it aside.

Soon she was choosing drinks at random, grabbing full cups, setting them aside, and starting again. The counter next to the station was almost full of cups of liquid before she stopped and turned her attention on the food menu.

"Okay, so Estelians get thirsty," Garcia said. "Good to know. But they don't eat. I know that. Everyone knows that."

Garcia ordered a hot sandwich and a side salad.

A panel slid open and her order was presented to her.

"Fuck me," she whispered as she lifted the plate and sniffed the food.

It smelled stale, but considering how hungry she was, it also smelled delicious. Garcia took a few cautious bites and almost swooned. Stale, yes, but it was food. Human food.

"No way. No way, no way."

She set the plate aside, shoving over a couple drinks to make room on the counter then backed away from the refreshment station.

The vid screen to her left caught her eye and she looked over to see that the program had ended. In its place was not the previous menu she had chosen from, but the Estelian ship's insignia, spinning lazily in three dimensions projected a few inches out from the screen.

Garcia stared at the insignia. She knew that insignia. Everyone in the CSC corps knew that insignia. It was an insignia she never thought she'd personally see ever again.

Ever.

Despite her stomach's insistence that the plate of food that was perched on the counter was perfectly acceptable and should be finished, Garcia kept backing away from the refreshment station, her eyes locked onto the spinning insignia. When her butt hit one of the game tables, she cried out, spun, and sent the blade of the axe right into the middle of the table.

Garcia left the axe there, its handle sticking up and out at an angle, as she hurried towards the hatchway and out of the recreation room. When she was out in the corridor she quickly oriented herself, which wasn't hard to do since she knew exactly where she was and exactly where everything on the ship would be located.

After all, she had spent her first year out of training on a ship exactly like it.

Forty-Eight

The injector fell from Metzger's hand and he sighed with deep appreciation as he stood over the blasted bodies of the cadet mob that filled the hatchway to the simulation room. He looked down, his mind alive and reeling, and watched the spent injector tumble across a cadet's nose and lodge between the corpse's lips.

Something about the image of the dead cadet kissing the injector made Metzger feel sorry for the kid. The stupid cadet wouldn't be kissing anything anymore except for the afterlife. The thought tugged at him, scratching at the feeling of the fresh high. But Metzger shoved it away and convinced himself the cadet deserved to die.

All doublegangers deserved to die.

Metzger stepped all the way into the simulation room and then pressed his wrist. A map came up, showing him exactly what the layout of the simulation was and where he could find North and Linklater. There were plenty of Estelian traitors all around him, but those two were the only ones he cared about. They were his target and he would let nothing get in his way from taking them down.

A scream off to Metzger's right made him wipe away the map and grab up his scorcher. It wasn't until he heard a second scream that he realized what was happening right in front of him. He'd been so engrossed in studying the map, and riding the exhilaration of fresh pharma, that hadn't realized there was quite a bit of death and destruction he would have to wade through to get to his targets.

"Better get started," Metzger said as he opened fire.

He knew the basic direction he needed to go, so he aimed his scorcher that way and held the trigger down, wiping his path clear with every plasma bolt that barked from his scorcher's barrel. Cadets, and even some station personnel that seemed to have stumbled into the simulation bay, turned and roared at him, coming together in a show of psychotic solidarity at their new foe. Metzger just grinned at them as he casually swung his scorcher from left to right, right to left, obliterating the attackers the second they were in range.

His scorcher beeped and he looked down to see the bolt count at zero. He ejected the power cartridge and then slapped in a new one, drawing from the absurd amount of ammunition strapped to his belt.

Metzger pressed the trigger again just before three cadets reached his position. Two of them lost their heads in a spray of blood and the third spun about, his hands clutching at the gaping hole that went completely through his chest and out his back. The young man had a split-second to actually press a hand inside himself before collapsing onto the gore-covered ground at his feet.

"You need to die," Metzger said, taking aim at a cadet that was crouched over another, his mouth stuffed full of the dead woman's entrails. The cadet didn't even see the plasma bolt coming. "And you need to die." Metzger swung about and vaporized the legs off of a master sergeant that was just standing there, his hands raised in the air, his mouth wide open and issuing a war cry that turned into a wail of agony. "And you. And you. And you."

Metzger fired bolt after bolt into the mayhem and madness. Cadets fell like sheaves of wheat before the scythe that was Metzger's scorcher. He barely had to aim, the battlefield was so full of targets to hit. A head and shoulder gone, an arm, a leg, belly after belly, faces burned off, chests torn through.

Metzger did not slow until he had traversed the entire battlefield without getting a single scratch. None of the cadets or personnel even got within five feet of him. Many tried, but all died quickly and horribly.

The valley below Metzger was green and lush and untouched. The horrors of battle had been kept to the rocky and barren plateau that it bordered. Metzger smiled at the beauty of it all and then smiled at the simple path that cut right down the middle of the valley.

"I'm coming for you, boys!" Metzger bellowed. "I am so coming for you!"

He slung his scorcher across his back and felt at the pouch at his waist. He pulled out another injector and almost did a little jig in anticipation of getting his head right. Those stupid cadets had ruined his previous buzz. He needed to make sure his head was clear for what came next.

"Oh, yeah, baby," Metzger sighed as yet another dose of pharma entered his bloodstream. "Oh, you are so good to me."

Metzger tossed the spent injector over his shoulder, rolled his head on his neck, savoring the cracking of vertebrae, then lifted his scorcher and marched down into the valley.

"Yea, though I walk through the valley of the shadow of death, I will fear no evil, because evil should fucking fear me!"

Forty-Nine

"Last missile is being locked in by Demon right now," London said over the comm. "You coming out of there, boss?"

"Yeah. Give me a minute," Valencio said.

She had counted how much ammunition and missiles had left Phobos' hidden cache and knew it wasn't anywhere near what they would need to take out the Estelian armada. Even if all the fighter skiffs unloaded on the armada at once, and hit their targets, they could only hope to take out a couple of battleships and maybe a destroyer and a cruiser. That would leave at least another cruiser and a couple of destroyers. And, if the last scan she saw was correct, more than one squadrons of quads.

"But I need to take them all out," she said. "Perpetuity won't last against even one destroyer. Maybe a cruiser, but not a destroyer."

She finished her task and then sprinted to her skiff, hopping into the cockpit and closing the hatch in one fluid movement.

"Boss?" London called.

"Coming," Valencio snapped. "Keep your shirt on."

"Are you sure? Because I do work out and these abs are something to look at," London said.

"London?" Valencio growled.

"Right. Not appropriate at this time," London said. "Got it."

Valencio launched her skiff from the landing bay and sped out to meet her squadron. She flew right into the middle of them and couldn't help but smile at the sight of the heavy missiles locked under the wings of each fighter.

"I'm going to be completely honest with all of you," Valencio said over the open comm. "I don't expect any of us to live very long once the Estelians get here. This red planet before us will be the last planet you ever see. I would advise you gaze upon it and appreciate it for what it is."

"What is it?" Richtoff asked. "I just see red and orange."

"You can totally see more than that!" Zenobia said. "Check that out over there! That's the Newman Colony! And right there is the Greer Colo—"

From the surface of the planet, right where the Mars colony Greer should have been, was a bright flash and a massive fireball. It had to be massive if it could be seen from where the squadron waited.

"What the fuck just happened?" London asked.

"The same thing that happened with the platforms," Richtoff replied. "People have lost their minds."

"Motherfucker," Zenobia sighed. "That really sucked to look at."

"Listen up, folks," Valencio said as she struggled to keep a sense of strength in her voice despite the demoralizing sight of the still burning fireball that had been Greer Colony. "What you see there is what is going to happen to the Perpetuity if we don't stop the Estelians. We are vastly outnumbered, and grossly underpowered, but we have something that the Estelians don't have. We have position."

Valencio tapped at her control screen and brought up a map of the area surrounding Mars. The platforms and the two moons came into view. She pressed her wrist and then started to draw on the map with her fingers.

"You should be seeing what I am seeing," Valencio said. "We have the planet, the platforms, and the moons to work with. The platforms are obviously compromised and not our allies, but they do have some firepower. We need to use that firepower against the Estelian warships. If the timing is right then these platforms here, here, and here will be in sight when the Estelians punch into Mars space. Our goal is to draw the Estelians into battle and direct them this way. If we can get them close enough that the platform cannons can reach then we'll use ourselves as bait to get the platforms to fire, hopefully sending stray bolts at the Estelians."

"Captain?" London said, his voice cautious and careful. "I think I have some bad news."

"What is it, London?" Valencio barked. "I'm in the middle of something here."

"I'm pretty sure everyone on the platforms is dead, boss," London said. "I've been monitoring their comm and I haven't heard a single voice in close to an hour. If they aren't dead then they are being very, very quiet."

"Shit," Valencio said. She almost punched her control console then stopped and smiled. "No. No shit. This is better."

"It is?" London asked. "How?"

"We can take control of the platforms and use their weaponry against the Estelians without resorting to subterfuge," Valencio replied.

"Oh, good, I hate resorting to subterfuge," London said.

"Wouldn't that mean we'd have to board the platforms and operate the cannons ourselves?" Zenobia asked.

"Not if we set them to auto," Valencio said. "It would be a risk to us since the cannons could easily target us just as much as they target the Estelians, but we were going to deal with that anyway."

"Great," London said. "How do we make this happen?"

"Someone has to go on board the platforms," Valencio said. "That person will need to manually enter a defense protocol. Being a TO from Perpetuity, I have the codes for that protocol."

"Yeah, but boss, we're going to need you up here," London said. "You've gotta lead the squadron when the Estelians get here."

"I know, London," Valencio said. "That's why I'm sending you the codes now. As soon as the platforms show up, you need to hustle and get those abs of yours onto the first one. Go straight to the bridge and enter the code. The automatic defense system will take over from there."

"There's one problem with that, Captain," Zenobia said. "The defense protocol will be in place when London leaves that platform. He'll be the first target the cannons will lock onto."

"Yeah, I was kinda thinking the same thing," London said.

"Then you better move ass when you leave the first platform," Valencio said. "You're always bragging about how well you can fly that cargo skiff. Time to prove it, Warrant Officer London."

"Wonderful," London sighed. "Just fucking wonderful."

Fifty

The forest was dense with tall trees that towered above North and Linklater. They had to be close to seventy meters high at least. But despite the over-arching canopy, there was still plenty of underbrush that proved to be a thick barrier for the two officers.

"No way to go around," Linklater said. "Gotta go through."

"You giving yourself a pep talk?" North asked as he kicked at a thorny branch that grabbed at the leg of his uniform.

"Just reminding myself why we didn't skirt the forest," Linklater said. "Gotta go through if we want to get to the lake before Metzger catches up with us. You'd think not hearing scorcher fire would be comforting, but it's not. I am not delusional enough to think the man was killed by all those crazies. He stopped firing because he's hit the valley."

"That's probably a pretty good assessment," North said. "Which means we only have a few minutes, maybe half an hour if we're lucky, to get to the lake and get set up."

"You really think this will work?" Linklater said. "This is a simulation bay, not the actual planet it represents."

"And you happen to be the tech officer that designed this protocol," North said. "We get to the lake and you can take it from there. All we have to do is make sure Metzger goes down to the shore once you've reprogrammed the levels."

"When I do that then this place becomes just as deadly to us as it does to him," Linklater said. "We're probably going to die too."

"I don't want Metzger to die," North said. "Not right away. I have to find out from him if he has the medal or if it's in security somewhere. Once he tells me where it is, and he's subdued, then I don't give a shit if he lives or not."

"I do what you want and he's probably going to die," Linklater said. "Just being realistic."

"That's the risk we have to take," North said. He stopped as the light in the forest grew brighter. North pointed ahead to a break in the trees. "Here we go."

The two men stepped from the shade of the forest and into the glaring reflection of the huge lake before them. North squinted and shielded his eyes with his hand as he walked from the soft loam of the forest floor and out into hard and rocky beach that lined the lake.

"Not much transition here," North said. "Pretty sure there was more vegetation at the lake's edge than this."

"There was," Linklater said as he looked about the beach for the exact spot he needed. "But erosion and damage from the solar winds has cut back on any greenery exposed to the suns."

North reluctantly looked up in the sky at the two orbs that shone down on the simulated planet. One was a bright orange, similar to the sun that Earth's solar system was anchored by, while the other was a deep red and seemed to flicker every few seconds. He squinted then looked away.

"Is that it over there?" North asked, pointing to a boulder that had moss on the forest side, but was bare and smooth on the side facing the lake. "That looks like your signature?"

Within the moss was an almost imperceptible "ML"-Linklater's initials.

"Perfect," Linklater said as he hurried over to the rock. "Good eye. I would have wandered for a while. These suns are killing my head."

"You built the simulation," North said. "You could have dialed back the brightness a bit."

"I didn't expect to be in here," Linklater said. "And it wouldn't have been an authentic training experience if the suns weren't so bright."

A far off scream caught their attention and they both looked back towards the forest.

"I think we're pretty far from authentic at this point," North said. "Even if we wanted to recreate the Battle of Strell, it wouldn't be anywhere near as bloody as what is happening back there."

Linklater pressed his hand to the moss side of the rock and a small panel popped open. He dug around in a pouch on his belt and pulled out a set of fine tools.

"Are those solid metal?" North asked. "Seems a bit old fashioned."

"I always keep a set on me," Linklater said. "Just in case my interface isn't working right. Good thing, don't you think?"

"How will you know if you've gotten it to work?" North asked, stepping closer to the water's edge. "There's no way we can test it without the trap springing on us."

"You'll find out pretty soon if you don't stay back from those waves," Linklater said. "This isn't going to take me long. It's actually only a matter of moving around a few switches into a specific pattern. It's easier from my control room, that's for sure, since it would have been just one command. But I made sure there was a manual backup here just in case of some type of tech issue or I needed to talk a master sergeant through shutting it down."

"If there was a tech issue then how would you communicate with the master sergeant?" North asked.

"Don't start poking holes in my redundancies," Linklater said. "Just be grateful I can do what I'm doing right now."

"I'll be grateful once we have that asshole where we want him," North said. "Are you sure it's going to be exactly like it needs to be?"

"I'm sure," Linklater said. "Are you sure you can handle Metzger when he gets here?"

"Not a problem," North said as he watched a far off ripple out in the lake begin to get closer.

Linklater closed the panel and put away his tools. He stood up, stretched and walked over to North.

"We are screwed, aren't we?" Linklater said.

"Oh, ye of little faith," North smiled.

"Yeah, we're screwed," Linklater grumbled. "I'm going to go hide now. Just use the thing to distract him. If it grabs him then he's a goner and you won't get any info. You know what these things can do."

"I got this, don't worry," North said. "I didn't become Chief Training Officer without having an innate sense of timing."

"I figured it was because you were just the only one that applied," Linklater said. "It was the only reason that made—"

Linklater went flying into the water as a plasma bolt hit the ground right at his feet.

"Hey, North," Metzger said from the edge of the forest, his scorcher trained right on the major. "You boys should really chat less. I pretty much heard everything you said."

He walked down from the forest and onto the rocky beach.

"Sounds like you boys have something in store for me," Metzger continued. "I have no idea what it is since I don't recognize this simulation. But I can't wait to find out."

North tensed to run, but Metzger shook his head and kept walking forward.

"No, North. Just no," Metzger growled. "You're going to stand right there and keep your Estelian spy mouth shut."

"Metzger, listen," North started but then found himself diving to the ground as Metzger sent a plasma bolt at his head.

"No listening," Metzger said. "Not to your doubleganger lies. You just keep that abomination of a mouth shut and turn around. On your knees, scum."

North did as Metzger ordered. He turned around to face the lake and got down on his knees. He looked out and saw the fear on Linklater's face as the lieutenant sat in the shallows of the lake. North knew there was nothing he could do to alleviate that fear. He just hoped Metzger would make a mistake so he could make a move before the thing he and Linklater had summoned got too close.

Fifty-One

Garcia knew she could get things up and running on the cruiser when she got to the bridge. She just hoped that the cruiser would last that long. Several more impacts against the hull could easily be heard. They had to be severe for the sounds to travel all the way to the heart of the ship and into the central lift shaft. Garcia wondered how much time she had left before she'd have to find a new safe haven.

Not that she felt safe on the CSC Norland.

Her first assignment right out of training had been to serve on the Norland. She wasn't a pilot then, just an ensign that worked the flight decks. She had spent hour after hour, shift after shift, watching fighter skiff pilots go out and come back. She'd watched even more go out and never come back.

Even knowing that the odds were against a fighter pilot living through a mission, Garcia hadn't wavered in her desire to hop in one of the skiffs and take to the vacuum. She hounded her CO, relentlessly putting in request after request to attend pilot training.

Garcia laughed to herself as she thought how being a pilot used to be a privilege, now it was open to whoever fit the physical requirements. All that time arguing for her chance at glory, starting with the skiff squadrons and working her way up to the quads, and it meant nothing since a farmer from the middle of some nowhere system could score high on a test and end up with wings on her uniform in mere months.

The lift doors opened and Garcia stepped out into the corridor, her mood less than pleasant.

"Makers, this place," she said, trailing her fingers along the wall as she walked towards the bridge hatch. "I can never shake this place. I know it's not the real thing, that the DGs set it up to look like the Norland, but damn... This place sucks."

She placed her wrist to the panel next to the bridge hatch and it popped open instantly. Pushing the hatch aside, she stepped onto the bridge of the Norland, her eyes going wide at what she saw and her hand going to her nose at what she smelled.

There were people sitting at each station, even one sitting in the command chair, but it was obvious they were no longer living. The smell alone alerted her to that.

Before her, past the rows of consoles, was the main view window, a five foot thick piece of plastic and glass interlaced with billions of reactive diodes that could change the window from real and into a vid screen at the push of a button.

Garcia stared at the scene before the Norland. All the wreckage and debris that swirled about in the vacuum. Slowly, she walked past the corpses, past the command chair and the dead captain that occupied it; past the ensigns assigned to handle the weapons systems, navigation system, communications. She approached the view window and looked out at the death and destruction before her.

She'd been in battles before, she had even been out in the very wreckage she was looking at, but it all seemed different from up on the bridge of the Norland. It seemed more intense, more drastic, more pointless.

Her eye caught sight of the hundreds of bodies that floated along, bumping off of and being torn apart by the battle debris. She watched as two bodies collided then went spinning off in different directions, quite possibly the last human interaction they would ever have.

Human interaction…

Garcia spun around and stared at the corpses. They were Estelian corpses. Doublegangers having taken the form of true humans. No one knew what a real Estelian looked like; one had never been captured in its natural state. She walked amongst the corpses, marveling at how real they looked. Even through the decay, Garcia could see the blemishes and scars that had marked the creatures' skin, just like the blemishes and scars that marked her own.

"So real," Garcia said. "So close to human. But not quite, you DG fuckers."

Yet…

Garcia had begun to move the corpses from the communications console, hoping to see if she could get a message out to the CSC that she was alive, but something stopped her. She held the corpse by its shoulders and narrowed her eyes as she looked into its mouth.

Braces.

The Estelian woman, if they had sexes, had braces on its teeth. Garcia had almost missed it since the braces were nearly invisible, but the light from the view window had caught them just right, giving off just the barest of reflection.

"Why the hell would a DG need braces?" Garcia asked. "Why go to that kind of trouble to replicate humans that much?"

It didn't make sense to her. Why put braces on someone that would be seated at a communications console on a cruiser? Detail was one thing, but no one would have given a second thought if the woman didn't have braces.

"Not a woman," Garcia said. "An Estelian."

That wasn't the only thing that bothered Garcia.

"How did you die?" she asked. "This ship was hit, but not enough to kill everyone on the bridge."

A gas? Some sort of toxin that also made the bodies decompose rapidly? Maybe Estelians committed suicide at the first sign of defeat?

All questions she asked herself as she looked around the bridge, her need to contact the CSC overpowered by her need to figure out the mystery that gnawed at her. She left the woman with the braces and went from corpse to corpse, studying the bodies closely. She took shallow breaths as she opened uniforms, pulled up sleeves, removed boots.

A man with a cybernetic eye. A woman with a prosthetic leg. A man with a port in his chest for easy access to his artificial heart. A woman missing most of her torso, nothing but wires and tubes enclosed in a plastic frame for a midsection.

Garcia hurried back to the woman with braces and examined her more closely. She found ports in the back of the woman's head; ports she knew were used to stimulate brain activity in wounded soldiers that had suffered severe head traumas.

"What the holy hell…"

She moved the woman out of the way and activated the communications console. The ship's transmitter was completely offline, but the receiver was in good working order. She started to scroll through any messages received and was puzzled by the lack of language. All she saw were command codes; codes given to systems for remote operations. She knew them well since she'd had to learn how to operate and fly a skiff or quad remotely. All pilots did in case they needed an immediate evacuation off a hostile planet they'd landed on and weren't close to their fighter.

Garcia backed away from the communications console, confused and alarmed. She bumped into the command chair and spun about, coming face to face with the man that was supposed to be the captain of the Norland. Except the man didn't have any eyes and was missing a large portion of his lower jaw.

Swallowing hard, Garcia reached past the captain's corpse and activated the log controls on the arm of his chair. An image popped up of a man talking, giving a basic, boring general report on the status of the cruiser and its crew. The image was not of the man that was seated in the chair. And the time stamp that scrolled by at the bottom of the image was nowhere near the current time.

In fact, as Garcia did some quick calculations, the time stamp matched closely to the time when the CSC Norland had been reported destroyed by Estelian forces during the Battle of Lost Skies. That battle had been over six years earlier. Even if the Estelians had captured the Norland and were using it as their own, which they had been known to do with other ships, why wasn't there a new log by the new Estelian captain?

Or if they didn't use logs like humans did then why wasn't the last log of the battle itself? Why was it a simple status report? All CSC warships went into automatic record mode so that each and every moment of a battle was saved for study and posterity.

And hadn't Garcia seen the last broadcast from the Norland, the last captain's log, just like the millions of other humans had when the defeat of the CSC at the Battle of Lost Skies was announced?

Too many questions. Garcia's mind swam with them, reeled from them, tried to reject them. She wanted to think there was some easy explanation. There had to be. She was on an Estelian ship, she was dealing with Estelian corpses, she didn't know the first thing about the alien technology the DGs employed. It was all a trick, all an illusion designed to mess with her head, to break down her confidence.

It was all designed…

"…to look like an attack," Garcia whispered.

She gasped as the words left her lips. She turned quickly, throwing up the couple bites of the stale contents of the dinner the refreshment station had provided her, throwing up food that had probably been in stasis since the Norland had been lost.

Because Garcia, at that moment, had zero doubt in her brain that she was on the actual CSC Norland.

She hurried back to the communications console and scrolled through the log, checking the details of the code received. She hunted for the information that would tell her what she needed to know to confirm her worst fears. After several minutes of checking and double checking, Garcia had her answer.

It was not an answer she liked, but it was an answer.

Fifty-Two

"Everyone hold," Valencio said. "You wait until I give the order. Do not fire until I say so. I want evasive maneuvers first. Fly around the attack. Weave between the ships when they get here. They will open fire on us as soon as they punch through. Do not return fire. We have limited ammunition. They do not. I want chaos, not a slaughter. Just keep from getting killed."

"You sure about this, boss?" London asked. "I mean, we went to all that trouble of arming these skiffs, seems like a waste not to use those arms."

"We will, London," Valencio said. "But only when we need to."

Valencio bristled at London's words. He knew what she had planned and he was trying to talk her out of it. In any other situation she would have let him. More importantly, in any other situation, she would never have created the plan she did.

But there was no going back. Even if she wanted the skiffs to return to the Perpetuity, she had no idea what waited for them there. While the skiffs waited for the Estelian armada to appear, Valencio had ordered London to try one last time and contact the Perpetuity. She had to try to find someone reasonable to speak with.

London had found plenty of people to speak with, none of them reasonable. He quickly reported back the same type of interaction they had had with the colonel on the Mars platform. Everyone had accused London of being an Estelian spy and traitor. Many threats were made, most involving the removal of his genitals and their storage in various orifices of his body.

As far as Valencio was considered, they were on their own and possibly the last defense that Earth had. That was the justification she held onto as she thought about what she was about to do to her squadron of cadet pilots.

Before she could dwell much further, the Estelian warships punched out of interspace just off of Mars, their cannons firing immediately just as Valencio had expected.

"You know the plan!" Valencio shouted as she flew her fighter skiff towards the battleship that led the armada. "Get in there and make those warships fight themselves! Dive! Dodge! Twist and turn! You keep those flight sticks moving at all costs! Never slow! Never sit still! Never give them an easy target! CSC OR DIE!"

"CSC OR DIE!" Zenobia yelled.

"CSC OR DIE!" Richtoff shouted.

"CSC or die," London said, not quite as enthusiastically as the others.

A few of the cadet pilots echoed Valencio's call to action, but most were so green that they didn't even know the battle slogan despite the CSC's continual attempts at indoctrinating the human populations of all the systems.

"You have this, cadets!" Valencio yelled. "I believe in you!"

She banked her skiff and ducked below a barrage of plasma bolts. Valencio rolled and then pulled up, changing the trajectory of her skiff so that she was facing one of the destroyers that had punched through. The plasma cannons from the cruiser behind her followed then stopped firing as the destroyer in front of her came into the line of fire.

Valencio had hoped that she could instigate some friendly fire between the warships and have a few take each other out. It would have made things so much easier if at least one of the ships would have gone down that way, but Valencio knew it was a long shot. Too many safety protocols built into the systems.

A muted scream over the comm then an explosion to her right caught Valencio's attention. She banked again, taking her skiff into a steep dive and watched as one of the cruisers began to list to the side, a good sized hole in its aft section.

"It's working," London said. "First casualty down and damage is done. You know the others are going to figure this out soon. Zenobia is gonna be pissed off and Richtoff could easily start firing on you."

"They already know," Valencio said. "I'm not proud of what I'm doing, but I'd be downright suicidal if I had hidden it from those two."

"Well, I'll cut you some slack then," London said. "Not much, but some."

More cannon fire caused Valencio to pull up and bring her skiff into a sharp, spiraling climb. She watched the plasma bolts fly past her cockpit and gritted her teeth until she thought one would crack. The bolts slowed then stopped as she got out of range.

There was another explosion and Valencio checked her console as she brought her skiff back around.

Three more cadet pilots were lost, two in vain it looked like. One got through and collided close to the battleship's bridge. There were massive sparks arcing out from the damage, telling Valencio that the battleship's crew was having a hard time sequestering systems. If that kept up then maybe her training squadron could disable the armada without all dying.

She didn't get her hopes up.

"Boss!" London yelled. "Incoming!"

Valencio's attention went back to her console as she flew through the next wave of plasma bolts. Her scanners lit up with dots indicating the quads had arrived. Not having the same power capacity as the bigger ships, the quads couldn't punch as efficiently, meaning they had to hang in interspace longer before reaching their destination.

"How many am I looking at?" Valencio asked.

"Looks like the Asteroid Belt stations thinned them somewhat," London said. "But not as much as they should have. It's a full squadron."

"Shit," Valencio said as she changed directions once again so that she could face the incoming quads and engage them immediately. "Richtoff. Zenobia. On me. We need to deal with these quads or they'll cut our cadets down in no time."

"Already on the way," Zenobia said.

"Same here," Richtoff replied.

"London? Hang back," Valencio ordered. "You stay out of it and be our eyes and ears. I want to know the second things go our way. Or the second you know the day is lost."

"I think the day is already lost," London said. "But that's just my opinion."

"Noted and ignored," Valencio said. "Just keep your eyes open and mouth shut, alright?"

"How am I going to tell you if the day is ours or if it is lost?" London asked.

"London," Valencio growled.

"Right, shutting my mouth," London said.

"And don't forget about the platforms," Valencio said.

"Not likely going to forget that," London said. "Yay."

Fifty-Three

"I ain't gonna kill you right away, North," Metzger said from directly behind North. "I need to know how deep this all goes. I need to know how many more traitors are on this station."

"Coop, you have to listen to me," North said, still on his knees, his eyes going from Linklater then out at the ripple in the lake that was getting closer. "I'm not a traitor. It's the pharma. The stuff is messing with your mind."

"The pharma is all that's keeping me clear," Metzger said. "I don't know why, but if I don't keep taking it then I start to get fuzzy. Did you put something in the water, North? Did you? Or in the food? You drugged the whole station didn't you and want to blame it on the pharma. I'm right, aren't I? I know how much you like that pharma. Is that why you took it so much? To counteract the poison in the water? The poison in the food?"

"There is no poison, Coop," North said. "I haven't had any pharma in hours. It was messing with my head too so I stopped. You have to trust—"

"Not a fucking chance!" Metzger yelled as he slammed the butt of his scorcher down on the back of North's head. "No way will I ever trust a DG!"

North collapsed onto the beach. His face hit hard and he felt the rocks slice open his cheek. He started to push himself up, but a boot firmly placed to his skull stopped that. He felt Metzger lean in and knew that all it would take was one hard push and his brains would be leaking everywhere. But Metzger eased up and North only suffered through a ton of grit grinding into the wound on his cheek.

"Who are the other traitors, North?" Metzger asked as he tapped the barrel of his scorcher against North's shoulder blades, bouncing back and forth from one to the other like he was ticking off eeny-meeny-miny-mo. "Just give me some names, North, and I can make this easy on you."

"Let Link go," North said. "He has nothing to do with this. I forced him to come along."

"Is that right?" Metzger laughed. "The guy sure didn't seem like he was forced to do anything. He killed my guards without even thinking about it."

"They were trying to kill me!" Linklater said, glancing over his shoulder at the lake as he sat in the shallows.

"What the fuck are you looking at?" Metzger barked.

"Nothing," Linklater said, turning his attention back to Metzger. "It's just been a long time since I saw a lake is all. I haven't had leave in close to—"

"Oh, shut the fuck up," Metzger sighed. "I do not care when you last had leave, Linklater. No one cares when you last had leave. You may be an officer, but fucking A, man, you are one boring motherfucker. Have you ever even been laid? I can't imagine any woman, or guy, wanting to fuck such a boring piece of shit like you."

"That's a little personal," Linklater said. He struggled not to look back over his shoulder again.

"Jesus, dipshit, what the hell is bugging you so much?" Metzger said. "You afraid of water? You think a fish is going to jump out and kiss you? Ha! That's the action you get! You fucking kiss fish! Did I interrupt your date? Is that why you came running in here? For a date with a fish?"

Linklater just blinked as his mouth tried to form some type of response.

"Now you look like a fish," Metzger chuckled. "Motherfucking fish kissing— HOLY FUCK!"

The thing that came out of the water was not a fish. It looked absolutely nothing like a fish, whether the fish was Earth based or from one of the many planets in the colonized systems. No, what came out of the lake had arms and legs, six of each, and a mouth so wide that it looked like its head was made of two saucers.

A hundred black eyes blinked in unison as the saucer mouth opened and a loud roar came up from the thick throat of the monster. The beast stood almost ten meters tall and was close to three meters wide across its massively-muscled chest.

"North!" Linklater screamed. "Bartram!"

Then he was gone as the monster scooped him up with four three-clawed hands and jammed him inside the multi-toothed saucer mouth. Blood flew everywhere, spraying out of the beast's maw and splattering the shallows. A long geyser arched out into the air and painted North's face.

"Oh, Makers, oh, man, oh, shit, of fucking god shit," Metzger whimpered. Even the pharma was no match for the terrible sight before him. "What the fuck, North? What is it? Oh, fuck, oh, god, oh, shit."

North didn't answer. He didn't even take the time to wipe his friend's blood from his face as he shoved up from the beach, knocking Metzger off balance. North lunged to his feet, his fist already swinging around before he was fully upright. He caught Metzger in the gut then sent an uppercut at Metzger's chin.

But despite the terror and pharma coursing through his veins, the sergeant-at-arms was always ready for a fight. He couldn't comprehend what had happened to Linklater, but he could comprehend what was right in front of him. He blocked the uppercut to his chin and lashed out with his own fist, nailing North in the wound on his cheek.

North spun about from the blow, droplets of blood flying out away from his cheek, and saw that the monster had quickly realized that its meal was not over. Six powerful legs broke into a run and came up from the water at a blinding speed. North let the momentum of his body take him back down to the beach just as the creature reached him and Metzger.

"No!" Metzger yelled as he opened fire with his scorcher. "You ain't real! This is a simulation!"

The monster cried out and stumbled back then regrouped and came at Metzger even faster.

"NO!" Metzger screamed just before two hands grabbed him, lifted him up in the air, and tore him apart, right down the middle.

The scorcher clattered onto the rocky beach and North scrambled for it. He grabbed up the weapon, rolled onto his back and took aim at the monster's belly. North fired until the weapon clicked empty.

Not surprising to North, since it wasn't his first encounter with a creature of that type, whether simulated or real, the monster stayed on its feet as it stumbled about the beach, its entrails dropping from its belly in horrid, smelly clumps.

North scrambled away on his hands and knees to avoid being trampled as the monster continued its death throws, black blood gurgling up out of its throat like a burbling fountain. With a final choked bellow, the creature collapsed onto six knees then fell over on its side. North ticked off the seconds, counting down from sixty, then the simulated monster faded out, leaving only Linklater's masticated corpse behind.

"I have never seen anything like that before," a voice said from the edge of the forest. "But I guess it stands to reason that with no simulated digestive system to hold the remains, the real body would be left behind. Fascinating."

North looked back and sighed.

"Ngyuen," North said.

"Yes," Ngyuen said, a pistol in her hand. "Me."

Ngyuen motioned with the pistol towards Metzger's halved corpse.

"You mind checking his pockets?" Ngyuen said. "Pretty sure he has what we are both looking for on him. I'd rather not get all bloody, if I don't have to."

North glanced over at the Metzger's body and shook his head. "I don't think so. Go find it yourself."

"North," Ngyuen said, her voice even and calm. "I know you just lost the closest thing you have to a friend on this station, but that doesn't mean you don't have more to lose." She cupped her free hand by her ear and listened. "Hear that? That is the sound of death. While there may not be any survivors left in this simulation bay, that doesn't mean there aren't people still alive on Perpetuity. So, unless you want the entire station to sound like death, you will crawl over there and retrieve Terlinger's medal for me."

"How the hell are you going to stop everyone from going crazy?" North asked. "The pharma is spiked, Ngyuen."

"Yes, I am fully aware of that, North," Ngyuen said. "Who do you think spiked it? Now, hurry along, please. I don't have all day. Taking down the CSC is full time work."

North gaped at Ngyuen for a second then crawled over to the right half of Metzger's body and began to go through the bloody and torn uniform.

Fifty-Four

Having finished stacking the corpses in the corridor, Garcia stepped back through the hatch and onto the bridge. There were so many thoughts swirling about in her head she didn't know where to start.

Her eyes drifted from one console to the next. She could get the thrusters back online and then get through the debris field. But that would mean she'd need to make sure the interspatial drive was working first if she intended to punch through the solar system. She had no idea how long all of that would take and she needed to make sure the Perpetuity knew the truth

She needed to make sure Earth knew the truth.

Garcia's eyes landed on the communications console. The transmitter was offline, but she had enough know how to get it going as long as the controls weren't locked. She had no reason to believe they would be since the crew was nothing but corpses. Don't really have to lock out corpses.

She took a seat and began to go through the diagnostics system to make sure she didn't miss anything. It took her longer than she wanted, but everything checked out. Garcia keyed in the commands to bring the transmitter array online and leaned back as the system did its work. Several minutes later, the system finished and all lights on the console turned green.

Garcia pressed her wrist against the interface and started to speak.

The console lights turned red.

"What the hell?" she snapped.

She pulled her wrist back and the console lights turned green again.

"Shit," she said. "Fucking feedback."

Garcia knew there were only a few things that could cause feedback like that and none of them had to do with the system itself.

She glanced at the view window and sighed.

"Guess I'm going for a walk outside."

She stood up and turned to leave when the whole ship shuddered. The shuddering was joined by a loud wrenching sound as Garcia braced herself against the console. Half the consoles around her started to light up red.

"Ah, shit," she said as she rushed over to security and brought up external vids of the ship. "Oh, super shit."

A massive chunk of one of the destroyers was scraping along the hull of the cruiser, tearing off metal as it went. Garcia watched in horror as an airlock burst open and atmosphere vented into the vacuum before the ship's failsafes kicked in and sealed off that deck.

"Okay," Garcia said as she moved from the security console and over to the helm. "I guess I call home later. Time to get the fuck out of this shit."

She brought up helm controls and began to power up the thrusters. Unfortunately, only one thruster was still intact and it refused to obey.

"Come on! Come on!" Garcia shouted as she slammed her fist against the console. "I just need enough juice to get away from this space junk!"

She attempted to reroute power from the damaged thrusters and into the intact one, but every command she gave ended in frustration as the helm controls slowly started to blink out red. No matter how fast she moved, she wasn't fast enough and within minutes the entire console was frozen, a dead hunk of metal and plastic that refused to respond.

Garcia stood up then was sent flying to the floor as the cruiser shuddered again. Claxons blared for a brief moment, indicating the hull had been breached, but then quieted down once the ship's failsafes kicked in yet again. Garcia was very aware that the failsafes had their limits. The ship could only lose so much atmosphere before life support completely gave out. That would be fine for the corpse crew, but wouldn't be so great for her.

"Think, think," she muttered. "What can I do? How do I move this stupid ship with the helm locked?"

She rubbed at a spot between her eyes that throbbed with pain. A pressure headache was quickly being added to her list of what a crappy day it had been.

"How do I fly this thing without flight controls?" she muttered again. "How, how, how…"

She looked at the navigation console and the bright green lights.

"Hold on," she said. "This thing was headed somewhere. The battle put it into defensive shutdown. All I have to do is point it back in the right direction."

She hurried over to the console and began checking the navigation systems. Everything was in order, including the destination coordinates. All she had to do was tell the navigational processor that the ship was no longer at battle stations and it should continue on its journey.

Garcia looked out the view window and gulped. She'd never attempted to punch before with so much traffic. Ships usually needed some space from other entities to allow for quantum deviations. Otherwise the interspatial pull could meld two entities together.

Another loud wrenching noise, followed by warning claxons, told her that two entities were about to merge anyway.

"Ah, fuck it," Garcia said as she strapped herself into the seat. "I always wanted to know what it would be like to die during a punch. I wonder if I'll get an express pass to the afterlife?"

She activated the interspatial drive and clutched at the armrest of her chair as the whole ship began to buzz and then shake.

"Well, that's not good," she said, just before the Norland blinked out of existence.

Fifty-Five

North looked at the blood slick medal in the middle of his palm. It felt so much heavier than the last time he held it. The weight of so many lives taken had been added to it.

"What's so special about this medal?" North asked. "What does it do?"

"It unlocks the CSC's secrets," Ngyuen said. "It tells the galaxy how all of you have been fooled for centuries."

"You spiked the pharma on the station, sending thousands of people into homicidal killing sprees for what? So you can work some Estelian espionage?" North asked, his eyes still on the medal. "How long have you been a traitor?"

"You don't know what you are talking about," Ngyuen laughed. "None of you Estelians do."

"Estelian?" North barked, finally looking up at Ngyuen. "How the hell can you think I'm an Estelian? Metzger thought I was an Estelian spy too, so why the hell did you kill him?"

"Oh, you're not a spy," Ngyuen said. "You're a full-blooded Estelian. As for Metzger, he was too. But I had him under my control for a while. All I needed was the pharma to kick in and he became my willing puppet. A lot of this would have been avoided if you'd played along as well, but that blow to the head you took in Terlinger's office ruined things."

"Blow to the head?" North asked then he reached up to touch his forehead. And the spot where the small bit of metal had been removed. "Wait? You put that there?"

"I did," Ngyuen said, waving her pistol at North. "Get up, Major. I'm tired of looking down at you."

North stood up and gripped the medal tight. "How did you get that thing under my skin?"

"During the explosion in the recruit bay," Ngyuen replied. "That actually wasn't planned. Just an overzealous patriot willing to die for humanity's cause."

The words the suicide bomber had spoken echoed through North's head- *"Death to the Estelian impostors! Long live the Earth colonies!"*

"Humanity's cause?" North asked, his hand gripping the medal even tighter.

"Careful there, Major," Ngyuen said. "How about you toss that medal to me so I can finish my job?"

"Never," North said. "You'll have to kill me and pry it out of my hand, you fucking doubleganger."

Ngyuen sighed. "You still don't get it. Aren't you listening, North? I'm not Estelian, *you are*. All of you. The whole damned CSC is Estelian. I'm human. I was born human out in the colonies and I have been fighting alongside my brothers and sisters since I could walk. The CSC was corrupted over a millennia ago, you fool. The Estelians won and made it to Earth. That chip you have in your head? Yes, that thing. It's what convinces you that you're human. Apparently, doublegangers fight better when they truly believe they are human."

"You lie," North said. "I know I'm human. There is no way I'm going to believe you. I've fought Estelians! I've fought real doublegangers with my bare hands! I've watched friends and comrades cut down! Butchered by the scum you work for!"

"You fought humans," Ngyuen said. "They weren't the false race, you were! Same with all of those friends and comrades!"

"NO!" North roared. "I know what I saw! I know what I did! I know who I am!"

"Bring me the medal, North," Ngyuen said. "I'd rather not shoot you. I actually have always liked you. You're a fair DG and I'd rather hand you over to my superiors than kill you on this simulated beach."

"No," North replied. "You're going to have to shoot me. I won't be a party to your lies."

Ngyuen watched North for a couple seconds then raised her pistol up. "Very well. I should have expected this. It's too bad you won't be able to see the secrets that medal will unlock. You'd know the truth then."

North stared at the barrel of the pistol. He was about to close his eyes when he caught sight of a shimmer by Ngyuen's shoulder.

Then the corporal's head turned violently to the left. North flinched at the sound of her neck snapping. He realized what had just happened and looked about for a weapon before the shimmer could attack him.

Then it was no longer a shimmer, but a person standing over Ngyuen's corpse dressed in a sheer black material. The person pulled off a helmet and tossed it aside then yanked down his face mask.

"Dornan?" North gasped. "What the hell?"

"Hey, Major," Corporal Dornan nodded as he raised his hands up. "I'm not here to hurt you. I am here for the medal, but you can hang onto it while we get to the server tower. I'll even let you send out the transmission."

North just stared at the man.

"Right, yeah this is going to be hard to hear," Dornan said. "But Ngyuen was correct when she said that medal unlocks all the CSC's secrets."

"Wha…? She…wha…?" North stammered.

"Yeah, she was right," Dornan said. "She just had no idea what those secrets really are."

"Then…then why did you kill her?" North asked.

"Because she was nuts," Dornan said. "She spiked the pharma and ended up killing most of the station. The bitch deserved to die."

Dornan turned and started to walk into the simulated forest then stopped.

"You coming? I really do need that medal," Dornan said.

"We're going to the server tower?" North asked.

"Yep," Dornan nodded.

"Linklater wanted to go to the server tower," North said, glancing at the mangled remains of his friend. "He said the medal was a key to unlocking something Terlinger had set up."

"Link was right," Dornan said. "I would have liked for him to be with us when we destroy everything the galaxy has ever known about this war."

"Then why the hell did you attack us in the corridor?" North asked.

"I didn't know who you two were working for," Dornan said. "It wasn't until I heard Ngyuen talking that I knew you were clean."

"Clean? Clean how?" North asked then reached back and felt the back of his head. "My chip? Do you mean my chip? Ngyuen said that the chips are used to—"

"No, Ngyuen was a brainwashed moron," Dornan interrupted. "The chips don't make you think you're human. You are human."

"So Ngyuen was a doubleganger. She was an Estelian," North sighed.

"Nope," Dornan said. "She was human too. Everyone is human, Major. There are no such thing as Estelians. There haven't been for a long time."

North felt his legs go weak and they almost collapsed under him.

"Pull it together, Major," Dornan said as he continued walking into the forest. "I'm not going to carry you. It's been way too exhausting of a day for that. Keep up and I'll explain everything on the way."

Dornan disappeared into the shadows of the forest and North watched him go. He looked down at the medal in his hand, looked over at Ngyuen's corpse then at the remains of Metzger and Linklater.

"Hold up," North called as he started to jog after Dornan. "Corporal! Wait up! That's a goddamned order! Slow the fuck down or I'm gonna kick your ass out into the vacuum the first chance I get!"

"There's the Major North I know," Dornan called back. "Come on! We don't have time for me to wait!"

Fifty-Six

Valencio's heart nearly broke every time she watched a cadet pilot lose control of his or her fighter skiff and went flying into an Estelian warship. Not that she had much time to watch the battle rage around her or time to watch her cadet pilots sacrifice their lives. She certainly didn't have time to worry about a broken heart. She was too busy trying to avoid a broken skiff as she dodged and flew around the Estelian quads.

Unable to match the quads' firepower or all out speed, Valencio had to rely on her skiff's agility. It was smaller and quicker, able to duck bolts and swerve away from missiles with the flick of her flight stick. But the advantage was slight and Valencio knew that using that slight advantage was all that would keep her alive.

Yet, as she sent a wave of plasma bolts into a passing quad while simultaneously sending her skiff into a power dive to escape the six disruptor missiles on her tail, she couldn't help but notice there was a pattern to the quads' attack. The quads were good, but they were too textbook. It was as if the Estelian pilots refused to take any risks, refused to fight on instinct and go for the kill even if the odds were against them.

"Demon?" Valencio called out as she flew under one quad then up and over another, banked her skiff to the right, curved around a third quad, then let her last missile fly into a fourth, ripping it in half and sending it careening into a fifth. "Demon, you seeing what I'm seeing?"

"We're getting our twats handed to us," Zenobia replied.

"No, the battle pattern they are using," Valencio said. "It's classic second tier tactics. We would have been teaching our cadet pilots the same thing in a week."

"Well, it's working," Zenobia said. "They've got me cut off from the rest of the squadron. Every time I try to get back to the cadet pilots to help out, my way is blocked."

"I see it," Richtoff stated.

"Of course you do, brown-noser," Zenobia replied. "Fuck!"

Valencio watched Zenobia's skiff get clipped by a plasma bolt and six quads descend on her position.

"I'm coming!" Valencio yelled, but she wasn't.

The quads around her own skiff closed ranks, forcing her to do an overhead roll and change directions immediately or get cut in half by a wall of plasma bolts.

"Demon!" Valencio yelled.

"Hey, boss? We got company," London said. "The platforms' ETA is five minutes, tops."

"Not now, London!" Valencio shouted. "I need to get to Zenobia!"

But she could see it was too late. The Estelian quads had crippled Zenobia's skiff enough that the vehicle lost its advantage. Without the ability to fly around the quads, the fighter skiff was easily separated from Valencio and Richtoff, forced out in the open where the quads no longer had to take caution when they fired for fear of hitting each other.

It was over in a flash as three missiles and a sun's worth of plasma energy obliterated Zenobia's fighter skiff.

Valencio screamed over the comm until her throat was hoarse. She pushed her thrusters to full and roared at the quads that had killed her comrade, sending plasma bolt after plasma bolt at them. Quad after quad exploded, the fire extinguished by the vacuum almost as soon as it erupted from the broken metal. But no matter how many she killed, there were still more. So many more.

"On your three!" Richtoff yelled over the comm. "I got it! I got—"

Richtoff fired two missiles, destroying the two quads that were coming at Valencio from her side and below. But in her haste to save her commander, she missed the three quads that attacked her from above.

Valencio screamed again and slammed her fists against her control panel as Richtoff's skiff was ripped apart. She took out one quad, but couldn't engage the others without being destroyed herself. She angled her skiff in a long arc, hoping to draw some after her so she could backtrack and send them into each other. None of the quads took the bait.

"Where the fuck are you going, cowards?" Valencio shouted. "Come back and fight me!"

"It's the platforms," London said, his voice choked with emotion. "They're going after the platforms in case the weapons are online and can take out the warships. I won't be able to get there, boss!"

With the quads changing their targets, Valencio was able to pursue them and pick one off here and another off there until she was back in the thick of things with her cadet pilots. She tried not to focus on the fact that only eight cadet pilots were left and instead focused on the fact that of the Estelian warships that punched into the area only one battleship and two destroyers were left.

Her cadet pilots had done her proud even if the destruction was caused more by a lack of training and careless flying than actual skilled attacks.

Valencio flew in front of the eight fighter skiffs and took the lead.

"We concentrate on the battleship first," Valencio said. "If we can focus our fire on the aft section, we could rupture the containment around the thrusters' power cores and get them to detonate. Our plasma cannons are too weak on their own, so when I fire I want all of you to aim for the exact same spot. You hit that spot enough and we'll take the thing out. Understood?"

The responses from her cadet pilots were less than enthusiastic, but there was nothing Valencio could do about that. She didn't have the luxury of coming up with a rousing call to arms speech. She probably didn't have the luxury of living through the hour.

Finding the spot she wanted, Valencio pushed her thrusters to full then aimed straight for the battleship. She waited until she knew she would hit her target perfectly then unloaded everything she had. It took less than forty seconds for her skiff's weapons system to be completely depleted. Valencio pulled up on her flight stick and hoped that the cadets could at least come close to where she hit.

Valencio banked hard and changed her trajectory so that she was aimed directly for the bridge of one of the destroyers. Her only weapon left was her own skiff and she knew that she couldn't live with herself if she didn't give the same sacrifice so many of her cadet pilots had already given.

"Get ready to kiss my albino ass, you doubleganger fucks," Valencio snarled. "Fire all you want, but you won't get to me in time."

The destroyer's plasma cannons took aim and glowed red. The vacuum erupted in a blaze of plasma bolts, but Valencio was surprised that they didn't come from the destroyer. The plasma cannons on the destroyer in front of her were ripped apart as the platforms' plasma cannons hit their mark. It looked like the platforms had their weapons systems on auto already.

Valencio barely got out of the way of the deadly barrage and could almost feel the heat of the plasma bolts on her ass as she rolled her skiff over and dove down under the destroyer, watching as flames erupted from its belly. The warship slowly broke apart, a series of small explosions sending chunks of metal into the vacuum.

Chunks of metal that came right at Valencio.

"Fuck," she swore as she flew left, flew right, climbed, dove, flew right again, all in order to get out of the growing sea of debris coming off the destroyer. "Fuck!"

A sparking strut and hunk of an airlock clipped Valencio's left wing, sheering most of it off and sending her into a spiral. She couldn't tell which direction was which and soon her world was a swirling mass of stars, Mars, platforms, debris, and warships. Valencio squeezed her eyes closed afraid she would vomit in her helmet.

Then it stopped.

She felt her skiff lurch and shudder and suddenly she was no longer in the fighter, but flying through the vacuum, strapped to her pilot's seat, her cockpit hatch exploding away from her, leaving her completely exposed and unprotected. Completely exposed and unprotected in an ocean of battle debris that threatened to shred her to bits at any second.

"I got you!" London yelled. "Just hold tight, boss!"

Valencio tried to orient herself, tried to see from which direction London's cargo skiff was coming, but all she saw was junk and wreckage. Then her visor dimmed to almost black as the battleship far above her exploded. Even the vacuum couldn't kill the flames fast enough, the detonation was so great.

"Good for you, cadets," Valencio whispered. "Your lives were not in vain."

"Right behind you, boss," London said.

Valencio tried to look over her shoulder, but her seat was yanked back so fast that her chin smacked into her chest and she saw stars.

"Fuck, London," she gasped. "You almost broke my fucking neck."

"Sorry," London said as Valencio was reeled into the open cargo hatch of the skiff. "Sometimes I don't know my own strength. It's my abs, you know."

Once secured in the cargo bay, the hatch closed and Valencio felt the skiff pressurize around her.

The hatch from the cargo bay to the skiff's cockpit opened and Valencio quickly unhooked her harness and jumped up on shaky legs. She stumbled her way into the cockpit and plopped down in the co-pilot's seat.

"Thank you," she said, her hand squeezing London's shoulder. "I mean it."

"No problem," London said. "What is a problem is that the platforms have gone dark. They aren't firing on that destroyer anymore."

"Shit," Valencio said. "Then it's up to us."

"I'd love for it to be," London said. "But this baby is out of ammo. No plasma, no missiles, nothing."

"Then our aim better be good," Valencio said nodding to the destroyer far above them. "We'll only have one chance. If this destroyer gets past the Perpetuity then all is lost. It can set its core to critical and point straight at the Earth. Even if it explodes before impacting with the planet, it'll end up poisoning the atmosphere. Humanity will have to hide underground for a hundred years to stay alive."

"So, what you're saying is we have to kill ourselves to stop the Estelians," London said. "Two lives to save billions."

"That's what I'm saying," Valencio replied.

"You sure?" London asked. "You could be saying we should punch out of here and go find a nice, quiet colony to drown our sorrows on. I know of a few bars in the Truglio System that would never even bat an eyelash at the fact that two healthy, service age folks like us aren't out fighting for the cause."

"You'd rather hide and die like a coward?" Valencio growled.

London sighed. "No, of course not. I just thought I'd throw the idea out there. You're my CO, so if you'd wanted to hide and die like cowards then I'd have to follow your orders."

"Take us at the destroyer," Valencio ordered.

"Aye aye, boss," London said and hit his thrusters.

He aimed directly for the Estelian destroyer's belly, his lips mouthing a silent prayer over and over.

Then the destroyer flickered and was gone.

"No!" Valencio said. "It's punched! Follow it! Take us to the Perpetuity now!"

"I can't!" London yelled. "I don't have the power to punch all the way. We'd only get halfway."

"Then take us halfway!" Valencio growled. "We'll refuel at the supply rocks!"

"By the time we do that the destroyer will already be at the Perpetuity," London said.

"Just do it!" Valencio shouted.

London stopped arguing and engaged the interspatial drive. Nothing happened.

"Why aren't we punching?" Valencio asked.

"Drive is down," London said. "We don't have the power to punch out."

Valencio did have the power to punch the console in front of her, which she did over and over until she couldn't move her arm.

"You're going to need ice for that," London said, staring at Valencio's limp fist. "There's some in the back. You go get it while I try to hail the Perpetuity."

Valencio didn't move, just held her fist to her chest while London tried to get the Perpetuity on the comm.

"We're jammed," London said. "The station's communications system is locked down tight. I'm trying every protocol I know as well as all the sub-channels. Nothing is working."

Valencio nodded towards the platforms that still floated above Mars. Some were taking severe damage as wreckage crashed into them, but one had gotten clear and continued its orbit around the red planet.

"Take us there," Valencio said. "Get me to the main comm console and I can override the Perpetuity's jam. I can't do it from here, this skiff doesn't have the right interface. Get us there now and we may have time to warn them of what's coming."

London nodded and sent the cargo skiff flying out of the wreckage and to the only whole platform left.

FiFty-Seven

"Why is this here?" North asked as he followed Dornan from the server tower shaft then to the hatch that opened onto the hidden communications room. "Has this always been here?"

"It's been here since Commandant Terlinger took over the Perpetuity," Dornan said, his hands on the wheel of the hatch. "He knew the right time would come when we could release the truth to the galaxy and let humanity know the real war it has been fighting."

"Couldn't he do that at any time?" North asked. "Why wait?"

"Because he needed to be able to prove the claim," Dornan said, as he spun the wheel and the hatch popped open. "Now he can." Dornan looked at the hatch then at North. "What you are about to see and learn will destroy everything you know. It will destroy everything all of humanity knows. There will be chaos, there will be rioting, there will be mass deaths. But if we can get through this as people then we will truly know freedom for the first time since the war with the Estelians began. Possibly for the first time ever. Ready?"

"Just open the hatch," North said. "I'm ready."

Dornan pulled the hatch all the way open then stepped into the small room. He stopped short and North bumped into him as he followed.

"What?" North asked then saw what Dornan was staring at. "Oh. Seeing that does destroy everything I know."

Before them, seated at the console was Wendt, dressed only in a pair of boxers.

"Hey," Wendt said, holding a wrench above his head. "I'm really hoping you guys aren't here to kill me. But if you are, just know I'll take at least one of you down with this thing. I'm in maintenance. I know how to use a wrench."

"What the hell are you doing alive?" Dornan barked.

"He was with Linklater," North said. "This is what Link was trying to tell me. It's why he wanted the key too."

"You survived the gas," Dornan said. "Good for you."

"You sent that shit at us?" Wendt snapped then jumped up from his seat, ready to swing the wrench at Dornan's head. "You fucker!"

"Whoa! Same side!" North said, jumping between the two men. "Calm down!" He turned and looked at Dornan. "Did you really try to kill them?"

"I didn't know what they were up to," Dornan said. "I couldn't take the risk of them finding this place."

"Well, we did," Wendt said. "And I've already figured out you have a data loop transmitting and receiving continuously. I just don't know what's in the data."

Dornan watched Wendt for a second then nodded. "You're about to find out." He held his hand out to North. "The medal, please."

North handed him the medal and Dornan tried to step past Wendt, but the maintenance chief wouldn't move.

"Wendt, let him by," North ordered.

"But how do you know this guy isn't an Estelian spy?" Wendt asked.

"There are no Estelian spies. There are no Estelians," Dornan said. "It's all bullshit. All of it. We've been fighting each other for centuries upon centuries all so the people in power could keep their place. War is profit and profit must be had at all costs. The ones in control never had to sacrifice, they never do. What was the death of billions upon billions when it meant they could stay in charge and their descendants could stay in charge?"

"Bullshit," Wendt said. He looked at North. "You fought out there. You killed Estelians. You know they're real."

"I killed doublegangers. Things that looked exactly like humans," North said. "No one I know has ever actually seen an Estelian in their raw state."

"Because we wiped them out in less than a decade of war. The combatants on both sides of this war for nearly two thousand years have all been human," Dornan said as he held up the medal. "This will unlock all the information to prove that."

"All humans?" Wendt asked. "Why? Why would we do that?"

"Because once the war was over, once we'd beaten the Estelians, the outer colonies wanted more," Dornan said. "They had banded together, learned to organize and work as one. Back then the conditions were horrible. People were basically slaves sent out to mine and reap whatever raw materials they could from the outer systems. After fighting for humanity's freedom, they realized humanity was them and they needed to keep fighting."

Wendt shook his head. "I... I don't..."

"The CSC created the idea of doublegangers," Dornan sighed. "The outer colonies' rebellion was classified as alien corruption. The enemy now looked like us and they had to be stopped at all cost."

"But the colonies weren't stopped," North nodded. "They kept fighting."

"Oh, no," Dornan said. "They were wiped out pretty quickly. They didn't stand a chance against the CSC. But the powers that be saw a never ending chance to keep the profits going. If the enemy looked like us then the war didn't have to ever end. As long as humans bred then there was a perpetual supply of fighters. For both sides."

Wendt eyed Dornan for a second then gripped his wrench tighter. "That doesn't hold up. In two thousand years, someone from the colonies would have told us. They would have exposed this. That's too many people that knew the truth."

"But no one knows the truth," Dornan snapped, brandishing the medal in Wendt's face. "The colonies don't think they're fighting the CSC anymore! They think they are fighting the Estelians that took over Earth! They think they are the last hope for humanity's survival! What I hold in my hand will unlock the data loop and send it all out into the galaxy! The truth that there are no Estelians will finally be revealed and humans will stop killing humans!"

"You're being a bit optimistic," North snorted. "I know humans. They'll always kill each other."

"But not because of a grand, constructed lie," Dornan said. "If people decide to kill people then at least they'll know it's people they are killing, not some extinct race of aliens that haven't existed for a very long time."

North raised a finger to ask, about to make a point then smiled.

"Something happened, didn't it?" North asked. "Something out in the colonies happened. The CSC won too well, didn't they? They wiped out the competition."

"Yes," Dornan said. "Only a small fraction of the CSC actually knows the truth. A few generals fought the good fight too well and won. It's not the first time. It's happened before, on both sides." He tapped the back of his head. "That's why we have the interface chips."

North shook his head. "All the recruits we were about to train, they were going to be sent out and turned into Estelians, weren't they?"

"To us, yes," Dornan said. "Their chips would be altered and they would have become the other side so the CSC would have someone to fight again and the profits would keep rolling in. But to the recruits, we would all of a sudden become the Estelians. Their chips would overwrite their minds with the narrative the CSC wanted them to know. It would be as if they'd never even thought any different. The war would have new players and go on. Business as usual."

"Jesus," Wendt muttered then sat down. "That's heavy. And that medal will tell everyone that?"

"The medal will unlock the data and send it out," Dornan said. "It'll be what tells everyone—"

The communications console beeped loudly and Wendt turned and looked at it.

"It's picking up an emergency message," Wendt said. "Coming in on a command backchannel."

"Bring it up," North said.

"We don't have time for this," Dornan said.

"We make time," North said. "People may not understand what's real, but they are still people. We help who we can."

"Fine," Dornan said. "You do that while I get this ready."

North nodded and Dornan moved past Wendt to the console. He inserted the medal and the entire console interface changed. North stared at it for a second then looked at Wendt.

"You're going to have to let the emergency message through," North said. "I have no idea what the hell is going on with this shit."

"Uh..." Wendt responded, looking just as confused.

"Here," Dornan said, tapping at the interface. "You now have your message."

"Perpetuity! Perpetuity, please come in! This is Captain Deena Valencio! I am calling to alert you to an Estelian destroyer punching towards you! It is en route and will appear any second now! Perpetuity? Perpetuity? Do you read?"

"Shit. The armada. One of the warships made it," North said. "How do I respond?"

"You can't," Dornan said. "You'll destroy the data loop."

"At least we know that the destroyer isn't actually Estelian," Wendt smiled then frowned immediately. "Not that it makes a difference. A destroyer destroys."

"Not if I can help it," North said as he moved towards the hatch. "I may not know how to work that convoluted communications interface, but I do know how to work this station's defenses." He smiled at Dornan. "You get the data out there and I'll get the Perpetuity's weapons system online. How long do you need?"

"Fifteen minutes, maybe twenty," Dornan said.

"I'll get you that much time," North said. "I may not be able to get you more."

"Wait, what does that mean?" Wendt asked. "If you can't get him more time then doesn't that mean the station gets destroyed?"

"Yeah, it does," North said. "We're talking about an Estelian destroyer. This station has limited capabilities compared to that thing. If their crew is even remotely competent then they'll blow us out of the vacuum pretty damn fast. I need to make sure it's not less than twenty minutes fast."

"But we can tell them the truth, right? If Dornan gets it out there then they'll know not to kill us," Wendt frowned. "Right?"

"All I can do is release the data," Dornan said. "It's up to each person to believe it. The truth means nothing unless people choose to believe. Some will, some won't. Words, even with the data collected in this transmission, will not be enough. Many will need actual proof. Proof they can actually touch and feel. It'll be far from over once I start transmitting."

"Shit," Wendt said.

"Come on," North ordered. "You're coming with me."

"I am?" Wendt asked.

"You are," North said, tapping his wrist. "My interface keeps crapping out. I'll need you to get things working for me."

"Fine," Wendt said. "Better to die doing something than sitting around here in my underwear." He looked down at his boxers. "You think we could stop and get me a uniform?"

"No time," North said.

"I didn't think so," Wendt sighed. "Let's go."

Fifty-Eight

London stared at the corpses all around the Mars platform's bridge.

"Jesus, they butchered each other," London said. "At least they blew the quads out of the vacuum first."

"Automated," Valencio said as she pushed away from the communications console and rubbed at her temples. "The weapons system kept firing until it was empty."

"Looks like the crew did the same thing," London said, nudging a scorched corpse with the toe of his boot. "Why would they do this?"

"I'm guessing it's the pharma," Valencio said. "Look at all the injectors. If you were thinking of having a boost, you may want to think again."

"Good call," London nodded. "My mother always said pharma would lead everyone down a path of destruction. She'd love seeing this."

"She'd love seeing a bridge full of dead bodies?" Valencio asked.

"Well, no, probably not," London said. He turned away from the corpse-covered floor and glanced out the bridge's view windows. It was nothing but battle wreckage for as far as he could see. "You think the message got through?"

"I hope so," Valencio said. "If not then we may be all that's left of the Perpetuity."

"We could make our own training station right here," London said.

"Who'd we train?" Valencio asked. She looked down at the bodies. "Them?"

"I'm going to shut up now," London said. "Maybe I'll go find us something to eat. Hungry, boss?" Valencio rolled her eyes. "Not hungry. Got it."

He walked out of the bridge, picking up a scorcher and putting it to his shoulder, just in case. The corridor was littered with plenty more corpses and injectors.

"Damn. Pharma would hit the spot," he muttered.
"No pharma!" Valencio yelled from the bridge.
"I know!" London said as he kept walking.

Fifty-Nine

North and Wendt reached the Perpetuity's bridge just as the destroyer punched into the vacuum. It loomed in front of the station, its hull scarred from battle.

"Wendt, I need weapons now!" North ordered as he was about to sit down at the weapons station console.

"Then move," Wendt said, shoving North to the side.

North watched out the view window as the destroyer began to turn, setting itself for the best firing position. "Wendt!"

"I'm working on it!" Wendt said. He swiped at the console interface, entering commands, rerouting protocols, tearing down firewalls. "Shit! It's not letting me in! It really needs command authority! This shit is not messing around!"

Then Wendt spun in his seat and looked at North. He smacked his forehead and shook his head back and forth.

"I'm a moron," Wendt said. "It would be way easier to just fix your interface. Get over here."

North stared out the view windows.

"North? Get over here," Wendt said then turned back to see what North was watching. "Oh, shit…"

The destroyer was firing all plasma cannons directly at the Perpetuity. Plasma bolts were flying straight for the station.

"You may want to hang on," North said just as the bolts hit their target.

The station shuddered and claxons rang out. The lights on the bridge flickered then dimmed as dust fell from the ceiling.

"North. Your interface," Wendt said. "We need that up and working."

North moved to Wendt and the sergeant grabbed his arm. He studied North's wrist for a second then set a pouch of tools on the weapons console, pulling a very sharp blade out.

"Where the hell were you keeping that?" North asked the man that sat there in only his underwear.

"You don't want to know," Wendt said. He looked up at North and frowned. "This will hurt."

Then he sliced into North's wrist, set the blade aside and grabbed up two other tools from the pouch. He began digging around until he found what he wanted.

"That...can't be...sanitary," North said through gritted teeth. He really wanted a hit of pharma, but he had to push that thought from his mind fast before it took him over.

"Don't worry about infection," Wendt said as he worked. "We're going to die when this station blows up. We just need you to keep that from happening long enough for Dornan to do his thing."

Wendt kept working as another round of plasma bolts hit the station. The claxons got louder and the lights grew dimmer.

"Done," Wendt said. "Now hold still."

North didn't have time to reply or react as Wendt placed a small box against North's wrist that had a button on top. Wendt pressed the button then dragged the box along the incision on North's wrist.

"Motherfucker!" North yelled. "What the hell is that?"

"I use it to splice cables together," Wendt said. "I figured it would work on skin. Looks like it. Give your interface a try."

North reluctantly pressed his wounded wrist. His interface image popped up and he grimaced, which was about as much of a smile as he could muster.

"Good work," North grunted. "Move."

"North?" Dornan called over the comm. "Can you read me?"

"I can now," North said. "How are you doing down there?"

"I need five more minutes," Dornan said. "Is that possible?"

North brought up the weapons system controls and then looked out the view window.

"Shit," North said. "Five minutes may be too long."

"Oh, Makers," Wendt whispered as a battery of missiles shot across the vacuum towards the Perpetuity. "We are so dead."

"What did he say?" Dornan asked.

"Never mind," North said as he targeted all of the Perpetuity's weapons on the incoming missiles. "Just keep working."

North fired and watched as the station's cannons tried to take out the missiles. They managed to stop half of them. The rest kept coming.

"You still want me to hold on?" Wendt asked. "Because I don't think it's going to matter."

The missiles hit and the claxons stopped. The lights flickered and went out before the backups kicked in, shading the bridge in a red glow. North watched in horror as the weapons console shorted out then one by one all the different systems consoles shorted out.

"We might as well be in the mess hall for all the good this place will do," North said. "Better pray to the Makers again. We're done."

North and Wendt stared out the view window at the destroyer, ready for the next attack. It came quickly. More plasma bolts flew out from the warship and ripped into the Perpetuity. North held onto the console as the whole station shook. There was a loud crunching noise and North's ears popped.

"We've lost pressurization somewhere," North said. "We're leaking atmosphere."

Then it felt as if the wind had been knocked from his lungs as he stared at the impossible sight before him. Out of nowhere, a cruiser punched into the vacuum, right next to the destroyer. But it wasn't just a cruiser. Attached to its side, and quickly flying off in the direction of the destroyer, was what looked like the wreckage from a warship of some type. It was too mangled for North to tell what type, but he could care less as the wreckage collided with the attacking destroyer, tearing it in half and sending it careening off away from the Perpetuity.

"Hot damn!" North shouted. "Would you look at that?"

"Yeah, that's great," Wendt said. "But what about us? What's that new ship going to do to us?"

"I don't know and I don't care," North said. "Dornan got his five minutes." North activated his comm. "Dornan? You there? Dornan?"

"Systems are down, North," Wendt said. "The comm is offline for the whole ship."

"I know where a comm will work," North said. "Follow me."

"How about I just stay here," Wendt said. "The view is nice."

"Where I'm going could mean we live," North said. "Not sure why I didn't think of it sooner."

"Live?" Wendt exclaimed. "You lead, I follow."

Sixty

The cargo skiffs sat there on the flight deck, all waiting for their next missions. Unfortunately, only one would ever see the vacuum again.

North opened the back hatch and gestured for Wendt to get inside.

"Get the comm up and find out if Dornan was successful," North ordered.

"What are you going to do?" Wendt asked as he hurried inside the cargo skiff.

"Get some supplies," North said, nodding to the pallets of crates off to the side of the deck. "We're leaving this station now and we may be out in the vacuum a while. I want to make sure we have enough fuel cells and ammunition to survive."

"Food and water would be good," Wendt said.

"Not from those crates," North frowned. "We'll have to deal with that later."

"Okay," Wendt said.

North had to make his way around and through a couple dozen corpses to get to a pallet jack. It looked like the flight crew had turned on each other, using whatever was at hand to crush skulls, break bones, and tear open throats. North was well past being shocked by the horrors, though. It had been that kind of day.

He grabbed the handles of the first pallet jack he could find, studied the stenciling on a stack of crates, then slipped the jack under and rolled the crates backwards until he could get around the corpses and turn the pallet towards the cargo skiff.

By the time he'd gotten the pallet on the skiff, Wendt was standing at the cockpit hatch, his face white.

"What?" North asked. The station shuddered and his ears popped again. "Shit. What is it, Wendt?"

"You better come talk to Dornan," Wendt said.

North set the pallet down and shoved the jack out of the back of the cargo skiff. He pushed past Wendt and into the cockpit then activated his comm, piggybacking off the skiff's communications system.

"Dornan? What's the news?" North asked.

"I got...it...out," Dornan said, his voice weak and short. "But...it...didn't go...far."

"What does that mean? It didn't go far? How far did it go?" North asked.

"Don't know," Dornan said. "I'm still...trying...to...transmit. But...console took...a lot...of...damage."

"Dornan? How much damage? Dornan? Listen, we'll come get you," North said. "You hang tight. We have a way off the station. We'll get the message out ourselves. Can you lock onto me and send it to this skiff?"

There was no response.

"Dornan? Hold tight! We're coming!" North shouted.

The entire station shook and the struts over the flight deck began to groan.

"We have to go, Major," Wendt said. "We can't go back down for him."

"We have to," North insisted. "Or this was all for nothing."

"He said he got the message out, he just didn't know how far," Wendt said. "That means someone heard it."

"We need everyone to hear it!" North said.

A warning beeped in the cockpit and North glanced around until he saw what it was.

"Shit," he said. "Incoming."

"Then we really have to go," Wendt insisted. "We won't hold up against that other ship."

"Okay," North said then double checked the scanners. "Wait. The missiles aren't coming from the other ship. They're coming from Earth!"

"Well, looks like we know someone down there heard us," Wendt said. "Can we go now?"

"Yeah," North said. "Strap in."

Sixty-One

The cargo skiff shot out of the Perpetuity, a small dot against the crumbling wreckage of the massive station.

North kept the thrusters pushed to full, aiming the cargo skiff out and away from the cruiser that loomed over it. He had no idea where the cruiser had come from, but considering he didn't know who to trust, he couldn't take the chance of being set upon by the warship.

Not that he expected to stand a chance against the cruiser if it decided to open fire on the skiff. He knew he and Wendt would be vaporized instantly. But he banked on the fact that the cruiser looked as damaged and beat up as he felt. All he needed was for it to just stay where it was and not attack for five minutes so he could get the interspatial drive on the skiff up and going.

"Where are we going to go?" Wendt asked, his eyes wide and locked onto the cruiser in front of them. "We can't just fly around forever. Should we put out a distress signal?"

"No!" North barked. "We stay off the comm. The CSC didn't send missiles at the Perpetuity because they wanted witnesses." North looked at the scanners and frowned. "This is going to be tight. Strap in."

"I am strapped in," Wendt said as he tightened his harness.

"Then double check your flight suit," North said. "When the Perpetuity gets hit with those missiles, there will be a million projectiles filling the vacuum. Most of them exploding out towards us."

"And if this skiff gets nailed? Then what do we do?" Wendt asked. "Float around until we can—"

"Hello!" a voice called over the comm. "This is Captain Deena Valencio calling for Major Bartram North! Hello! Come in, Major!"

"Valencio?" North replied.

"Major North? Is that you?" Valencio asked.

"It's me," North said. "How the hell did you reach me?"

"Warrant Officer London has a way with the comm system," Valencio said. "He went through my interface for your personal signal then sent out a comm blast."

"It was nothing," London said. "Rudimentary—"

"London, can it," Valencio barked. "Listen, Major, we heard the broadcast. It made it to us before it cut off. It was...confusing."

"No shit," North said. "I'm still trying to figure it out."

"London was able to capture it, and the background data stream that was with it," Valencio said. "We need to know what to do with this."

"Background data stream?" North asked.

"All kinds of charts and reports. Vid logs, troop and command interviews," London said. "There is stuff in there going back over a thousand years. It'll take a lifetime to sift through it all."

"If you heard it then you know you may not be able to trust me," North said. "And I can't trust you."

"I know," Valencio sighed. "But...but we don't have much choice. We're on a Mars platform and London is fairly certain the structure was damaged by the Estelian armada. Or sabotaged by the crew. We can't tell which."

"By the crew?" North asked. "Jesus, did they go insane too? Are there pharma injectors everywhere?"

"Yes," Valencio said. "They're all dead here."

"Same with the Perpetuity," North said. "Listen, Valencio, I'm in a cargo skiff and about to punch—"

The Perpetuity went up like a super nova behind the skiff. North and Wendt found themselves tumbling end over end as the blast rolled through the vacuum. The major struggled to get control of the cargo skiff, but he couldn't get the thrusters to respond. The tumbling continued and North thought it wouldn't stop.

Then the debris from the Perpetuity began to pelt the skiff, knocking it this way and that. The tumbling turned into rolling, turned into shaking, to shuddering, turned into crumbling. North screamed as the cockpit broke apart around him, sending him and Wendt out into the deadly chaos of the vacuum, only their flight suits to protect them from instant death.

North reached out and grabbed a chunk of paneling from the skiff that was still bolted to a heavy strut. He locked one glove in place then reached for Wendt. The sergeant stretched out his hands, trying to grab for North's hand, but a hunk of metal slammed against his legs and sent him flying away.

"Wendt!" North yelled. "Try to grab ahold of something!"

"Good idea, Major!" Wendt said as he scrambled about, his hands flailing as he tried to find something his gloves would stick to. But everything moved too fast, racing past him at deadly velocities. "I'm really trying here, I promise!"

Then a sheet of metal cut through Wendt's legs, slicing them off below the knees. North's comm was filled with the man's screams.

"Wendt! Oh, shit! Wendt!" North yelled, watching helplessly as the man's blood floated out into the vacuum in undulating globs. "Wendt!"

North tried to reach for him, but Wendt was tumbling away, farther and farther, headed straight for the cruiser. The good thing was North could see Wendt's suit sealing up and blood was no longer pouring out of the man's severed legs. The bad thing was, as he watched Wendt tumble off, he saw a cargo skiff launch from the cruiser, aimed right for him.

"Valencio? Valencio, can you hear me?" North called out. "I have no idea if you can hear me, but you need to take that message, take that data, and go. Get out into the galaxy, go to other systems. Spread the word. Don't trust anyone. Never stay in one place for too long. Get that message out then go. They will hunt you, they will find you eventually, so you have to act fast. Do whatever you can to tell humanity the truth."

North's comm crackled in his ear and he had no idea if his transmission made it to Valencio or not. He hoped it did. He hoped she and London could get on some ship and go. But, he was afraid they couldn't go anywhere or she would have never reached out to him.

North had to let it all go. He had to just have faith that someone, somewhere, whether it was Valencio or maybe some brave soul down on Earth, someone would carry the information, the truth, to the people. That hope echoed in his head as he watched the cargo skiff spin about and the back hatch open to catch Wendt inside perfectly.

"Someone knows how to fly," North said to himself as the hatch closed and the skiff changed directions.

North braced himself for whatever was next as the skiff came closer and closer to him.

Sixty-Two

Valencio hurried around the flight deck, yanking off parts from other skiffs as London called out their names.

"Coolant coupling!" London yelled. "This one is shot! Also a single pronged pressure valve! External! An internal one will rupture the second we hit the vacuum!"

"All I see are tri-pronged!" Valencio yelled, her hands working a driver as she took a coolant coupling off a cargo skiff. "These cargo skiffs are ancient!"

"The CSC wasn't interested in upgrading," London said. "There was a memo that only military vehicles would receive upgrades."

"Are you kidding?" Valencio cried as she got the coolant coupling free and jumped down from the skiff. She ran it over to London, who was strapped to the side of their cargo skiff, a tool pouch at his hip and grease coating his flight suit. "All vehicles are military vehicles! This is fucking war!"

"Apparently, it's not," London said. He took the coupling from Valencio and placed it against the skiff. "Thanks. You hear anything from North?"

"No," Valencio said. "His comm went dead. It's just us."

"Not for long if we don't get this skiff up and out of here," London said. "Life support is almost depleted and the bottom discs are already beginning to separate from the platform. Each level will automatically seal itself off as it is compromised, but the platform can only take so much before it rips apart. There's just too much junk out there colliding with us."

"If we get this skiff up and running, how will we get through the junk?" Valencio asked. "We won't have enough space to punch out."

"We're probably going to die," London said. "But at least we won't do it sitting on our asses."

"North was counting on us," Valencio said. "Humanity is counting on us."

"I'm guessing you aren't as used to disappointing people like I am," London said. "Karma really is a bitch if this is the lesson you learn before you kick it."

"We aren't going to kick it," Valencio said. "We have more than enough fuel cells loaded onto the skiff. We'll just boost the thrusters so we can get clear of the debris field and then punch all the way out of the system. We are going to live."

"I like your optimism," London said.

"It's not optimism," Valencio snapped. "It's a plan."

"Well, do you plan on finding me a single-pronged pressure valve any time soon?" London asked. "Because optimism or not, this skiff isn't going anywhere without that valve."

"Yeah, yeah, I'll find you one," Valencio said. Her interface beeped and she stopped, pulling up an image on her wrist. "Shit. Shit, shit, shit!"

"What is it?" London asked.

"Proximity warning," Valencio said. "One of the armada's cruisers just punched into the space around us."

"That was a dumb thing to do," London said. "The wreckage out there will tear it apart."

Valencio studied the image and shook her head. "It's moving outside the debris field." Another beep and Valencio growled. "It just launched a skiff."

"Fighter?" London asked, stopping his work to look at the captain. "One missile and we are dead."

"Cargo," Valencio said. "It's making its way slowly through the wreckage and coming right for this flight deck."

London looked around at the cannibalized skiffs on the deck. "I could set half of these to blow. Take out our visitors as soon as they get here."

"That would take us out too," Valencio said. "No. I say we hide and wait. See what they want. If we get lucky, we can hijack their working skiff and get the hell out of here."

"Good thinking. That's why you're the boss. Better grab the data case," London said, nodding towards a small black box that sat atop a pile of supplies next to the back hatch of the cargo skiff. "If we bring anything with us, it's that."

Valencio hurried over to the case and tossed it into a pack then strapped it to her back. London hopped down from where he was working and picked up two scorchers, tossing one to Valencio.

"We wait over there," Valencio said, pointing her scorcher at a stack of crates up against the wall. "Let them come to us. If we can, we'll avoid them all together and just steal the skiff. If we can't then we kill them where they stand and steal the skiff."

"Steal the skiff," London said. "Kill them or don't. Got it."

Claxons rang out and large red lights started to spin above them.

"They're here," Valencio said as she jogged over to the crates, activating her flight suit's boots so that they magnetized to the deck. "Ready?"

London came up next to her and secured his own boots then looked at the captain.

"No. Not at all," London said. "But not like I have a choice."

Sixty-Three

The flight deck doors pulled apart and various parts of cargo skiffs came floating out.

"Jesus," Garcia said as she angled the skiff and reduced thruster power to avoid the majority of the parts. "Someone did not pick up after themselves."

She piloted the cargo skiff into the flight deck, let it hover for a second then landed it perfectly so North only felt the slightest bump.

"Nice landing," North said then pointed out of the cockpit view window at a rough looking cargo skiff a few meters away. "There. That skiff's from the Perpetuity. This is the platform. They have to be here."

"Try your comm now," Garcia said. "It should patch in with the platform's system and transmit. You find your people and I'll try to find as many supplies as possible."

"Sounds good," North said as he unstrapped his harness and pulled open the hatch to the cockpit. "Be careful. We don't really know if Valencio is to be trusted."

"I don't really know if you are to be trusted," Garcia said. "And you don't really know if I am either. But there's nothing we can do about it. All I know is I want to live and get the truth out to the rest of the systems. You seem like that's your plan too."

"It is," North said as he activated the back hatch. "But we have a lot of work before we can do any of that. Let's focus on the living part first."

The hatch opened and North stepped out. He looked about the flight deck, watching as stray skiff parts continued to float out into the vacuum. His eyes were too busy watching the debris field that swirled about between the platform and the far off cruiser to notice the movement on his right.

"This isn't going to be easy," he said to himself then activated his comm. "Valencio? This is Major North. Do you read me?"

North finally caught the movement and spun about, but realized he didn't have a weapon on him, not even a stun baton. He was suddenly facing two scorcher barrels and feeling way more exposed by them than by the open flight deck.

"North?" Valencio asked. "Is that you?"

"Oh, thank the Makers," North sighed. "I thought for a second I had made it all this way to die because I left my pistol in the skiff. It's been a really fucking long day."

"Hey, Major," London said as he came up next to Valencio. He reached out and lowered her scorcher. "Chill, boss. It's time to go."

"Can we trust you?" Valencio asked.

"You'll have to," Garcia said from the hatch, both her and North's pistols in hand. "We all have to."

"That was a lot of crazy shit in that broadcast," Valencio said. "You sure it's real?"

"It's real," North said. "When you get to the cruiser, you'll see how we know. Someone told me that the only way to convince folks will be to show them proof. Solid, tangible proof. That cruiser out there is the proof. We just have to take it to folks."

Garcia holstered her pistol and then walked out of the skiff and handed North his. He holstered it and pointed at the pile of supplies by the Perpetuity cargo skiff. "That all you could find?"

"All we could gather in the time we had," London said. "Which is almost out. When you opened the flight deck, you just shortened the life of this platform. The change in pressure means we have maybe fifteen minutes."

"Then lets load that shit up," North said. "It's time to get moving."

Sixty-Four

Valencio sat in the mess hall, an untouched tray of food in front of her as North finished telling her what he had learned from Garcia.

"The CSC was sending its own ships to attack Earth?" Valencio asked. "That's crazy."

"Everything is crazy," North said, his arms folded across his chest. "But, in the CSC's defense, I don't think they expected the armada to make it past Titan Base. Pluto and Neptune were sacrifices necessary to maintain the rouse, but the point was to scare Earth and get even more support for the ramp up in troop deployment. They needed as many bodies as possible to fill the fake Estelian side of the battle. Easiest way to get folks to sign on is to scare the living shit out of them."

"You're telling me that all of those warships my cadets died fighting were on auto and manned by corpses." Valencio laughed. It was a hollow, bitter laugh. "They died fighting fucking simulation programs?"

"Yeah," North said. "The CSC filled the warships and quads with corpses; casualties they had on hand. That way when the ships were destroyed, there'd be plenty of bodies to float around in the vacuum and make it all look real. If the data is correct then this is not the first time the CSC has done that."

"Hey," London said as he walked into the mess hall. "We're entering the first system. You guys ready?"

"We've already punched through?" Valencio asked.

"Yeah," London nodded. "Wendt may not have any legs, but his hands work just fine. He got the drive working perfectly. Probably better than before Garcia nearly destroyed it punching that destroyer along with her. No more shimmies, no more shakes."

"Then let's get to the bridge," North said. "Time to get to work."

North and Valencio followed London out of the mess and to the main lift. They rode in silence as the lift rose up and opened out onto the bridge corridor. The hatch to the bridge was wide open and North could see Garcia at the helm.

He walked in and sat down at the command chair then stood up and moved over to the navigation console.

"Major?" Valencio asked. "Everything alright? You are the ranking officer, you should have the command."

"No one should," Major said. "If this war is bullshit then so is our ranks. We're just people now. People trying to help other people."

Valencio nodded and sat down at the weapons console, bringing up the interface just in case. London took his seat at the communications console and checked the interface, making sure the broadcast was ready to go.

"It's safe?" North asked, looking over at London. "Sending the broadcast directly to folks' interface chips? It won't fry their brains?"

"What we're about to tell them might fry their brains, yes," London replied. "But the tech won't. We're using the same system the CSC uses to switch people from believing they are fighting Estelians in the colonies to believing the colonies are the ones fighting Estelians. I modified it so people wouldn't end up losing their own will. They get to freely believe what they hear or disbelieve. All that matters is they get the choice."

"Then let's make this happen," North said. "I have the next punch plotted in case we have to make a run for it. Valencio?"

"Weapons system up," Valencio said. "Scanners are clear though. No one is coming to greet us yet."

"Garcia?" North asked.

"Cruiser is steady and holding its position," Garcia said. "All thrusters are operational and can get us to a safe punch point in seconds."

"Excellent," North said then looked around. "Where's Wendt?"

"Sleeping," London said. "He said he'd catch the highlights later. He can work, but it takes a lot out of him."

"Understood," North nodded then looked out the view window at the planet far below the cruiser. "Time to send a message. London? Hit it."

London swiped at the communications interface and unleashed the truth.

Sixty-Five

LeAnne Stussi looked into the night sky, marveling at the vast, twinkling depth. A firefly sped past her and, like all six year olds, she instantly shifted her focus and chased after the luminescent insect.

"LeAnne! Time for your bath, sweetie," her mother called from the porch.

LeAnne slumped her shoulders in disappointment, but knew not to argue or there wouldn't be stories before bed. She used to get to watch vids, but those days were gone.

It had been a year since the broadcast had stunned the planet, had sent everyone panicking. LeAnne hadn't understood any of what had been said, all she understood was that the CSC had taken all vids, all communications offline after the broadcast.

The planet had grown so quiet.

Her daddy had said the CSC tried to suppress the communication grid so people couldn't talk and discuss the broadcast. He'd said they wanted everyone in the dark like always.

LeAnne looked about at the night shadows and the smelled the fresh, summer air. She didn't know why being in the dark was so bad, she'd always loved the dark.

Her mother called again and she ran to the back steps, but turned once more to look up at the stars. Her father came around the corner of the house, setting aside a shovel and other tools the darkening evening had forced him to abandon. He put his hands on his daughter's shoulders.

"Whatcha lookin' at, Little Sweets?" her father asked.

"Just the stars," she answered thoughtfully. "Hey, Daddy?"

"Yeah, baby?"

"Do I still have to be a soldier to go up there?" she asked, pointing to the inky blanket of stars. "To go up into the dark?"

"No, sugar," he answered, leaning in to kiss the top of her head. "Not anymore."

"I want to go up there now!" she exclaimed, showing six year old impatience and enthusiasm.

Her father laughed and scooped her into his arms.

"How about you take a bath first, okay?" he chuckled, carrying her into the house.

The porch door swung shut behind them, the muffled slam swallowed by the cool, still summer night air.

And the stars twinkled down, their truth ready for LeAnne to discover one day. When she was ready to make that choice. A choice given to her by the will of a few brave souls on a mission that would never end, could never end.

For the truth had to be told in perpetuity.

Jake Bible, Bram Stoker Award nominated-novelist, short story writer, independent screenwriter, podcaster, and inventor of the Drabble Novel, has entertained thousands with his horror and sci/fi tales. He reaches audiences of all ages with his uncanny ability to write a wide range of characters and genres.

Jake is the author of the bestselling Z-Burbia series set in Asheville, NC, the Apex Trilogy (DEAD MECH, The Americans, Metal and Ash) and the Mega series for Severed Press, as well as the YA zombie novel, Little Dead Man, the Bram Stoker Award nominated Teen horror novel, Intentional Haunting, the ScareScapes series, and the Reign of Four series for Permuted Press.

Find Jake at jakebible.com. Join him on Twitter @jakebible and find him on Facebook.